A spicy whiff of aftersha[...] as I assumed. An intruder [...] and shaved, anyway.

I put down the pepper spray to pick up Chakra, who licked my arm as I nuzzled her. "You scared off that big bad intruder with your howl, didn't you, sweetie?"

Between my fear for her and the potential, albeit aborted, attack on my person, the episode left me trembling.

It took a minute for me to unlock my elbow and loosen my white-knuckled grip on the crowbar before I could lower it to my side, though I wasn't ready to let it go.

My heart, echoing in my head, slowed by the beat, thanks to our safety and Chakra's soothing presence.

As an aftermath to the adrenaline rush, I began to relax and shiver.

A husky, "Bravo," was whispered in my ear.

Chakra howled, jumped ship, and ran for cover.

With a honed fight or flight instinct, I screamed and wielded the crowbar, intending to beat the speaker to a bloody pulp . . .

PRAISE FOR

A Veiled Deception

"Whimsical, witty, and wonderful . . . Sure to enchant readers everywhere."

—Madelyn Alt, national bestselling author of *Where There's a Witch*

"A wonderful book. A great setting, an intriguing mystery, and characters so well developed that even the villain has elaborate layers make this a winner." —*Romantic Times*

"[A] stunning start to a new and magical mystery series . . . Phenomenal." —*Fresh Fiction*

Larceny
AND LACE

❧

ANNETTE BLAIR

BERKLEY PRIME CRIME, NEW YORK

THE BERKLEY PUBLISHING GROUP
Published by the Penguin Group
Penguin Group (USA) Inc.
375 Hudson Street, New York, New York 10014, USA
Penguin Group (Canada), 90 Eglinton Avenue East, Suite 700, Toronto, Ontario M4P 2Y3, Canada
(a division of Pearson Penguin Canada Inc.)
Penguin Books Ltd., 80 Strand, London WC2R 0RL, England
Penguin Group Ireland, 25 St. Stephen's Green, Dublin 2, Ireland (a division of Penguin Books Ltd.)
Penguin Group (Australia), 250 Camberwell Road, Camberwell, Victoria 3124, Australia
(a division of Pearson Australia Group Pty. Ltd.)
Penguin Books India Pvt. Ltd., 11 Community Centre, Panchsheel Park, New Delhi—110 017, India
Penguin Group (NZ), 67 Apollo Drive, Rosedale, North Shore 0632, New Zealand
(a division of Pearson New Zealand Ltd.)
Penguin Books (South Africa) (Pty.) Ltd., 24 Sturdee Avenue, Rosebank, Johannesburg 2196,
South Africa

Penguin Books Ltd., Registered Offices: 80 Strand, London WC2R 0RL, England

This is a work of fiction. Names, characters, places, and incidents either are the product of the author's imagination or are used fictitiously, and any resemblance to actual persons, living or dead, business establishments, events, or locales is entirely coincidental. The publisher does not have any control over and does not assume any responsibility for author or third-party websites or their content.

LARCENY AND LACE

A Berkley Prime Crime Book / published by arrangement with the author

PRINTING HISTORY
Berkley Prime Crime mass-market edition / August 2009

Copyright © 2009 by Annette Blair.
Cover illustration by Kimberly Schamber.
Cover design by Rita Frangie.
Interior text design by Laura K. Corless.

ISBN: 978-0-425-22911-8

BERKLEY® PRIME CRIME
Berkley Prime Crime Books are published by The Berkley Publishing Group,
a division of Penguin Group (USA) Inc.,
375 Hudson Street, New York, New York 10014.
BERKLEY® PRIME CRIME and the PRIME CRIME logo are trademarks of Penguin Group (USA) Inc.

PRINTED IN THE UNITED STATES OF AMERICA

10 9 8 7 6 5 4 3 2 1

Author's Note

Mystick Falls and its role as Mystic's governing body, the Phantom Coach Road, and the carriage house on Bank Street, home of Vintage Magic, are figments of my imagination. I took the liberty of eliminating River Road and located Mystick Falls in a nature sanctuary across the Mystic River from the seaport. The river, the seaport, and its ships, historic downtown Mystic, and Mystic Pizza—of movie fame—are real and well worth a visit. Though I throw in a real Mystic shop name, on occasion, characters come with fictional shops.

One

I find that it is vital to have at least one handbag for each of the ten types of social occasion: Very Formal, Not So Formal, Just a Teensy Bit Formal, Informal but Not That Informal, Every Day, Every Other Day, Day Travel, Night Travel, Theater, and Fling.
—MISS PIGGY

If I hadn't asked my New York cronies to mention my grand opening in their national fashion magazines, I might be able to breathe as if I *weren't* wearing Scarlett O'Hara's corset.

Thirteen days before Halloween. Thirteen days to open Vintage Magic, my dress shop for timeless classics and designer originals.

What was I doing to make it happen? I was driving home to Mystic, Connecticut, from New York after working out my contractual two weeks' notice, rather than forfeiting the bonus I needed to turn my building *into* Vintage Magic.

As I drove, grinning witches and twinkling pumpkin lights mocked me. I needed a tucking miracle.

My name is Maddie Cutler, well, Madeira, a former New York fashion designer, and I can fix anything, with the possible exception of cloning myself. So you can imagine my frustration two weeks ago at having to hand my shop's renovation reins over to my father.

Harry Cutler, staid academic, planned ahead. His oldest daughter, creative free spirit—that would be me—did not, which is how I got myself into this.

The silver lining? I passed my departing construction crew near Mystic Seaport. Finished. Finally. And only three weeks late.

The flaw in the fabric? A faxed report from the construction crew's night watchman. A rash of bumps in the night and running feet into the early hours of the morning. Note from said watchman: *The Mystick Falls police are getting ticked at being called every night "with no perp to show for it."*

I did not need any more grief from my old nemesis, Detective Sergeant Lytton Werner, also known as "the Wiener," thanks to a certain third-grade brat—that would also be me.

My complicated relationship with the local police aside, did the bumps in the night worry me? You bet your French knickers, they did. Why this sudden interest in a building that had been boarded up and left undisturbed for more than half a century?

I hoped never to find out.

Tomorrow I'd start moving in my stock and setting up my displays. How long could it take? I'd only been collecting vintage my whole life. Oy.

As I turned onto Bank Street, I heard raised voices in the distance, which anyone who passed the playhouse across from my shop heard at one time or another. Broderick Sampson, the curmudgeon of an owner argued with everyone. Just another sign I was home.

I pulled into the crowded lot behind Mystic Pizza to view my building from across the street. I had always admired the original copper weathervane, a ship in full sail time-coated a soft green, but I loved the new Victorian streetlamps brightening my parking lot and the spotlit old-fashioned tavern sign hanging above the door: Vintage Magic in bold white on a dark eggplant-colored shield. Behind the shop name stood a pale lavender side silhouette of a woman who could be Jackie O., the sixties being such a popular vintage.

I finally uncrated my squalling kitten, who would rather have been riding shotgun from the armrest, and she came to make her own assessment.

I refused to stress over the parking-lot debris marring the scene: empty wire reels and a mountain of boxes at my front door. You'd think the crew would have cleaned up.

The yellow fur ball purred and curled against my solar plexus chakra, an intuitive move on her part. She had the uncanny ability to calm me. Because of it, I'd named her appropriately. "What do you think, Chakra? Beautiful?"

She approved with a soft meow.

Genuine delight washed over me.

No more weather-ravaged, raw wood shack, though we hadn't replaced a splinter that didn't need it. No windows existed on the building's main floor, but I didn't want sunshine fading my vintage treasures, anyway.

We'd replaced the people door, but the huge, tall, front-facing double doors beside it, built for horse-drawn hearses, were now sealed . . . though the same could not be said for a similar door at the side of the building.

In front, however, their sheer size in lavender with eggplant crossbeams, made the sage building pop. Magical colors, according to Aunt Fiona, lawyer, godmother, and witch. Sage: the herb to clear negative energy and the color for prosperity; lavender for harmony; purple for wisdom.

In this incarnation, Vintage Magic oozed character and charm, leaving its days as a morgue, then a funereal carriage house, to the history books.

I moved Chakra from my lap, drove across Bank Street, and pulled straight into my smooth new tarmac parking lot.

I had yet to see the transformation inside.

Between the New York job and condo to sublet, I hadn't been back in the last two weeks. But the minute both were done, I'd packed seven years of my life into a funky rental and beat my ETA by an hour.

As a result, Dad, Aunt Fiona, Eve, my best friend, and Nick, my hunky Italian boy toy, weren't here, yet. They were due soon to crack open the secret room with me; secret being relative.

Dolly Sweet, friend and centenarian, who'd deeded me the place for the price of taxes, forgot to tell me about the second-floor storage room, its doors cut so seamlessly into a wall I'd missed it on my pre-ownership tour. Like the rest of us, Dolly couldn't wait to find out what she forgot she sold me.

Sure, reports of bumps in the night made me think twice about viewing even the bottom floor alone. But this was *my* building and I was the only one who *hadn't* seen its transformation.

Besides, I had four things on my side. A key. A can of mace. Spiked heels. And a watch cat. Who could ask for more?

I was going in.

The key my father sent me slipped into the lock like a

knife through flan, or cheesecake, or tiramisu. Hmm. I forgot to eat today. Forgot to sleep last night, too, I was so busy packing.

My stomach growled as I stepped inside, the scent of fresh paint filling me with a giddy Christmas-morning rush. Chakra jumped from my arms and hit the floor with a whomp to scope out the place.

The panel of switches and dimmers behind the enclosed stairway, near the door to my horse-stall dressing rooms, allowed me to flood the room with a soft wash of indirect pale pink light. I'd asked for a hint of art deco in the mahogany trim and it looked sensational, better than my sketches.

Crazy-quilt ideas for finishing touches, decorating, displays, and shop layout filled my mind.

I grinned as I perused my linen-paneled, three-thousand-square-foot dream-come-true. Vintage Magic.

The mahogany, waist-high hearse stalls against the back wall remained intact and set the style, while a cart of matching movable lower walls awaited placement along the front and sides. I'd be able to see my customers in whatever fashion type or designer nook they perused.

Unexpectedly, the wind grabbed the front door and slammed it.

I jumped and Chakra howled.

A metallic clank hit the floor above us.

My heart skipped a beat. Chakra flew into my arms, her fear becoming mine as I shivered in my Jimmy Choos.

Scrap! A bump in the night and no watchman in sight.

Two

Balanced emotions are crucial to intuitive decision making.
—DONNA KARAN

I stood glued to the spot, adrenaline rushing through me while hair-raising pinpricks ran up and down my arms and legs.

An unnatural silence followed, thick and heavy with jeopardy.

It couldn't be a lagging construction worker. I'd told them *not* to touch the upstairs.

I could call 911, wait for the police, who were so sick of coming here they might take their time. In which case, I'd chance losing the intruder. Or I could try getting a visual and a description, which would give the police something to go on.

Since the perp was a documented runner, I decided to investigate. I wiped my sweaty palms on my skirt, propped open the front door, and hung my Lucite box bag on the outside knob, in the event a quick getaway became necessary.

Slipping from my Jimmy Choos, I put Chakra on the floor and picked up a shoe. "Follow my lead," I whispered.

With a spiked heel in my right hand and a vial of pepper spray in my trigger-happy left, I went boldly forward.

I flipped the switch for the enclosed stairs, expecting to light the upper level, as had happened on my tour. Instead, a single token ten-watt lightbulb went on at the bottom of the stairs, and the second floor remained black.

Scrap. I'd had the circuit split. It seemed a waste to light so many square feet with one switch . . . except when you were about to confront a bump in the night.

I caught movement above, stealth slithering across the ceiling, just enough to make me tremble and hesitate, but not enough to make me stop.

This was *my* building, dammit. I felt violated. Angry. Furious. I was a woman of action.

Impetuous had its perks. If a member of my family found themselves in this situation, they'd call *me*.

Acting first and thinking later worked for me. Mostly.

I looked up, beyond ceilings and roof and wind-scuttling autumn clouds. Please let this be one of those times.

Chakra kept a step ahead of me, lying low as if sneaking up on a mouse.

The first stair squeaked, sending a trickling stream of icy perspiration down my back.

I raised my can of pepper spray and took the stairs more carefully, more quickly, silently repeating my mantra: I can *fix* anything.

I can fix *anything*. I *can* fix anything.

Each ancient stair voiced a whispered protest. Squeal,

creak, groan, squeak. Holy Harrods, I should've had *them* replaced!

I can fix this. I can. I can.

I believed that.

The Little Engine That Could had nothing on me. So why was sweat ruining my Prada blouse? Talk about the last straw. The blouse *hadn't* been a fashion-week freebie. It cost a fortune!

I charged up the rest of the stairs, slapping the wall at the top for a nonexistent switch plate.

Full stop. Except for my heart.

Double scrap! "Split the circuit," I'd said, *and*, "Don't touch the upstairs." Wooly knobby knits, why did two and two only make four when you couldn't see your Jimmy Choos in front of you?

Light behind me. A black hole before me.

Chakra sitting on my foot, scared meowless.

My knees turned to jelly, it was so tucking dark. I wiggled my toes to prod Chakra to her feet and, chin high, I stepped from the stairwell into a still-as-death room.

My eyes adjusted to the darkness, which was useless as I scanned the back of the room before I rounded the stairs and faced front where the sound had originated.

The wide-open room appeared empty, except for the caskets on pedestals in the dark back corner and, in shadow at the far side, the antique hearse, brought up from downstairs.

In the vast expanse, light from the parking lot spilled in, casting long window shadows across the floor and illuminating what I'd missed on my initial visit. The once-invisible doors cut into the wall to the storage room were now delineated by giant gouges and splinters.

I moved close enough to see that the lock held and in my stocking feet stepped on something hard, uneven, painful.

Losing my balance, I dropped the pepper spray.

Chakra pounced on the small vial rolling away from me, and I didn't want her accidentally setting it off and hurting herself, so I put down my shoe and ran to grab the pepper spray.

Once I did, the sound of footsteps came closer from the far end of the back wall behind the caskets. I grabbed the object I'd stepped on, raised the crowbar as high as I held the pepper spray, and braced myself for the intruder, his approach slow, intense, threatening.

He must have gotten close because Chakra's banshee howl seemed to ignite the invisible runner to action.

Footsteps, no longer muffled, rattled down the stairs at a fast clip and slammed out the front door.

Relief washed over me in dizzying waves, and though I mourned the loss of my Lucite bag, likely bleeding value in the parking lot, Chakra and I were safe.

A spicy whiff of aftershave reached me. Probably a male, as I assumed. An intruder with class? Well, one who bathed and shaved, anyway.

I put down the pepper spray to pick up Chakra. She licked my arm as I nuzzled her. "You scared off that big bad intruder with your howl, didn't you, sweetie?"

Between my fear for her and the potential, albeit aborted, attack on my person, the episode left me trembling.

It took a minute for me to unlock my elbow and loosen my white-knuckled grip on the crowbar before I could lower it to my side, though I wasn't ready to let it go.

My heart, echoing in my head, slowed by the beat, thanks to our safety and Chakra's soothing presence.

As an aftermath to the adrenaline rush, I began to relax and shiver.

The husky "Bravo" whispered in my ear made Chakra howl, jump ship, and run.

Me? I gave in to my honed fight-or-flight instinct, screamed, and wielded the crowbar, intending to beat the speaker to a bloody pulp.

Three

I've been strong and determined all my life about many
things I've wanted.
—CALVIN KLEIN

❧

"I'm already dead, Madeira," Dante Underhill said. "You
may now put down the crowbar."

It took a minute for his words to penetrate my panic.
I stilled and focused. No blood. I covered my heart with a
hand to keep it from beating from my chest. "Dante!"

This building, once the Underhill Funeral Chapel carriage house, had gone into hibernation when the last Underhill quit this earthly plane, though he can't seem to leave
the building . . . or so *he* says.

I know. Shiver. And I mean that in the most titillating of
ways. I gave him a withering glare. "You scared me!"

He bowed. "My apologies."

His outdated manners short-circuited my anger.

Chakra sat on my foot and looked up at him.

I put down the crowbar, picked up my cat, and huffed.

"What's the point in having a ghost if he doesn't give you a heads-up when there's a break-in?"

Dante raised a brow. "I was thinking only of you. The thief might have been able to see and hear me, like the plumber I scared to death—"

I scowled.

He shrugged. "I was planning to appear at the very moment your luscious skin most needed saving."

"Compliments will get you nowhere," I said, though my congenital vanity probably gave me away. "You mean," I attempted to clarify, "*if* the intruder had attacked me, and *if* he or she could have seen you, their fear would have frightened them away and saved me?"

Dante raised his empty hands. "That's all I've got, Twinkle Toes, a store of scary spirit energy."

I covered one stockinged foot with the other. "I guess. But you could have warned me downstairs that I wasn't alone."

"You would have given us both away. You scream every time I appear."

"I do not."

"Do, too, and your cat seems to take after you."

I ignored that. "Did you see the intruder?" I asked. "Who was it? A he or a she? Anybody you recognized?"

"I have no idea who," Dante said, "but *he* wanted in your storage room in the worst way."

"No bloody kidding," I snapped, indicating the damage. "How *would* I manage without you?"

Dante's chin dimple deepened, but he was smart enough not to smile outright.

I refused to be charmed. "Don't ever sneak up on me from behind, again. From now on, you appear facing me, or I'm calling Ghostbusters."

What a cocky grin. Mr. Delicious tipped his hat, and Chakra tried to catch it.

"Wait, it's a man, you said. Has he been here before? Same man?"

Dante nodded. "He's been trying to get in since you left. Welcome home, by the way."

"Thanks." I ignored the heart flutter his welcome induced.

Dante Underhill had died young, relatively speaking. Gorgeous man. Loved women. Broad shoulders, sturdy chest, charm, charisma. Think: Cary Grant in a tux, tails, and a top hat, but dead—fifty, sixty years' worth.

I'd had the weird ability to see ghosts from the cradle, every one the silent type.

Dante, however, had been chiseled from a different hunk of spook. He spoke to me the day I toured the building, and I about jumped from my skin that time, too.

Not many people can see him, but when they do, he says hello. He's a people person, to the detriment of that one poor plumber.

"Now my intruder's gone," I said, "I want to see my dressing rooms."

Dante shook his head. "Aren't you going to call the police?"

I shrugged and turned toward the stairs. "I'll see what Nick thinks."

Dante obediently appeared before me. "Who's Nick?"

"FBI," I said.

"Like J. Edgar Hoover?"

"You have been here a long time."

The sexy specter furrowed his brows. "Why's that Dick fellow coming here?"

"Nick with an N, and he's mine," I said, without elaboration.

"You're married? Of course you are."

I raised a brow. "Why do you say 'of course?'"

"Well, look at you. You're so, so deliciously . . . marriable."

I took that as a compliment, since he was looking at me as if he had a sweet tooth and I was a drizzle of hot fudge. He'd used "marriable" in lieu of an earthier word. "So was Dolly, but you didn't marry her."

"Dolly," he said, sigh wistful, expression sensual. "Being with Dolly was like touching the stars and catching fire."

"A scenario I know well." My echo of his sigh annoyed him.

He faced me all the way down the stairs—a bit disconcerting, but I'd asked for it, while he grilled me with personal questions I refused to answer. So much for checking out my dressing rooms. Only one way to stop his interrogation: leave.

"Are you married or not?" he finally asked.

"Not."

"The cad," he said.

And I laughed. "You should know."

I found my vintage box bag on the floor inside and undamaged, gratefully grabbed it, slipped into my Jimmy Choos, and went out the front door.

I expected to see Dante in the doorway—which was as far as he could go—his hands on hips or in some other similarly chiding pose, but he'd disappeared.

I did not expect to see a loiterer across the street leaning on a lamppost—a rather stupid move, standing under a bright light. But between his spot-bleached black jeans, leather vest, T-shirt, and green toque, I could pick him out in a lineup, if I had to, which just might become necessary.

Given his belligerent stance, I wondered if he was trying to scare me away.

As if in answer to my unspoken question, he stepped off the curb in my direction, but I stood my ground, took out my cell phone, and hit speed dial.

The slacker backed up and walked away before Nick answered his phone.

"I'm at Vintage Magic," I said. "Are you coming?"

"Are you wearing your lucky panties?"

"Stop being such a tease. I *mean*, when can you meet me here?"

Nick sighed. "I'm flying out tonight, ladybug, on assignment, but I can stop at your place for a minute on the way to the airport."

"Bummer," I said.

"Tell me about it. I had a helluva private welcome-home celebration planned."

I felt lonely and he hadn't left yet. "I'll bet you did. See you in a few?"

"Sure thing."

I looked back across the street. No more loiterer. At my open door, still no ghost.

I wondered—a bit late, perhaps—about the wisdom of buying a haunted building. I'd acquired it in my usual, perverse way, by acting first and thinking later. Dante, I'd considered a bonus after the fact.

That was then. This is now.

An owl hooted, and Chakra came to sit on my foot.

I picked her up and we both calmed. I wondered if our "familiar" attachment had to do with any untapped, otherworldly talents I might own.

I came by my ability to specter-speak naturally, only *one* of the arcane endowments from my late mother—a broom-carrying witch, as it turns out.

That black cat out of the bag—as far as my father is concerned, as in: he can't know that I know—I'd learned recently from Mom's best friend and soul-mate witch, Aunt Fiona. She hadn't exactly mothered us over the years, unless you counted my craft, needlework, and early sewing lessons, but she'd always been there for us.

So far, I haven't shown any signs of spell casting or moon dancing. Except in my recurring dream of being held in my mother's arms while we danced with Aunt Fiona under a full moon, a dream I usually have before a significant life change. But the jury's still out on whatever witchcraft or magic I might harbor.

What kind of witch, I ask you, owns a *yellow* cat?

For fun, I'd recently haunted the occult section of a bookstore, thinking a spell for kissing toads into studs could be fun. I mean, if somebody had to do it, I was up for the job. Other than ghost gab and a weird clairvoyance around certain vintage clothing items—an aptitude I discovered when my sister Sherry was accused of murder—I don't know what other metaphysical skills I might possess. But I'm game to find out.

Four

Design can have such a positive impact on the way people live and on their relationships and moods.

—GENEVIEVE GORDER

I took Chakra to make use of the sand near my driveway before we checked out the boxes by the front door. They were stuffed with old clothes and notes from Mystick Falls neighbors, friends who didn't want me to fail and must have known I was coming home today. Gossip travels the fast lane in Mystick Falls.

The brunt of the donations might best be used for dust rags, which would hurt their feelings, though I did spot the occasional treasure.

I was up to my elbows in old clothes when Eve, my best friend, a platinum blonde two weeks ago but a raven-haired vixen today, pulled up in her Mini Cooper convertible, top down.

As she got out, her Hells Angels jacket fell to the ground. She picked it up and tossed it in her backseat.

"You're early, Cutler! Don't deny it," Eve said with a one-fingered scold.

I went to meet her. "I know. I've already been inside."

"You know that I like to be first on the scene," she griped. "You said to meet you at nine, and it's only eight thirty."

"Don't get your knickers in a knot, Meyers. I was glad to have some alone time to wallow."

She gave the building a dubious glance. "In misery?"

"In possibilities, brat. It's a showpiece, and you know it."

She shrugged, toying with me, and looking good in the boot-cut black jeans I'd designed and stitched for her. She wore them with a delicate, black silk baby-doll cami and clunky Doc Martens.

The walking "fashion don't" with the huge heart, who'd watched my back and saved my butt more times than I cared to remember, handed me a caramel latte and an Allie's maple frosted doughnut.

"Yum. Thanks. You've been to Rhode Island?"

"New England educators' meeting."

I opened the cup's sippy slot, recaffeinated, munched on the primo treat, and sighed in appreciation, while Chakra curled around our legs.

Eve drank her coffee black, the way she wore her clothes, and she did both with gusto.

"Your hair looks great," I said. "I like the cut, but now it's the same color as your clothes."

"It's a confirmed fact that sports teams who wear black are more intimidating, like warriors prepared for battle."

"So that's why you wear bold and black, so people will take you seriously and appreciate your brain?"

"Well," she said, looking me up and down, "when a man

starts by looking at your spikes and works his gaze up your bare legs, it's not your brain he's thinking about."

Our arguments about her single color apparel choice of black could go either way, but I conceded defeat. "Eve one, Madeira zero."

She bowed regally. "You're hardly a zero, my friend," she said, "but I hope whatever's in your surprise storage room is worth the trip."

"It must be. Somebody just tried to break into it, but Chakra and I scared him away."

Eve stepped closer, horror etching her features.

Uh-oh, I thought. I should have kept my mouth shut. "Meyers, *swear* you won't tell. I don't need a lecture from the men in my life."

"Somebody broke in? While you were *here*? Who? Why? Are you all right?"

"I didn't see who, and how the Hermès would I know why? I'm fine. Don't I look fine?"

"Did you call the police?"

"What do you think?"

"Oh," Eve said, "not calling is why you expect a lecture, and I wouldn't blame the men in your life. You really should have dialed 911."

"I do *not* need an investigation further delaying my opening."

"It's not the investigation, it's the *investigator* you don't want to deal with," she said with a smug expression, knowing me too well.

"Exactly. Better I should stay away from the Wiener."

"I'm sure he feels the same about you, with good reason."

I crushed my napkin. "Thanks."

"Who else are we waiting for?"

I checked my watch. "My dad and Aunt Fiona should be along in a bit."

Eve sighed. "And Nick, I suppose?"

"Yep. He just went home to change."

She gave me a bland look. "Gee, and I thought he needed a full moon."

"Eve one, *Nick* zero."

Nick Jaconetti, my on-again, off-again since high school, ticked Eve off with his very existence.

In the seven years I'd worked and lived in New York— Eve with me for two of them—Nick had visited only once, though I often saw him at family gatherings. This time, when I went back for two weeks, he visited me twice. I smiled.

"Gross!" Eve snapped. "You and Nick are on again, aren't you?"

"Al-mo-osst."

She frowned. She and Nick had a snarky, grudge-rooted relationship, because she thought he took me for granted, and he thought she was a pain, but they put up with each other for my sake, more or less.

To my surprise, Eve handed me her cup and abandoned me to run across the parking lot. "Vinney?" she called to the guy on the sidewalk in front of the old playhouse.

Vinney? Wearing a green toque and bleach spots on his jeans? The belligerent lamppost leaner was Eve's Vinney? If so, this was no time mention my suspicion that he might be the one trying to break into my storage room.

The playhouse, which still held theatricals on the main floor and rented its ballroom upstairs for special events, looked closed, except for lights in the back office on the main floor behind the stage. Broderick Sampson's latest sparring partner seemed to have left, since all was quiet. Also known as McScrooge, the curmudgeon was working late again, probably stacking his gold coins.

"Yo, Vinney!" Eve tried, again, her hands cupped around her mouth.

The toque wearer kept walking, head down, hands in his pockets, as if Eve couldn't possibly be talking to him.

She came back, her expression puzzled, and took out her cell phone, but whoever she called didn't answer.

"Is Vinney your hunk du jour?" I asked, getting an affirmative nod.

No surprise; Eve was a man-magnet, though I didn't have a good feeling about this particular catch. "What happened to Ted?"

"Ted was just a fling. I'm not a keeper."

I sucked in a breath. "Did *he* say that?"

Eve looked up from her phone. "No, I did. Ted didn't dump me. I dumped him." She clicked her phone shut, slipped it into her jeans pocket, and took back her coffee.

"Guess that wasn't him across the street, then?"

"But it was." She looked over there, as did I, but the loiterer had vanished. "Never mind," she quipped. "I'll beat him up later."

Suspecting that her Vinney might be *my* intruder didn't count for much with no proof or motive behind it. "You're a keeper, Meyers," I said. "And don't you forget it."

"Yeah, yeah. What about Dolly? Is she coming to see the secret room?"

"She's not up to it tonight. I'll bring her tomorrow."

Eve ran a hand through her hair, leaving the short, ebony spikes in fashionable disarray. "For a hundred and three

21

years old, Dolly sure gets around. I wanna be her when I grow up."

Eve glanced at her diver's watch, then picked up Chakra, one-handed. "Hi, baby girl." Chakra and Eve were pals. "Probably past Dolly's bedtime, anyway," Eve added.

"True."

Dolly Sweet and the late Dante Underhill had been lovers, mid-twentieth century, a huge secret that everybody in Mystick Falls knew, even before he left her his building and his fortune.

Dolly was dying to see Dante again.

Five

I want to do my best to take care of the planet by designing with recycled and eco-friendly materials. I think we all have to start with what we know . . . I design clothing, so I figured I'd start there.
                                                    —DEBORAH LINDQUIST

❧

"I'll bet this place was beautiful in Dolly's day," Eve said examining my building, known for years by the locals as "the Shack." As of last month: "Maddie's Shack."

"Hell, I'll bet Dolly was beautiful in Dolly's day," she added, taking another sip of her coffee.

"Beauty-pageant beautiful." I'd seen her wedding pictures. "But, Eve, you should know that I thought this place was beautiful when we were kids."

She spewed a mouthful of coffee my way.

I jumped back in time to save my Prada blouse, pencil skirt, and spikes, but not my rare Lucite box bag.

"Watch it," I said. "This is a valuable collectible." I wiped it with my napkin.

"Sorry." Eve chuckled as she dabbed coffee off the

protesting Chakra. "Speaking of collectibles—not. Here comes Jaconetti."

Nick's refurbished military surplus Humvee had alerted us both to his approach before he turned the corner.

"Good thing he makes his own fuel for that guzzler," Eve said, wincing at the sound.

"The bio-diesel? Yes," I said over the roar as he drove into my parking lot and took up two parking spaces. "He makes it in his garage with used French fry oil and a couple of reagents. Imagine. Very eco-friendly."

"That's me," Nick said. "You're eco-friendly, too, lady-bug. You recycle clothes." He swooped in for a *hell-lo* kiss and communicated the added longing that went with a good-bye. A kiss, very well executed. Gentle but hungry. Respectable, yet French.

Nick and I shared a long-standing relationship built on a white-hot charge of spontaneous combustion and a mutual fear of catching fire.

I could live with that.

Eve could not. She faked a gag.

Nick pulled from the kiss and gave her his "Evie eye."

She shook a finger his way. "You get five points for fuel conservation, Boy Toy, and minus ten for noise pollution."

Nick shook his head. "Love you, too, Meyers."

I chuckled, leaned into him, and noticed, in one of my upstairs windows, Dante crossing his arms and frowning down on us.

Hah, a jealous ghost. What a spook.

A minute later, I spotted Dad's six-year-old Volvo, and behind him, Aunt Fiona in her 1963 Corvette Sting Ray. The ultrarare one with the split window. I wasn't sure what the original color might have been, but sunshine over the years had mellowed it to a warm purplish red.

I surmised that her car was one of *two* reasons why she and Dad didn't get along. One: she and my mother were witches together, which/witch Dad would rather forget and didn't know I knew. And two: Aunt Fiona owned a car that my practical (read: stuffed shirt, though you didn't hear that from me) father coveted, but would never lower his frugal, Connecticut Yankee standards to buy.

Both reasons amused me.

After quick hellos, conversation being stilted between Dad and Aunt Fee, we headed for my shop. "Nick?" I asked. "Can you help me take in these boxes?"

"What are they?" Eve wanted to know.

"Vintage—and I use the word loosely—donations from our neighbors."

Everyone grabbed a box and together we brought them in. "Put them in the first hearse stall," I said.

After we finished stowing boxes, my father indicated the interior of my shop. "So what do you think?"

No longer the storm cloud who'd growled when I told him I was quitting my well-paying, prestigious job in New York to open a vintage dress shop, he asked my opinion with pride.

"Dad, it's gorgeous."

If I hadn't been forced to work out my two weeks' notice, he might never have approved my foray into self-employment. But making him Clerk of the Works while I was gone netted me a beautiful building and a father who now respected my career move.

He rocked on his heels. "Amazing what a construction

crew forced to answer to a stubborn academic can accomplish."

Nick slapped him on the back.

"I didn't know you had it in you," Aunt Fiona said. "Good job, Harry."

Working together had equalized our relationship. Dad wasn't treating me like his ten-year-old mothering her siblings, and I wasn't feeling sorry for him.

The exercise had taught me that his aimless-widower and absentminded-professor routines appeared only when his comfort was at stake. A ploy I would swallow no longer.

Harry Cutler was as vibrant and sharp as ever. He'd proven it by acing my renovations. "Did you have a hard time getting the hearse upstairs?" I asked. "I wish I'd seen it."

My father looked toward the anomaly in my ceiling. "All I did was watch," he said, but it was amazing.

Huge, double doors were cut between the two floors. Upstairs, you could grab iron rings to haul each half door back and look down on the first floor.

The block and tackle hanging from the ceiling above the double doors were used to haul things, like hearses, up there for storage. The construction crew had done exactly that before beginning construction on the lower level.

As a result of the architectural anomaly, I'd given up on the idea of having a finished ceiling down here and had the exposed boards cleaned, stained, and finished.

I liked the look.

"That hearse is incredible," my father mused. "The workmanship is impeccable."

"It's collectible," I said, tongue-in-cheek. "I'll give you a great deal."

Dad about choked, but when he recovered, he wore a familiar expression. "From the day you're born till you ride the hearse, ain't nothin' so bad it couldn't get worse. Author unknown."

"A quote for every occasion," I said. "I shouldn't be surprised that you have one for a hearse, as well."

Eve hooked an arm through mine and dragged me toward the stairs. "So let's go crack open the secret room, already."

"Scrap," I said. "We may need a flashlight or nine. There's no electricity up there, now that the circuits are split."

Nick snapped his fingers. "I'll be right back."

He returned with a good-sized box and set it on the floor by the stairs. "These are NiCad Fluorescent Area Lights, but I've used them, so I don't know how much battery time they have left. Here's where you switch them on. I hope they help." He checked his watch and kissed me. "Gotta go, ladybug. Got a plane to catch."

"Stay safe," I said, nervous as always when he and my brother, Alex, his partner, went off on an FBI assignment.

My father nodded. "Tell my son to take care, too. Alex and I talked on the phone this afternoon, but tell him, again, will you, Nick?"

"Yes, sir," Nick said, shaking my father's hand.

Scary when you didn't know what kind of danger they were getting into. Nick kissed me once more outside, a ravenous "I'll miss you like hell" kiss.

I really didn't want to let him go—we were like ships passing in the night—but I didn't have a choice. "Will you be able to call this time?" I asked.

"I will if I can. I don't know yet where we're going."

"And if you did, you wouldn't tell me."

He tapped my nose, traced my lips, and walked away.

I stood in the doorway until his Humvee disappeared, then I turned to the people I loved, standing at the bottom of the stairs, watching me with concern.

"I'm fine," I said. "Alex and Nick will be, too. Let's go open the secret room."

Six

For me, elegance is not to pass unnoticed but to get to the
very soul of what one is.   —CHRISTIAN LACROIX

❧

My father, carrying the box of NiCads, indicated that we
ladies should precede him up the stairs.

"Ever the gentleman, Harry," Fiona said, going first.
She liked getting her kicks by baiting my father with slip-
stitched compliments that he could take either way.

The day he started giving her as good as he got would
be the day he saw Aunt Fiona for the first time.

"Dolly thinks I'll like what I find," I said to break the silence as I reached the second floor. "She just can't remember
what it is."

Everyone there had already seen the hearse, the row of
vintage caskets, and the ancient oval metal tub—once
skirted and filled with ice to set beneath caskets at home
wakes—so no one was skeeved by the knowledge of their
presence in the shadowy darkness.

Eve rubbed her hands together. "Open the damned doors."

"Wait," my father said, putting the box of lights on the floor. "First we need to *see* the damned doors. He stood the giant flashlight-type thingies around the room, with two by the secret doors, switching them on as he went, turning the room to near daylight.

"Figures," Eve said, hands on her hips. "Leave it to Jaconetti to carry around a box of florescent phallic symbols. I'm surprised they don't flash his name."

"Eve!" Aunt Fiona gasped, though she was grinning.

One of the lights went out immediately.

"Any batteries in that box, Dad?"

"Afraid not." My father frowned. "What the devil?" He stared aghast at the storage room entry and indicated a free-hanging splinter the size of his arm. "These doors didn't look like this earlier."

"What time earlier?" I asked.

"I left with the construction crew around seven thirty."

"And I got here a little after eight, so the intruder didn't waste any time."

Eve and I glanced at each other. Fiona caught the glance. My dad didn't.

"Somebody must have broken in," I said.

Aunt Fiona stared into my eyes. "Madeira? You don't sound too surprised."

Scrap. "Okay, somebody did break in. But he's gone now, so it's all good."

"He?" my father asked.

I huffed. "Judging by the sound of him thumping down the stairs? Yes, it was probably a man." A half-truth. "Someone with a heavy and robust build. I didn't see him. It was too dark."

"Madeira!" my father and Fiona snapped, in sync for once.

Eve chuckled. "Our Miss Fix-It chased him away by herself."

I picked up my baby cat and the butterflies in my middle stopped fluttering. "Chakra helped."

My father frowned. "Was the outside door open when you got here, because I locked it when I left."

"Locked. I had to use my key."

Given Dad and Aunt Fiona's black looks, it was a good thing I was too old for a spanking. They made me recap every detail.

By the time I finished, another of Nick's lights went out while my Dad walked the perimeter of the room, hands fisted. "Here," he called from the corner behind the caskets.

"What'd'ya know?" I said, coming up behind him. "An open window. Is there a ladder out there?"

"No," my dad said. "He was a resourceful burglar. Probably the same one the night watchman heard. There are two huge wooden wire reels below the window, stacked, one atop the other."

Dad turned back to me. "You need to be proactive, Madeira. Get an alarm system. Now."

"I was proactive. I chased him away. But yes, I agree on the alarm system. I should have had it done during the construction, but this is Mystic, after all. I didn't think it needed to top my list. I was wrong."

"Can you afford the expense of an alarm system right now?" Aunt Fiona asked.

I sighed. "I expected to bleed money for a while. I'm okay, and I love this place. I really do." Ghost, burglar, lack of second-floor lights, and all. "Now can we open the storage room?"

"You need new locks on these windows, too," my father said, checking them all. "Are you sure you don't need an investor?"

"No. Thank you, Dad. Just make a note. Window locks, an alarm system, and reel removal."

He pulled out his trusty notebook and started his list. He enjoyed this partnership, of sorts, as much as I did. I'd accepted his presence and his expertise, yes, but I would *not* accept his money.

"Time for the grand opening," I said. "We should have brought trumpets." I attempted to insert the key that Dolly said would fit the lock. "Scrap! My key doesn't work!"

Another NiCad fluorescent went out.

"Mad, didn't you get a *new* front door?" Eve asked. "Which key are you using?"

I sighed. Either my intruder upset me more than I thought, or my lack of sleep was catching up with me. "I'm using the new one, of course, also known as *the wrong one*."

"What did you do with the original, Madeira?"

My father's tone made me feel like a child. "I gave it to *you*."

Aunt Fiona smothered a chuckle.

Dad shot her a look as he unhooked a hefty key ring from the key safe on his belt and began flipping through, somehow managing to identify most of them.

I held up a fluorescent to shed light on his quest as he tried several before one finally turned in the lock.

"Woo-hoo!" Eve's shout echoed in the cavernous room.

"Don't take that key from the lock," I said, grabbing a bottle of Red Passion nail polish, industrial strength, from my purse. With the brush, I dabbed a spot on the faded tab that once identified the key. "Now we'll always be able to find it."

My father cleared his throat at my efficiency after his scold. "I'll have a copy made for you tomorrow."

"Thanks, Dad."

Dante appeared, probably because he was curious about the polish.

When Aunt Fee grinned his way, he winked at her, and she blushed.

Once the nail polish dried, I let the key disappear into my father's stash. God knew, nothing could be safer.

"Madeira," my father said, stepping away from the doors. "Care to do the honors?"

I tried pushing, until Dante told me to pull. The squeal level of the doors scraping the floor reminded me of fingernails across a chalkboard, or harbingers of doom. I shivered as Eve pulled the other half door in the opposite direction.

When they finally stood open, they revealed a darker pit than any I'd seen tonight.

The last of Nick's fluorescents died as we stood there, unable to see our hands before us.

"Faulty phallic symbols," Eve said into the darkness. "What does that signify?"

Fiona giggled and Dante chuckled.

"Madeira," Dante said. "The switch is a flat-topped, round button to the right of the doors."

"Got it." Some minutes after I pressed the button, a pair of long old-fashioned fluorescent bulbs clickety-click-clicked, teasing us with the possibility of light, as they repeatedly glowed and dimmed, while emitting a weird smell.

"That fixture needs a new ballast," my father said.

I was sure the fluorescent tubes would need replacing before we could see the storage room properly, but the fixture finally clicked one last time and shed a modicum of light, however uneven and dim. "Dad, will you add fluorescent bulbs to our list?"

He raised his notebook in a "will do" salute.

At first glance, the room might be someone's attic—cluttered, musty, and dusty. Lots to see in the disorderly, pack-rat stash, including the additional hearse that Dolly hinted was here. But I could focus on only one thing: a set of perfectly aligned white enamel body drawers, four by four along the back wall.

"We brought those up for storage," Dante said beside me. "This wasn't the embalming room."

"Do I want to know where it was?" I replied without thinking.

"No, you don't," Aunt Fiona said, a warning in her look.

"Downstairs," Dante said. "In the basement."

My head came up. "I forgot about the basement." The construction foreman said it existed but was inaccessible, and since my funds were limited, I'd told them to stick to the main floor.

"Madeira?" my father asked. "Are you talking to yourself?"

Great, I was so spooked by the body drawers, I'd answered a ghost that only Fiona and I could see and hear. I'd have to get better at ignoring Dante. "Yes and no, Dad. I just realized that the morgue and embalming room must have been in the basement."

"You're right," Dante added. "But you can only get to the basement via the casket lift in this room, behind the debris toward the front. It's sealed on the main floor just below, in your dressing room."

I wanted to tell Dante that he could have warned me, but I guess ghosts lose their people skills after a while. At some point, I'd build a stairway to my basement, beneath the stairs that led up here. After I did, I could enlarge this room and my dressing room . . . and find out what lurked below. Shiver.

Aunt Fiona nudged my chin up with a finger and looked into my eyes. "You *knew* the building's history, dear, when you accepted Dolly's terms. You shouldn't let a little thing like body drawers throw you. You're thrilled to have the place, remember? And you're in it for the long haul."

She was right, but I had no chance to acknowledge it because a sluice of ice water ran up my spine, as if someone had stabbed me in the back with an icicle. The sensation brought a shivery, stomach-churning knowledge that had nothing to do with body drawers or embalming rooms and everything to do with—I whipped around to look behind me.

Three side windows, with shared frames between them, overlooked West Main Street and the playhouse beyond. In this instance, a nightmare.

The sight tripped my heart and parched my throat.

"The playhouse is on fire!"

Seven

I want to create theater, clothes are theater.
—JEAN PAUL GAULTIER

❧

"A small fire, thank God," my dad said, after a second of visual confirmation. "Let's try to keep it that way." He took the stairs as fast as my intruder had.

"I didn't know Harry could move that fast," Fiona said as she took out her cell phone. "911," she explained before she spoke to a dispatcher and gave the address.

I caught her arm to stop her as she headed for the stairs. "Smoke with your asthma? You'll end up in the hospital, Aunt Fee. Wait here."

"Thank you, sweetie. You're right." She slipped her phone back into the colorful Louis Vuitton bag I'd given her.

"Sampson might still be at the playhouse," I said as Eve and I went downstairs. "His lights were on earlier."

Broderick Sampson had been baiting the locals worse than usual, lately, with his plan to sell to a department-store

36

chain and, as many had said, "ruin the quaint charm of historic downtown Mystic."

We cleared Vintage Magic in time to see my father reach the playhouse, where the fire looked worse. "Wooly knobby knits, if the fire doesn't get him, smoke inhalation will! Dad, don't go in!" I shouted, but it was too late. If he heard my warning, he ignored it.

Eve and I crossed the street, looked up at the death trap's top floor, bright with fire, and followed my father in, if only to get him the Hermès out.

Right away, I heard him shouting for Mr. Sampson, and I followed the sound upstairs, while Eve started searching the main floor.

"Madeira," my father shouted when he saw me, "I have everything under control. Get out of here." One set of mile-high drapes burned while Dad was pulling down a set that wasn't. "Go see if you can find Mr. Sampson on the main floor," he shouted over the fire's roar.

"Eve's looking there. I'll check the basement."

"Be careful!" we both shouted as I sprinted down the stairs to the faint scream of fire trucks in the distance. I ran through the basement maze calling Sampson's name and passed a rack of prized vintage costumes. I checked the rest of the basement, but found no sign of Sampson. Then I took a half minute to throw the costumes into laundry carts, roll them out the door, and awkwardly drag them one by one, up the half dozen or so steps that led to the sidewalk.

I left them in the ATM lobby of the bank next door, and by the time I got back, red lights swirled around me, men shouted, the moment surreal and ghastly. Gathering my wits, I ran back to the playhouse and followed the sound of raised voices.

When I reached them, I stopped dead.

My heart hammered as I wiped my sweaty palms against each other and examined the faces around me: Dad, Eve, with tears in her eyes, Detective Werner, my nemesis, and half a dozen sooty firemen.

Tunney, the meat cutter, had blood on his apron and a meat cleaver in his hand, as usual.

Even when I was a kid and Tunney used to get down on all fours and pretend to be my pony, he'd worn a bloody apron. But he'd never looked this scared.

I forced myself to follow everyone's gaze to the floor and worked hard to resist retreat.

Broderick Sampson looked like he was sleeping.

I shuddered. He couldn't be— I gazed at my father seeking hope. "He'll be okay, right? Dad?"

"In on this one, too, Ms. Cutler," Detective Werner said. "And only home, what? Two hours?"

This one what? I retreated inside myself where it was safe.

"Looks like foul play," Werner said. "We don't know yet if anything is missing."

My father hugged my shoulder. "Mr. Sampson's gone, honey."

My stomach lurched. "Not murder. Not again."

Tunney looked at his cleaver, stood, opened his hand with effort, as if it had stiffened into a death grip, and he let the knife clatter to the floor.

"Was Sampson stabbed?" I asked, staring at the cleaver with disbelief. "He doesn't look injured at all."

I'd heard that even Tunney, our beloved butcher, had been loud and angry at the town meetings, but he didn't have a violent bone in his body. He made kids flowers from butcher paper, for pity's sake.

He wouldn't harm a bird . . . except that he did.

Tunney Lague was a big old teddy bear . . . who chopped animals into edible pieces for a living.

Eight

Little black dresses first began to appear around 1918-1920 and I have the feeling they came out of the mourning look of World War I.
　　　　　　　　　　　　　　　　　　　—KARL LAGERFELD

❧

Broderick Sampson lived around the corner from us in Mystick Falls, a widower rattling around in a big old place alone, until his younger sister showed up to keep house for him. Gossip is that Sampson and his sister didn't get along and that she showed after the planned sale of his playhouse to a world-class department-store conglomerate made the headlines.

Sampson hadn't grown up in Mystick Falls, so no one knew the sister, but he'd been here long enough for every-one to know and dislike him. He was a neighbor, but not neighborly, a hermit who barely spoke to anyone, turned off his lights on Halloween, and never bought a Girl Scout Cookie. Which didn't mean that he deserved to die.

"Did anyone hear or see anything?" Werner asked.

"I heard arguing coming from here when I got home a little after eight," I said.

"He was always arguing with somebody," Werner said, and everyone nodded.

"Detective," Eve said, "I saw someone leave here when I was driving over to meet Maddie. It was dark, though. It wasn't anybody I recognized."

"Could you tell if it was a man or a woman?" Werner asked, ready to make a note of Eve's answer.

"If I had to guess, I'd say a woman, because of the way she moved, but I couldn't swear to it. Dark pants, dark hat."

My mental suspect list started with Sampson's fellow shop owners, most angrier and more formidable than Tunney.

My father kept me up-to-date on local happenings and he'd said that many of the shop owners made veiled threats at the last Mystick Falls town meeting, while Councilman McDowell and the trustees looked fit to kill.

"Blunt force trauma to the head is my guess," a paramedic confirmed, though I didn't remember when they'd arrived.

Detective Lytton Werner took a pair of handcuffs from his back pocket.

"What?" I snapped. "You think Tunney held the knife by the blade to hit Sampson on the back of the head with the handle? He would have cut his hand if he did." I raised Tunney's hands, palm side up. "There. No fresh cuts."

Werner showed me the cuffs. "Madeira, do you mind? I have a job to do."

I reluctantly released Tunney's hands, but not before I squeezed them to show my support.

The detective brought one of Tunney's arms behind his back. "We'll let forensics find the answers."

"Tunney's no killer," I snapped.

"And what about the woman Oscar's seen coming and going from here?" Eve asked.

Oscar, from the hardware store, was second only to Tunney when it came to keeping tabs on his neighbors.

"Gossip," Werner said. "Useless."

"And what about the fire?" I added. "Shouldn't we get out of here?"

"Fire's out, Mad," Johnny Shields, firefighter, said. "Your dad put it out."

"Dad, are you okay? You didn't burn yourself, did you?"

"I'm fine, Madeira. I smothered the burning curtains with the other pair. You saw. It looked worse from across the street. The fire was confined to the ballroom."

"I'm glad." The place might have looked like a ballroom sixty years ago, but now it was just a big *old* empty space with a fancy tin ceiling and peeling wall murals.

Werner got down to business and cuffed Tunney while one of the uniformed officers bagged the meat cleaver.

Prime suspects didn't always get cuffed, I knew from my sister's experience, but Werner wouldn't use cuffs without just cause.

Though I knew I should keep my mouth shut, frustration got the best of me. "Tunney did not do this, Lytton, and you know it."

"I can't discuss a case, Madeira," Werner said. "Which you know very well."

"I'm outta here," I said. "The smoke is killing me." It was about as smoky as an ashtray full of ciggy butts, but that wasn't the point.

"You're a witness, Cutler," Werner called after me. "Again, dammit."

"I'm not any happier about it than you are, Lytton." By his own admission, Lytton Werner, also known as the Wiener, hadn't forgiven me for the nickname that still dogged him. Probably never would.

"You're *all* witnesses," he added. "I'll be in touch. You know the drill." Warning laced the detective's words.

"Tunney." I touched the meat cutter's arm before I left. "I know you didn't do it. Take care of yourself."

"Maddie," Tunney said. "I saw the fire and came running like you and your father did. Get me out of this, will you? Solve this case like you did your sister's."

"I didn't solve Sherry's case," I said, backing up, not daring to look at Werner. "Detective Werner did."

Tunney shook his head. "That's not what I heard."

"Then the Mystick Falls Information Network is as unreliable as ever," I said. Wooly knobby knits, I knew without looking that Lytton must be shooting daggers my way. Daggers? Oy. *Bad* pun. *Bad Madeira.*

"Tunney," I said. "You know town gossip. It's ruthless and useless. Besides, the case isn't mine. It's a police matter. I can't help you."

I had fallen into my first sleuthing experience when my sister Sherry, a bride-to-be, became the prime suspect in the murder of the woman trying to steal her fiancé. In my determination to set Sherry free, ghosts and skeletons fell, literally, out of closets everywhere and I didn't much like it.

Frankly, if I started digging in the dirt, again, I was afraid of what I'd discover about the deceased, the suspects, about the murderer, and most especially about myself.

A uniformed officer escorted Tunney to a squad car,

while my dear friend looked back at me, still silently begging for my help.

I shook my head in denial. "Get a good lawyer," I called after him. Poor Tunney.

Poor Sampson!

"Speaking of lawyers," Eve said, "Fiona must be wondering what's taking us so long."

"Tunney didn't do it," I told Eve as she followed me to the bank. "Are you all right?" I asked her.

"I'm shaking in my Docs," she said. "Queasy, too."

"I can imagine. I was a wreck after I found *my* first dead body."

"Your *first*? Are you planning to find more?"

"We should both bite our tongues." I shoved a cart her way.

She caught it and tilted her head. "You saved the *costumes*?"

I was pleased to have put a hint of amusement in her eyes.

"Thanks," she said. "I needed a reason to smile." Except that she wasn't smiling, quite.

Together, we pushed the carts across the street toward my shop. "I figure that I saved a slice of history. I also thought that Mr. Sampson would appreciate having the costumes, even if he lost the building."

"He'll never know," Eve said.

"Whoever inherits the playhouse might. His sister, I guess."

"He has a child somewhere," my father said as he came up behind us. "His wife gave birth after she left him. I'm not sure Sampson ever knew whether it was a boy or a girl. If he kept in touch, he wasn't saying."

"Of course he wasn't saying; he didn't say much, did he, unless he was arguing. He was *so* closemouthed that I thought he was a widower."

"The Sweets tried to set him up with a date once," my father said, "and Sampson confessed that once divorced was enough."

"I'm surprised the Sweets got that close."

"Please," Eve said. "Dolly and Ethel Sweet could sweet-talk a stump. Pun intended."

"Whoever is Sampson's heir," my father added, "if he or she doesn't want the costumes, they might sell them to *you*."

"Flirty draped silk! I didn't save them for myself. I respect vintage clothing. So sue me. If they come up for sale, I'll offer a fair price."

"Hey," Eve said. "Maybe Sampson's heir won't sell the playhouse to the chain store conglomerate and spoil the flavor of the historic district."

"I dearly hope that wasn't the point," my father said soberly.

That *would* be a good motive, I thought, though there could be others. The heir could have done it for the inheritance. Nah, too cliché. Who'd be so obvious?

Back at Vintage Magic, I wondered about Fiona when the second floor appeared so eerily quiet.

"Here," Dante said. "I've been talking to her to calm her down and keep her from jumping from her skin."

Neither my father nor Eve saw or heard our resident ghost, of course, but the minute he spoke, a casket in the darkest corner of the room erupted with sound and movement.

Eve screamed and backed up until she hit the stair wall.

I headed Dante's way and found Aunt Fiona a bit tied

up, literally, inside that noisy casket, her arms and legs bound with clothesline, duct tape over her mouth, a dingy T-shirt blindfold, and Chakra licking her cheek.

I put Chakra on the floor and removed the blindfold. "Aunt Fiona," I said, looking into her panicky eyes and stroking her brow. "I think we should get your hands free first so that you can take the duct tape off your mouth yourself. I'm afraid to tear the skin."

Aunt Fiona nodded, sought Dante with her gaze, and gave him a grateful look.

He tipped his hat. "You're welcome."

My father bent over the casket. "What did you do, Fee, piss off a ghost?"

Nine

You know, one had as good be out of the world, as out of
fashion.
                                    —COLLEY CIBBER

If my father hadn't jumped out of Fiona's way so fast, she
would have kicked him in the gut for that remark, or lower,
with both feet.

"Dad!" I snapped. "I know you and Aunt Fee like to
bait each other, but that was a rotten thing to say."

"Bound or not," he said, "Fiona Sullivan packs a wal-
lop."

Had I caught a touch of respect in his tone?

Dad tried to help us untie her but Aunt Fiona wouldn't
let him near her.

"My deepest apologies, Fiona," he said, standing back.
"That was unforgivable of me."

She growled beneath the duct tape and indicated, with
snapping, angry eyes, that he would be better off if she
stayed tied up.

"Are you all right, Eve?" I asked as she paced beside the casket.

She shook her head, looking a bit green. I'd never known Eve to be out of words.

"You're sick over finding Sampson, aren't you?"

She gave a half nod, her eyes bright.

I hugged her. "Stick around and we'll talk, 'kay? Been there. Done that. Hated it."

She blotted her eyes with the back of a hand, pulled herself together, and tried to help us.

"Poor Aunt Fiona," I said, tugging on the tightly knotted clothesline. Judging by the scuff marks on the casket lid, it looked like she might have been closed inside for a while, but she fought a good fight.

Eve gasped, shook her head, and whipped out a pocket-knife. "Sorry, I was distracted." Having the rope cut helped move things along.

Fiona sat up as quickly as possible, even before her legs were free.

I winced when she began to remove the tape, though she removed it slowly and only ended up with a split lip. I'd feared it would be much worse. "Dad, you have to lift her out."

"First, she has to promise not to knee me."

Fiona touched her jaw, exercised it, and raised her brow. "No promises."

Dad shook his head and bent over to lift her out anyway, brave man.

From the corner of my eye, I caught a stealthy movement in the storage room. "Stop!" I shouted and ran, in time to find an intruder straddling a window with a sack in his hand.

He threw the sack out the window.

"Vinney!" Eve yelled from behind me. "Don't. You'll hurt yourself," but he dropped from sight.

Eve and I ran to the window and looked down, but that fast, he'd disappeared. "Are you sure that was Vinney?" I asked. "Your Vinney?"

"Yes. No. I don't know."

"Vinney or not, I wonder if he could have been the same guy who broke in earlier?"

"It's possible," Eve said.

Probable, I thought, feeling personally bruised. My building and the vision I had of its future had been violated. I turned to take in the room, looking for answers, for a reason that Vinney, or anyone, would do such a thing.

What had he put in the sack? Had he taken something valuable? Whatever it was, it would have shattered on impact, unless it was soft and pliable. If you wanted something badly enough to steal it, I couldn't imagine that you'd want to break it.

"Damn," I said. "The guy wouldn't have gotten in, if not for the fire.

Eve shook her head. "Vinney might steal something, but I don't think he'd shut someone in a casket." She rubbed her arms and raised her chin. "Besides, I'm not sure it *was* Vinney."

Was she protesting too much? I wanted to share my theory with my father, but he and Fiona were arguing, years of animosity stiffening their stances, though they kept their voices low. This was the longest conversation they'd had since my mother died. And as long as Aunt Fiona was in fighting mode, she wasn't freaking over being shut in a casket.

Who knew, they just might clear the air between them.

"I'm probably just overthinking the situation," I told Eve. "Call it panic."

Bottom lip between her teeth, she gave me an imperceptible nod.

I picked up my cat, sighed, and rubbed my chin against her fur. "I'd like to know what the guy took, though." I looked around the storage room and noticed for the first time the glass-fronted top of a cabinet with stainless-steel instruments lined up on its glass shelves. Embalming instruments? I shuddered. Oy.

Dante appeared beside me, and Chakra howled my name, though perhaps not as loud as she had the first time she saw him. I opened the single cabinet drawer, between the top and base of the cabinet, and shuffled through the papers inside.

"Good," Dante said. "You need to go through them. There's an important packet in there for Dolly."

I sorted through until he pointed to Dolly's. I took the large envelope and put it in my purse. Then I rummaged through a closet full of vintage clothes, dresses, suits, tuxedos, and big black ostrich feathers. "Huh?"

"To dress the dead and outfit the undertakers," Dante said. "The black plumes were for the horses pulling the hearse."

I nodded. Of course; I'd seen pictures. Elsewhere in the room, I found trunks, urns, vases, spittoons, junk, beautiful and ugly, and some valuable antiques, too many things to identify. But I kept turning back to the body drawers. At fifth, or tenth, glance, I noticed a *new* imperfection in their alignment.

"Eve, the bottom right body drawer is crooked, and

there's something bright sticking out the side that wasn't there before the fire."

"You're right," she said. "The drawers were even before. Should we call the police now?"

"The Wiener didn't exactly welcome our presence across the street a little while ago. And if we call, we'll have to spill about the earlier break-in."

"Right."

Besides, I wanted to talk to Dante first. He must have seen what happened in here while we were gone, and he might know who did it. But I couldn't talk to him until he and I were alone.

I held Chakra closer and began to tremble against a chill that had nothing to do with the temperature. "Why would someone rob a *body* drawer?"

Ten

❧

Clear as day, or should I say, clear as night, I saw my re-curring dream. Me as a toddler, in my mother's arms, with Aunt Fiona by the river, dancing beneath the light of a full moon. Something, and I didn't know what, was about to turn my life in another direction.

As if tonight hadn't already been lively enough.

When my mother shivered for no reason, she used to say that someone had just walked over her grave, and for the first time, I understood what she meant.

Eve went to the body drawer, tugged on the silver han-dle, and broke it right off. "Drawer's jammed."

I scoffed. "No kidding."

She pulled on the front panel and I tried to help, but the drawer wouldn't budge.

I straightened, stepped away, and searched the room. "We need something to pry it open."

When nothing seemed appropriate, I knelt to see what was sticking out the side. "It's fabric, two kinds sewn together that I can see. Looks like it's jammed in the track on this side. Our only hope is to pull the drawer toward the opposite side to knock the drawer off its tracks, which I'd like to do without tearing the fabric."

"Easier said than done," my father griped, Aunt Fiona beside him.

Either they'd fought it out or stopped trying. Their poker faces revealed nothing. Nevertheless, they poised themselves beside Eve and grabbed the drawer to pull to the right.

"On three," I said. "I've got the fabric, and as soon as you give me room on this side, I'm going to try and slide it from the track and into the drawer."

"We understand," my father said.

I nodded. "One, two . . . three!"

I freed a bit of the fabric and shoved it in the drawer before the left side bounced back.

I yelped when the drawer caught my hand and took a chunk of skin with it.

Fiona checked my wound. "Mad. Are you okay?"

"Nothing an antibiotic cream won't fix. Warn me next time."

"That was my fault," my father said.

Fiona wrapped her scarf around my hand. "It was both of us."

Dad looked dumbfounded. He didn't know how to share blame, or anything else, with Fiona.

"Ready to try again?" I asked. "I think one more tug will clear the track so we can pull the drawer out."

Eve lay on her stomach on the faded old linoleum on my side, beneath my crouch, and when Dad and Fiona pulled, she helped by pushing.

I reached over her to slide the rest of the thick fabric from the track and shove it into the drawer. "Done!"

Everybody let go and Fiona and Dad fell to the floor, they'd been pulling on the drawer with so much effort.

As we watched, the drawer rolled open like a fine piece of machinery. "A quilt," I said. "That's what I suspected from the look of the fabric in the tracks."

Eve frowned. "I can't imagine why a guy would try to steal a quilt."

"I'm guessing he had what he came for in the sack," I said. "Notice that he left the quilt behind. What could you put in a sack that had been wrapped in a quilt?"

Aunt Fiona shrugged. "A million things."

The quilt was made of flannel, cotton sateen, gingham, duck, linen, some squares printed in chintz and calico, some in plain but faded primary colors. One of the squares had a button in a buttonhole. One, a pocket. Another, a piece of a collar. Some of the solid squares had been embroidered. Others were needleworked with nursery rhymes.

"I suspect that this was made from women's clothes, because of the colors and designs. The clothes belonged to a woman who didn't have wealth but joy of spirit. I can tell because the colors are so vibrant." The quilt gave up some of its secrets and I hadn't unfolded it yet. "Someone with time on her hands made it with love."

"I'm impressed by what you're getting just from looking at it," Aunt Fiona said.

"You must remember when people used to make quilts from old clothes," I said. "Waste not, want not? The clothes these squares came from must be about forty-five to fifty years old, but the quilt is closer to thirty years old."

"How can you tell?" Eve asked.

"Oh, the thread. It's polyester, or the squares would be falling away from each other."

"It's been here for about twenty-eight years," Dante said, "give or take a year."

Aunt Fiona and I exchanged glances.

"It's made of *vintage* clothes," I stressed, eyeing Aunt Fiona, because I was afraid to touch it and get a psychometric vibe/reading/vision—or whatever you wanted to call my gift of seeing the past in some of the vintage clothes I touched. Whatever its name, it was a psychic surprise from the universe, still too new for me to fully understand. Or take chances with.

Eve and Fiona knew about my gift, but my dad didn't. And I did *not* want to zone out in front of him.

"Sweetie," Aunt Fiona said, "why don't I take it out for you so you can look at the whole thing?" But when she started to move it, I heard a click.

"What?" my father said, stopping her. "Did we really hurt your hand so badly, Madeira, that you can't take it out yourself? If so, we should take you to a doctor."

"She's stressed," Fiona said. "You wouldn't understand."

"She's *my* daughter. *Not* yours."

"Oh, for goodness sakes," I snapped. "Stop arguing. Don't worry about it, Aunt Fiona. I can see it from here."

I looked more closely at the quilt edge against the drawer bottom—what I could see of it inside the drawer—to figure out what, from a quilt, could have clicked against the enamel. Buttons, maybe?

But that's not what I saw.

Nobody else was looking at it from the same angle as I was, because they were all on the opposite side of the drawer, so I shut it.

Now I *had* to see if the quilt would talk to me. "Dad, Fiona's had a hard night. Why don't you follow her home?"

My father had been caught unaware by the suggestion and said nothing.

"Aunt Fiona, if you're not up to driving, and Dad takes you home, I'll leave my rental here and take your car home, later, where it'll be safe."

"I can drive," she said. Then she wilted, almost theatrically. "No, I can't. Harry? Do you mind?"

"Of course not. Eve and Mad?" my dad asked. "Why don't you follow us? It's been a long day."

"In a while. Eve might need a stiff drink on the way home. That's how I felt after I found my first, and *last*, dead body."

Eve turned to look at me, and she knew, she *knew*, that I was up to something.

We listened for Dad and Fiona on the stairs, heard them going out the door. When a car started, I went to a front window in the big room to look out. My amusement worked like a release valve. "My dad decided to drive Fiona's car," I told Eve. "I wonder why."

But Eve wasn't about to be diverted. "What are you up to, Cutler?" she asked, following me back to the storage room. "Why did you get rid of them?"

I opened the drawer to reveal the quilt. "Don't scream," I said.

Eleven

I'm crazy, and I don't pretend to be anything else.
—CALVIN KLEIN

❧

I went to the closet and took out a pair of sturdy black feathers, and I used them to manipulate the tangled quilt until I revealed what I feared . . . bones.

Eve slapped a hand over her mouth and screamed behind it, then she slowly raised her head to face me.

"Someone," I said, "possibly Vinney, took something out of this drawer, or the drawer wouldn't have been disturbed, right?"

She nodded, hand still over her mouth. Then she sobered, lowered her hand, and released her breath. "Vinney might have kicked the drawer in frustration."

"And left the quilt stuck in the track where it wasn't before?" I pulled my gaze from the grisly sight, enough bones strung together to form the better part of a foot. "They might not be human."

Eve's shoulders relaxed. "Old Underhill might have had a dog that dragged the bones home."

"No dog," Dante said. "I'm allergic."

"He's allergic," I repeated.

"What?" Eve said. "Who?"

I gave her a bland look. "What?"

"How did you know that?"

"Did Vinney know that there wouldn't be a night watchman here tonight?"

Eve's shoulders went back. "What?"

"When was the last time you saw him?"

"Last night."

I sat back on my heels and Chakra crawled into my lap. "Did Vinney know what time I was getting home today?"

"I might have mentioned being glad that you were coming home for good."

"Did you mention meeting me here at *nine*?"

"I don't know. Why?" She was getting defensive and I didn't blame her.

"If he knew what time I was planning to be here, he might have been watching for the construction crew to leave, and when they did, he figured he had a one-hour window of opportunity."

"Vinney and I did talk, Madeira. But I don't remember precisely what I said. Whatever it was, it didn't feel like a state secret or anything."

"Sweetie, I just want to know. I'm not accusing you of anything. Just fitting puzzle pieces together. You've gotten me out of more scrapes than you've gotten me into, mostly."

Somehow, that struck us both as funny, and we laughed . . . hysterically . . . because that's what we were—hysterical. Eve sobered quicker than I did. "Honestly, now that we've found someone or something's remains, shouldn't we call the police, or something?"

"Yeah, I'm sure they'd be thrilled to come out this late for dog bones."

"Big bizarro dog," Eve said.

"Why don't you try calling Vinney again? See what he's up to."

She shook her head. "Wait. I remember now. I didn't need to tell him you bought the place. That nosey gossip columnist, Lolique, or whatever her name is, outed you."

"I guess I lived in New York for too long," I said with no clue as to who she meant.

"You know her," Eve said. "The councilman's flamboyant trophy wife. She likes animal prints, smokes like a chimney, and takes a perverse pleasure in revealing personal secrets in snarky ways in the newspaper?"

"We have a councilman who's married to a columnist?"

"McDowell. Wears a rug, is always in the news, though not the gossip column, and annoys the hell out of you."

"Oh," I said. "*That* councilman. The publicity hound."

"Right. His wife wrote about you buying the place and what you were going to do with it, adding an unfortunate amount of speculation as to how soon you'd fail. She's kind of a local personality."

"She sounds nice," I said, brow raised.

"Not. But the column about you opening Vintage Magic appeared about two weeks ago."

"So when did you meet Vinney for the first time?"

Eve thought about that for a minute. "I believe I might have met him the night the article came out." She sighed. "Nah. Our meeting was a coincidence. We were eating at

Mystic Pizza, at separate tables, with separate pizzas, and he smooth-talked his way over to my table. He paid for both pizzas."

"How gallant. Did he seem *immediately* interested in what was happening here? Did he know that we were friends?"

Eve sighed and sat back on her heels. "Yes. He was interested, said he had a thing for local history, and could I take him to see the place? I mean we could see it out the window from across the street as clear as day. But how *did* he know that I knew you well enough to *show* him the place, the rat? I'm usually smarter than to fall for a line."

"You were smitten. Forgive yourself. I do. He probably knew we were friends from the Mystick Falls gossip mill. Tunney or Oscar from the hardware store probably told him."

Eve huffed. "I'm going right over to Vinney's to give him a piece of my mind."

Her destination caught me off guard. "That's not a bad idea, but you're not going without me. First, however, since the quilt is made of vintage clothes, I'd like to take a minute to see if I can get any vibes like I did when I was working on Sherry's vintage wedding gown. However, I don't want to touch it any more than I have to, because I suspect that the rest of Big Foot here was wrapped in it. Under no circumstances do I want to see what the other side of it looks like, nor do I want to touch it."

"Eeeyeww."

When I nudged the quilt from the drawer to the floor with the feathers, the connected bones jiggled, so Chakra tackled them and batted them off the quilt quicker than I could stop her, not that I wanted to touch them. Didn't matter; she sent the foot—if that's what it was—flying beneath the body drawers.

"Out of sight, out of panic?" I suggested.

Eve scoffed and wiped her brow with the back of a hand. "You wish."

Chakra, who I was beginning to think understood my needs better than I did, returned to my lap.

"Thanks, sweetie cat. That was really skeeving me out."

"I can't believe you're going to touch that quilt," Eve said. "At least I'll know enough not to go bonkers when your mind disappears and your body stays behind. Mad? Could any of this be construed as tampering with evidence? Like at a crime scene?"

"What crime?" I asked, manipulating the quilt with the feathers to find the pocket. "Think animal foot."

"What kind of animal? And don't say a dog."

"A dinosaur or a bear?"

"Okay, I get your drift and I'm trying to work with it."

"Good. Let me try to read the quilt, then we'll go see Vinney, and after that, I'll call the police."

"You will?"

"Tomorrow at the latest."

"Madeira," she said, sounding very much like my conscience.

A scold, I didn't need. "Shh. I'm concentrating."

I slipped my hand into a pocket on one of the quilt squares, closed my eyes, got nauseous and dizzy, and found myself staring at an old wishing well made of round stones. I did not want to look inside the well, but I went closer, despite myself, and started to peek over the edge, when the air turned to ice.

"She's going to faint," Dante whispered.

I opened my eyes. "Eve!" I caught her before she fell.

Her eyes opened, and as I cradled her, Chakra licked her hand. Slowly, Eve's color returned. "I'm sorry," she said, sitting up. "But you didn't talk the last time you zoned in front of me."

"I talked? What did I say?"

"You wailed a soft and eerie 'Isobel' *twice*. What did you see?"

"An old wishing well."

"That's all?" Eve fanned her face. "That doesn't sound too frightening."

That's why I'd described it that way. She'd found a dead body. She'd had enough trauma for one night.

"Where did Isobel come into the picture then?" Eve asked.

I shrugged and hugged Chakra. "What say we go home and wait until tomorrow to visit Vinney? Better still, we go to the Sweets. I found something with Dolly's name on it earlier."

"Vinney probably won't be at home tonight. He works the late shift sometimes."

"Doing what?"

Eve tilted her head. "I never got that quite straight."

He's a third-shift burglar, I thought. "If he's not there," I said, "I guess it wouldn't be too smart to break in and look around, see if we can find a bag of something suspicious or . . . bony?" I looked straight at her. "Unless you have a key?"

Her color returned in spades, as did her smile. "I have a key."

Twelve

It always depends on how it's done—it mustn't be overtly
exhibitionist.
                                              —GIORGIO ARMANI

❧

We took my rental to visit Eve's skunk du jour so no one
could ID the car. Well, maybe we weren't exactly planning
to *visit* him. If he wasn't there, we'd search the place, scope
it out, or whatever the universe deemed appropriate.

How's that for justification?

We had to pass by the Sweets' house on the way, and
their lights were on. I had that packet for Dolly, and I was
pretty sure that if anyone had information that might help
me free Tunney of suspicion, it would be the Sweets.

Dolly once told me that they rarely slept anymore, except
for catnaps during the day, so with my usual quick thinking,
I pulled into their driveway on two wheels. "Do you want to
come in with me?" I asked Eve. "I'll only be a minute."

"No, thanks, Mad. It's been a draining night. I'll just
close my eyes for a few."

"Good. Rest."

The front light had gone on and now both Sweets were standing at the screen door waiting. "Madeira? Is that you?" Ethel asked. "Is something wrong, dear, that you're here so late?"

Dolly, the older at a hundred and three, was being held up by her daughter-in-law, Ethel, the younger at eighty-plus.

"Can we talk?" I asked, opening the door.

Ethel smiled. "Of course, cupcake."

I grabbed their arms and insinuated myself between them, where the scent of rose water fought with that of baby powder. I sneezed as I walked them to the sofa and sat them down.

Dolly had deeded me the Underhill building with Ethel's approval. Neither of them wanted to pay taxes on it any longer, so that was my price. I'd paid this year's taxes, which were, of course, for last year, but that didn't matter. It had been an awesome deal all around. They practically gave me the place.

"I have something for Dolly," I said. "And I have a couple of questions for both of you." I pulled out the envelope from my storage room cabinet that Dante indicated as Dolly's. "I found this in my storage room, Dolly," I said handing it to her. "It has your name on it."

Dolly's hand shook as she fumbled with it then she handed it to me to open.

After I did, she pulled out a card. "Oh!" she said. "Oh, I've never been so pleased."

Ethel took the card from her mother-in-law's hand as if it was her due. "A bronze casket and a cemetery plot? Beside your old lover? Are you out of your mind? You know the gossips around here."

Dolly cackled. "I won't be here to care."

"So you're happy about this, Mama? You don't want to be laid to rest beside your husband?"

"Your Edward's father was an idiot, Ethel. I'd prefer to spend eternity beside Dante. Consider it my last wish."

"Oh, please, you've had so many last wishes since you turned a hundred, I'm keeping a journal collection for your eulogy."

I chuckled, despite myself.

Dolly pulled me down to the sofa beside her and kissed my cheek. "Tell him I said yes."

"Mama, are you losing it?"

"You can tell him yourself whenever you want," I said.

"I could," Dolly said, "though I'd hate for him to see me this way."

Ethel made a weak protest, since we weren't making any sense, but I winked at her, so she stopped.

"What he'd see," I said, "is the girl he fell in love with."

Dolly giggled, the blushing centenarian, and Ethel rolled her eyes. "You said you had a question for us, cupcake?"

"A question and a request."

"Anything you want," Dolly said, hugging that envelope to her heart.

I hated to dim her joy but I needed answers. "Did you hear what happened tonight at the playhouse?"

"Of course we did. It's a shame about Tunney."

"And Sampson," I added.

"Sampson never did fit in here," Dolly said. "Transplants rarely do. He only lived here for thirty-three years."

Ethel nodded. "Grouchy, inhospitable man."

"Could Tunney have had a motive to do Sampson in, besides Sampson's sale to the conglomerate? I mean, since the whole town was mad about that. The playhouse fire started right before Tunney closes his market, and he said that he ran over to help like we did, but he was, unfortunately, still carrying a butcher knife when the police got there."

"Was there much blood?" Dolly was one for lapping up the gore.

Ethel sniffed. "*Certain* people go to the butcher shop *after* Tunney closes."

Huh? I felt like a bloodhound who'd lost the scent. "Really? Why?"

"You might talk to Sampson's sister, Suzanne, about that."

"Ethel," Dolly said. "You shush."

"I'm only telling our little cupcake."

They'd called me that forever, probably because I ate as many as they made over the years.

Ethel failed to look contrite, though she tried. "It's true that my suggestion is rooted in gossip. So go to the source."

I looked from one of them to the other. "The source of the gossip or the object of the gossip?"

"The object," Dolly said.

Oh scrap. If Suzanne Sampson was visiting Tunney after hours, presumably not for meat-cutting lessons, and she turned out to be Sampson's heir, Werner might be able to make a case against Tunney for conspiracy at the least. I'd go to the source, all right. Both of them.

Dolly patted my arm. "Don't assume anything, cupcake."

Hmm. I forgot how long the Sweets had known me. Long enough to read my fast track mind, apparently.

"Listen, Eve's waiting for me in the car. Do me a favor? Ask around about Vinney Carnevale? See what people know about him?"

"Why?" Dolly wanted to know, getting all perked up for more gossip.

"I know nothing," I said. "But by the time I do, I'm guessing you'll be way ahead of me."

Dolly chuckled as Ethel walked me to the door and watched me get into my rental.

"Eve? Wake up. We need to go see Vinney."

"Oh. Sure. Right." She closed her eyes again.

"You have to give me directions," I said.

"Got any toothpicks?" She blinked her eyes open and started directing me.

Vinney Carnevale lived on the outskirts of Mystick Falls, in an upscale fifties housing development that had seen better days. Among the fixer-uppers, however, his house stood out. "Looks like somebody spent a few bucks to update this place," I said as I parked the car. "Does he have money?"

Eve hooted as she got out on her side. "Not that I could see."

I'd actually turned off my headlights to drive down his street and up his driveway, until we reached his garage at the edge of his backyard, so we wouldn't be spotted by the neighbors.

"This is feeling clandestine," Eve said, opening my door.

"Ya think? I should have left the car out front for a quick getaway." I was either getting cold feet or my lack of sleep was catching up with me. I lay my head against the steering wheel. "There are no lights on inside. Maybe we should come another time."

Eve tugged me from the driver's seat. "I was coming

ANNETTE BLAIR

here tonight, anyway," she said, "until I began to suspect that he was a thief. Just think of this as being for a good cause."

I grabbed Chakra and followed her.

The minute she unlocked the back door, the smell of sausage and meatballs in a spicy tomato sauce that had probably simmered for hours hit me, made my mouth water, and turned me weak in the knees with hunger. I opened the refrigerator at the same time that Eve flipped on the kitchen light.

"Son of a stitch," I snapped, sprinting over to turn it off.

She flipped it back on. "Time to put on your big-girl panties, Mad, and help me search."

I opened the fridge. "I'm wearing them. They say 'kiss my sass.'"

"You should put those snarky puppies into production and sell them at your shop."

"Maybe I will. I have a T-shirt idea, too." I watched Eve go through Vinney's mail. "Is there an all-night hamburger joint between here and home?"

She opened a cupboard and handed me a box of cereal. "It would be *Boo* Berry," I said, downing a handful. "What *are* we looking for?"

"An old mailbag of bones?"

There went my appetite. "That's what that was. A *mail-bag.*"

Eve raised her brows. "That's what I said."

I followed her through the house, looking behind parlor furniture, in the bottom of the entertainment unit, inside a window seat.

In the bathroom, I checked his medicine chest for aftershave, unscrewed the cap, and took a whiff. "It was him," I said.

Eve looked from me to the bottle and back. "A million men wear that stuff. It's a drugstore staple."

"Fine," I huffed. "It could have been him."

We'd barely gotten to the bedroom when we heard sirens. "Scrap!"

Eve put her arm out in front of me, as if we were taking a sharp corner, and I might fall off the passenger seat and hit my head on the dashboard. "Don't move," she whispered. "They might not be coming here."

The knock at the front door made us both jump.

"We might as well be back in fifth grade hiding beneath Fiona's window," I whispered, tugging my hand from Eve's clammy grasp.

"Shush," Eve snapped. "And don't pee your pants this time."

"Brat."

Chakra hotfooted it from the bedroom. Oy. Then I heard her wildcat yowl, bombastic and echoing, a capacious version of my name that astounded my father every time he heard it.

"Mystick Falls police," someone announced.

They'd come in through the back door, which we left unlocked.

Are we smart burglars, or what?

Thirteen

Problems are only opportunities in work clothes.
—HENRY J. KAISER

"Climb out the window," I whispered to Eve as I made a running motion with my fingers before I went to meet the police.

In the kitchen, my nemesis, aka the Wiener, was aiming a gun in my general direction, so I stopped in the doorway between the kitchen and the hall. "Should I raise my hands?"

He scanned the room behind me. "Are you alone? Are you safe, Madeira? You're not being held hostage or anything?"

"I'm alone,.but am I safe from you?"

He lowered his gun. "Never. Sometimes I dream of getting my hands around your throat." He holstered the gun with a look of pure annoyance. "But in the dream, I'm a superhero whose voice hasn't changed yet, and you're carrying a Barbie lunch box."

I smiled fondly. "She always had the *best* clothes."

"What the hell are you doing here?" he shouted, making me jump. "I knew it was you the minute I heard that cat roar your name. Breaking and entering, Madeira? That's a new one, even for you."

Eve stepped up beside me. "This is my boyfriend's house."

Werner raised a brow my way. "You said you were alone."

"Eve hardly counts."

"That's true."

She rolled her eyes and held up her key. "We didn't break in. We're doing a sleepover."

Lytton smirked. "The three of you?"

"Of course not. Vinney works the night shift."

Lytton took out his notebook. "Where?"

"I really don't know," Eve said in all truth. "But honest, Lytton. I keep some of my clothes in his bedroom closet. Wanna see?"

"Sure. Why not. It's been a slow night."

I caught his sarcasm while Chakra jumped into my arms.

Eve waited for Werner and his officers to enter the bedroom, her hand on the closet doorknob. "I have two pairs of black jeans and three tops in this closet, and some undies in a drawer. Want to know what my sleep shirt says?"

"No," Lytton said, fingering a pillowcase. "This has blood on it." He signaled an officer and the guy confiscated the pillowcase and bagged it. "Why the blood?"

"Vinney cracked his head open something fierce last night. I took him over to Lawrence and Memorial for stitches. Check with the hospital. I signed him out."

Werner nodded to his officer to do just that. "Open the closet, Ms. Meyers."

Eve opened the door with a flourish, but the closet stood empty. "Hey," she said. "I liked those jeans!" Then she ran to the honey maple bureau and opened four empty drawers, bottom to top, not closing any. "Vinney stole my clothes, the rat! Arrest that man!"

Laughter caught in my throat and I coughed.

Werner started taking notes. "Mr. Carnevale's neighbor reported this break-in. He said that Carnevale told her he was going away early this morning, for an extended period of time, but he didn't say where or when he'd be back."

The gears in my mind started working as if they'd been oiled. Carnevale had moved out this morning, almost as if his last goal in Mystic was getting into my shop. But why would that be so important? And why was it necessary for him to run, because whether he got into my shop or not, he had planned to relocate.

"I *slept* here last night," Eve said with no thought but to exonerate us.

"Congratulations," Werner said. "You may well be sleeping in jail tonight." He urged us toward the kitchen.

At least he hadn't taken out his handcuffs. Yet. My father was not going to like bailing me out of jail. "But we had a key," I reiterated, "and Vinney knew she was coming here tonight. It's not our fault the guy's a lousy communicator."

On our way out the door, Werner behind us, I saw a quality sweater on the back of a kitchen chair, Armani, maybe. I didn't dare touch it, though I wanted to. "Eve, you forgot your sweater."

She stopped and I walked into her, pressing a finger into her ribs.

"Oh, right. Thanks, Mad." She turned back, saw it, and grabbed it.

Werner took it from her and looked it over: V-neck cardigan, primo label, black, thank goodness, and handed it back to Eve.

Yay, something of Vinney's to wrap my psychometric mind around. It certainly looked old enough to be readable. Older than Vinney, maybe.

Werner put us in the backseat of a squad car, the Wiener. How mortifying. "Can one of your officers drive my rental, Detective? I have to return it in good condition."

"Anybody else but you, Cutler—" He opened his hand. "Keys?"

Chakra caught his hand in a playful swipe. She liked him. Go figure a cat's taste in men.

He took her paw and shook it. "Nice to meet you. Again."

I gave him my keys, and he threw them to an officer, gave his own to another, stood a distance away to use his cell phone, then he got into the passenger seat of our squad car. "I want to keep my eye on the perps," he told the driver.

Did he wink? Nah, he couldn't have. Too human, though shaking Chakra's paw leaned in that direction and gave me a little flutter.

He'd saved Chakra once. Nick had dropped her the first time they heard her roar, but Lytton caught her. On the other hand, she was a cat. She would have landed on her feet. But Lytton had recognized her yowl as sounding like my name, like Fiona and I did, and he wasn't ashamed to admit it.

Too bad I had the unique ability to suck the nice right out of this man. I leaned my brow against the window beside me wondering if this would be a bad time to report my two break-ins. Probably. But the longer I waited, the madder the Wiener was going to get.

Guess I should stop worrying about whether to try to solve Tunney's case for now. I not only had break-ins against me to worry about, I had to deal with a breaking-and-entering charge of my own.

If I couldn't help myself, how could I help Tunney?

How could I not?

I wondered again who, or what, the foot bones belonged to. And why had I said "Isobel" without knowing it, when I was about to look in a well?

I shivered involuntarily and Eve tried to hand me the sweater. I reacted with horror by leaning as far back against the corner of the seat as I could, while I regarded her as if she had two heads.

"Oh," she said, realizing it'd be embarrassing if I zoned and called Isobel—or Ingrid, or Irmingard—in front of the Wiener.

"Oh, what?" Werner asked, but before either one of us could form a lie, a call came over the radio that he took, speaking in tongues, though I thought I caught the word "inferno."

"Detour," he told his driver, who seemed to get his drift.

Werner also took a call on his cell phone, gave them an "affirmative," and hung up.

At one o'clock in the morning, West Main Street beamed as bright as day. Brighter.

Fiery bright.

"My building!" I shouted and burst into tears.

Fourteen

Every single item you put on your body literally shouts out
your unconscious dreams and desires to the entire world.

—CYNTHIA HEIMEL

❧

"The playhouse is gone," I said on a sob as we parked at
the far end of my parking lot. "My building is next. Those
flames, they're licking their way across the street. Look at
them!"

"Madeira," Werner said, a bit too gently for my comfort
as he helped me from the squad car. "At least two fire
crews are hosing down the buildings around the playhouse.
See?"

"Mine will catch. It's old. I just got it, and I love it. And
Dante, I mean, you know, it's like an inferno." I wiped my
eyes in a bid for sympathy, though, truth to tell, I was scared
shirtless about the very good chance that Vintage Magic,
and Dante's essence, were both in danger of going up in
flames.

Where did ghosts go when the haunts their spirits were bound to disappeared?

Werner helped Eve out, too, and slapped the squad car roof. The driver backed out and took off.

"Ms. Meyers, I just got confirmation that you've been dating Vincent Carnevale for the past couple of weeks, so you didn't break any laws by using the key he gave you. The two of you are free to go."

"How did you find out so fast?" I asked. "It's the middle of the night."

"Mr. Carnevale is . . . known to us. I had the relationship confirmed at the station. I think you're well out of it, Ms. Meyers."

"Thank you, Detective," Eve said. "I think you're right. Mad, I'm going home. Are you okay to drive? Do you want me to take you home?"

"Nah, but thanks. I'm worried about my building. I'm gonna stick around until I know it's safe. Are you okay to drive after finding Sampson and all?"

"Yes. Call me craven but I want my mother. Oh, Mad, I'm sorry."

"It's okay, sweetie. You're allowed." I hugged her. "See you tomorrow."

"I can take you home, Madeira," Werner offered.

"I have to stay with my building. I'm going upstairs. I'll be in the room facing the playhouse. You'll see the light. So before *you* leave, tell one of the firefighters that if my building does catch a spark, to come and get me, 'kay? But tell them *not* to let it catch."

"I'm not going anywhere," he said walking me to my door.

I yawned. "Maybe I'll see you when it's over, then."

He scratched Chakra behind an ear and nodded.

"Chakra will protect me. Won't you, sweetie?"

I'd seen a bit of a softish center beneath Werner's hard outer shell tonight. Not as soft as caramel, but nougat, maybe, the kind that looks soft but can pull your teeth out by the roots.

Upstairs, I turned on the clickety light in the storage room and looked across the street at the playhouse, or what was left of it, through water-lashed windowpanes, thanks to our industrious firefighters.

Werner used his hands as he spoke and seemed to be directing the firemen to hose down my building.

The walls of Sampson's playhouse were falling in. No more top floor, and the main level didn't look like it would last much longer. For Tunney's sake, I hoped the local forensics team had come and gone before this second blaze.

I saw huge sparks, flaming splinters of wood, actually, headed my way, but most of them dimmed and went out before they reached my windows. Not quite insurance, but reassurance. They might hit, but they could hardly smolder on a wet surface.

Looking for something comfortable, like a padded chair, I went around behind the storage room hearse, a little smaller and a little older than the one Dad had hauled up from the first floor.

I moved some jadeite lamps, a couple of tall flower stands, more spittoons—clean, thank goodness—and to my surprise, I found a dusty fainting couch in pretty good shape.

I took the bric-a-brac off of it and pushed it over to the window. Then I took the tuxes from the closet and used them like a sheet.

"The couch was a cared-for treasure," Dante said. "It doesn't have cooties."

"I have allergies," I said, quoting him.

He chuckled. "Are you tired?"

"Exhausted. I didn't sleep last night because I was packing, and after work today, I drove home from New York. Now this."

"I can tell you a little about what happened here, earlier, but not much. It can wait until morning if you're too tired."

I got up, toed off my shoes, and nudged the quilt toward the couch. "Just tell me one thing. Did a body come wrapped in this quilt?"

"Yes and no. Bones only. They've been here about twenty-eight years."

"How can you be sure about time? How have you counted the years?"

"I count Christmases. The town dresses up for Christmas, so every time I see a Christmas display, I know it's been another year."

"How creative of you."

Dante accepted the compliment as his due. "The man who originally brought the bones was nervous," he said. "Very nervous. Like he'd killed someone."

I nodded. "A simple deduction when a man hides bones."

"He dropped some of the small bones on the way up and had to go back for them. All told, he fell down the stairs three times while he was here with very little help from me." Dante looked rather proud of himself. "On his running out, the guy took the worst tumble I ever saw. Judging by the way he drove away, I think he was scared. He drove right into that telephone pole on the corner. I watched the ambulance take him away."

"When he was here, did he see you?"

"Of course not."

"Yet you toyed with him. No wonder he was scared."

Dante's grin held a great deal of wicked pride. No wonder Dolly fell for him. "I got a good look at the bones he dropped before he went back for them. They were clean and dry before he put them in the quilt with the rest."

"I can't tell you how much better I feel now about touching this quilt."

"Why would you *want* to touch it? Does it have anything to do with the way you seem to go into a trance and say things you don't remember, like when you made your friend almost faint?"

"Let's save the whole story for another day, shall we?" I about begged. "In a nutshell, I'd rather touch a vintage clothing item likely to speak to me when I can't scare anyone by doing it. I mean, I'd rather not touch it at all. But I'm doing it for my friend who was arrested tonight, for poor Mr. Sampson, and for the person the bones belonged to."

"Why?" Dante asked.

"I've been involved in one murder investigation. Certain vintage clothes spoke to me then, and I believe that this quilt has something to tell me now."

Dante nodded, as if satisfied.

I got on the fainting couch facing him, my insides trembling at the thought of losing my senses to a dark past. Chakra curled into my middle as I lowered my hand, hesitated, and, finally, tucked it into a pocket of the quilt puddled on the floor.

"Go to sleep," Dante said. "I'll protect you."

"How can you protect me?"

"I've gathered a deal of energy over the years. I can

make a man trip over his own feet. Which can be fun when he's committing nefarious deeds."

"I'll bet. What else can you do?"

"Flicker the lights, break a window, take the cover off a casket when a woman's tied up inside."

"Cary Grant, my hero."

His chin dimple deepened with his frown. "My name is Dante Underhill, no matter who you and Dolly *think* I look like. I might be able to knock you off that couch, but you'll have to take my word for it, because if I showed you, I might not have enough energy left to protect you, in the event you needed protecting. Close your eyes, sweet friend."

"I'm not sweet," I said, doing as I was told.

"You were worried about me losing my building. I heard you say my name to that cop."

"You listen at windows?"

"I live for the sound of human voices," Dante whispered near my ear, and I felt a touch of ice on my brow.

No wonder Dolly fell in love with him, I thought again, as I spun into a nightmare I resisted, my world dark, my captor rough, my trust shattered . . . my body in a freefall.

I'll die when I hit bottom.

Please let me die.

Fifteen

Fashion is as profound and critical a part of the social life of man as sex, and is made up of the same ambivalent mixture of irresistible urges and inevitable taboos.   —RENE KONIG

❧

"Madeira, Mad, you're crying."

With the scent of smoke in my nostrils and the hard, cold earth at my back, I felt myself being lifted and rocked against a hard chest.

Hands large but tender stroked my hair. Strong arms enclosed me in a safe cocoon.

Maybe I didn't die.

I clung to my haven, but as I trembled from the cold, those same hands chafed my arms and my back. I warmed but held no control over my sobs, wasn't even sure they were mine.

Did they belong to the lady in the well?

Isobel.

Warmth began to seep deep into my bones, awareness,

too, just enough to appreciate the heart beating beneath my ear.

"I'm alive. You smell like smoke. You should quit."

"I hate to disappoint you, Mad, but it's me."

"You hate me."

"I hate what you said. Not you. We were kids."

"You can be sweet."

"You're talking in your sleep. I'll ignore that."

I didn't want to leave this new dream. "Nick smells different. Good, too, but different."

"You think I smell good, after all that smoke? And you know it's me?"

"You wear Armani's Black Code. You're taller, broader than Nick." I opened my eyes, despite myself, and raised my head. "Lytton?"

"You said you knew."

"In my sleep, maybe, but not awake."

"Was I at the bottom of that well with you?" he asked, smoothing my hair one last time as his hand fell away. "When you were asleep, I mean. You seemed to think I was."

The well? Oh God, the well. "My head hurts." I sat up. "The fire! My building?"

"The fire's out." Werner straightened, too, but I was still sitting on his lap. "You're safe. So's your building and your cat. It's nearly four in the morning."

"Hmm. I got up at four to go to work in New York two days ago, and I haven't slept since, except for now."

"Three hours sleep in two days?"

"Mmm." I cuddled back into him. "G'night."

Slowly, reluctantly, his arms came back around me and

he rested his chin on my head. "I couldn't leave with the light still on up here. Let me take you home?"

The idea of moving seemed impossible. I shook my head against his chest. "I'll just sleep here."

"In my arms? Or on the sofa?"

I raised my head. "The sofa. Of course, I meant the sofa." My eyes closed without my permission. I knew it, but I couldn't do anything about it. Lytton's heartbeat began, again, to lull me.

He stood, carrying me with him.

"What are you doing?"

"I'm going to put you in my car and take you home."

"Where do you live?"

His heart beneath my ear skipped a beat. "No. To *your* home."

"My father won't like that you arrested me."

I heard the rumble of a chuckle beneath my cheek as the lights went off behind my eyelids.

"My cat," I said, drifting.

I closed my eyes tight against a new flash of light.

"Chakra? Hey, what have you got, there? Madeira? We have to talk."

"Not tonight, 'kay?"

Werner lowered me, so I had to hold on tight to his neck or fall, then I felt Chakra's fur beneath my chin.

"Tomorrow then," he said.

"Whatever," I whispered, riding a cloud.

More lifting, up and down, drifting. Someone mumbling about keys, me holding tight again.

"Which room's yours?"

"Hmm?"

Light pricked at my eyelids, so I closed them tighter.

"What is the meaning of this, Detective?"

"Detective who?" I asked, my eyes still closed. "Dad?"

"Madeira, are you drunk?"

I saw my father in his pajamas, shocked out of his socks. Shock didn't come easy to Harry Cutler, a college professor who'd raised four kids alone.

I blinked against the light. Details came to me in pieces.

Why wasn't I standing? I looked at my ride. Werner?

"Daddy, he arrested me."

My father crossed his arms. "Why? What did you do, this time?"

I'd never heard Werner's full-bodied laugh before. A real wake-up call. "Sir," he said on a last chuckle, "could you just show me where her bed is?"

"I don't bloody well think so."

"She's getting heavy and I'm afraid—"

"I am *not* heavy."

Werner fumbled me and I slid down his body and landed on my ascot in the hall. "Ouch! That was rude!"

Werner, my father, and Aunt Fiona looked down at me.

"Aunt Fiona, what are you doing in my dream wearing Sherry's old bathrobe?"

My father ran a hand through his hair. "Fee was distraught after being shut in that casket. She couldn't stay alone. She's been having nightmares all night."

I'd never seen my father so discomfited. "How would you know?"

His ears turned red. I'd never seen that happen before, either. "It's not what you think," he said.

"How many times did you believe me when I used those words?"

Was I having a middle-of-the-night conversation with

my father in the Wiener's presence? "I'm hallucinating, aren't I?"

"Madeira, do you two know what time it is?" my father asked.

"Dawn," I said. "The playhouse burned to the ground. And I thought my building would, too." Tears slid down my cheeks, but I didn't know how they got there.

"She's sleep deprived," Lytton said, as he and my father each took one of my arms and between them, got me standing.

"I feel like a jellyfish. No legs." I leaned into Werner, who was forced to slip an arm around me.

"Harry," Aunt Fiona said. "She worked a full day in New York, drove home, and hasn't stopped since."

"That's right; I hasn't."

Lytton chuckled. "She's had a hard forty-eight hours, sir."

My father sighed. "This way to her bedroom."

I rode up in Werner's arms, mine around his neck, my head resting there.

He placed me on my bed and I missed his heartbeat. "Who moved my cloud?" The drifty, out-of-body sensation I remembered with fondness had passed. So I was forced to curl into myself.

"Fee will take care of her." My father's voice drifted away.

Aunt Fiona's perfume, like a blanket of warmth, covered me. For the first time in days, I drifted in dreamless and endless peace.

"Damned light, again," I snapped, opening my eyes, against my better judgment.

"Chill, Mad. It's about time." Eve handed me a latte. "Your dad said you've been asleep for hours. You don't look like you spent the night with the Wiener. Are the gossips wrong about that, too?"

Sixteen

Elegance is fluid. It consists of desire and knowledge, grace, refinement, perfection, and distinction.   —RENE GRUAU

❧

"Me? Spend the night with the Wiener!" I sat up fast. "Are you out of your mind?"

"Shush," Eve said. "They're saying that Fiona and your dad spent the night together, too."

Memory alert. I looked up, saw my dad coming toward the foot of my bed, and wondered how much he'd heard.

"Fiona was shut in a casket last night, Eve," he said. "I think you'll grant that she had a right to be upset."

Eve looked contrite. "Of course."

"I granted it from the get-go, Dad, but you mocked her."

"I've never been more sorry about anything. She's a wreck. That's why she stayed the night. In Sherry's room. I slept in my own."

I winked. "You should have put her in Brandy's room so

you could have experienced the full roller-coaster scope of the getaway tree."

Every one of his children who ever sneaked a date up to our rooms—and we all did—sent them home via the tree outside Brandy's room, which is how it became known as "the getaway tree."

Bit of a sore spot with my father.

The thundercloud himself handed me one of my mother's plates bearing one of Fiona's famous homemade cinnamon rolls. Hmm.

"It's three o'clock, Madeira. And Eve," he added, "for your information, Madeira spent a few hours at Vintage Magic last night, and after the playhouse fire was under control, Detective Werner brought her home."

A shred of memory rolled in, and I sat straight up to dislodge it, nearly spilling my latte. "Uh, where's Chakra?"

My cat jumped on the bed. "Oh, sweetie, thank goodness."

"No worries. She rode in with you and your knight. He's waiting downstairs to see you."

"Nick? Nick's home already?" I put my cup on the nightstand and jumped out of bed.

Eve chuckled. "Do you remember nothing about last night?"

"It's fuzzy, and what's with the gossip?"

"Jump in the shower," Eve said. "And come down as soon as you can."

Fifteen minutes later, wearing a black tent dress and two-tone flats, I sat across from the Wiener and my father in the gentleman's parlor. "I thought Nick was here," I muttered.

Eve shook her head almost in warning. "He's on assignment, remember?"

"Oh, *you* wanted to see me, Detective?"

"Ms. Cutler," he said, "before we left your shop last night—"

"*We* left my shop last night?"

Eve shook her head at me.

"What?" I asked.

"Selective memory. It's so accommodating. Mad's blocking it," Eve told Werner as she sat on the arm of my chair.

Werner looked confused, an emotion I embraced, then lightning struck. "That was *you* last night!"

Werner rubbed the side of his nose. "Guilty."

"For what?" I asked suspiciously.

"Please remember that I wasn't up there alone," he said.

What did I do, kiss him or something? Had I called him a Wiener? If not, I probably should have. I held on to the chair's arms as memory tried to rush me, but I managed to push it away. "Eve, what did you say about gossip? Never mind. Screw the gossip. I have to think."

I got up to pace, the heat in my face making me want to open a window, October or not.

Werner obviously took my movement as a sign to continue. "As I was saying, last night I saw your cat batting around an object of great interest. It seemed to come from beneath the body drawers in your storage room. Do you know what was under there?"

My heart stopped as I turned, but when Werner opened an evidence box, and I saw the skeletal appendage inside, some kind of trip switch got hit that restarted my heart double time.

I'm afraid it said a lot about our knowledge that neither Eve nor I ran screaming from the room, because my father sure looked poleaxed.

"Before you say anything," Eve warned, her hand on my shoulder. "He already *interrogated* me, and I caved like a kid caught with crib notes at a final exam. Detective Lytton Werner knows all."

Werner wore a look of smug satisfaction.

I crossed my arms. "Why ask me questions you know the answers to?"

"Details," he said. "Different people notice different things."

Okay, so if I told him the truth, I'd be fine. "Fine. Ask away."

"What I didn't tell Ms. Meyers," Werner said, "is that a body, charred beyond recognition, was found in the rubble of the playhouse."

"That's horrible." I swallowed hard.

"The bones, most of which have been broken, have to be sent to an FBI lab for DNA testing, but judging by the pelvic bone, a local forensics team was able to identify the remains as female between the ages of twenty and thirty, never had children. Death happened approximately thirty-five years ago. Cause unknown."

Nausea rose in me. I stood. "I need a cracker or I'm going to be sick." Wishing I'd eaten that cinnamon roll, I ran for the kitchen, but Fiona met me with a cracker box. I dug in, grabbed one, and inhaled it, letting it fill the caffeine-raw hole in my quivering stomach.

Werner watched with concern. Scrap, so did everyone else.

I ate another, and another, until the nausea passed. I

took a deep breath, kept the box, and returned to the sofa. "Sorry." I looked at the contents of Werner's evidence box and turned to Eve. "Probably *not* from a dinosaur, a bear, or a bizarro dog, then."

Werner raised both brows. "You thought it belonged to an animal?"

I could either nod here or be honest. "We hoped it belonged to an animal. We hoped *hard*."

"Hard enough," Eve said, "to go looking for Vinney Carnevale to ask him if he broke in, instead of calling you about them, because the guy who broke in looked a lot like Vin. I suspected," Eve added, "though I didn't say so, that he took the rest of the bones that belonged to that . . . set you've got there. We did plan to call you after we confronted Vinney."

"Animal bones." Werner closed the box and put it aside, praise be. "Puts a different spin on obstruction of justice and tampering with evidence and a crime scene," he muttered as he made a few notes.

What a relief. Eve and I weren't screwed then?

"Madeira, Ms. Meyers said that you had *two* break-ins last night. Why didn't you call the police the first time?"

"Dad?" I said. "Do you have that report from our night watchman?"

My father went for it and gave it to me.

I handed it to Werner. "That's why I didn't call for either break-in. You know, I think maybe it was Vinney who broke in both times *and* maybe while I was away. I also think that the first fire last night was convenient. I mean, it got us out of my building so something could be taken away in that old mailbag."

"For argument's sake, let's call the contents bones,"

Werner said, scribbling furiously on his notepad. "An old mailbag, *not* a sack."

"Oops," Eve said. "I forgot."

"Details. That's why I'm talking to Mad, er, Ms. Cutler, too." Werner read the construction company watchman's report, frowned, and held it up. "Can I take this?" he asked me.

"Sure. I have a copy."

"I'll make one for myself and return this; it's the original."

"Fine."

"Now, what do you need to know, Detective? I'll tell you everything." Except about Isobel and the abandoned well, because I didn't know if they meant anything at all beyond mixed messages and bad dreams. In my second vision, I didn't know if I'd been falling into the well I'd seen in the first.

Handing Werner clues—if they were clues—out of thin air would make him suspicious. When my sister was a murder suspect, I'd fed him the clues from my psychometric readings of certain vintage clothing items in a roundabout way. But I couldn't be that lucky twice.

Revealing my knowledge directly and prematurely would be like switching on a flashing neon sign: Maddie's Psychic. Maddie's Psychic. A nut. Not to be trusted.

Nobody would say as much but everyone would be thinking: "Sure, she can read vintage clothes. Get her a vintage straightjacket to read."

I dug into the box for another cracker, but Fiona traded me the box for a hot ham and egg sandwich on a roll.

"Bless you," I said. "I forgot to eat yesterday. Oh, this is delicious, like a handheld omelet."

She offered egg sandwiches all around, but only Eve took her up on the offer.

"I have to get down to my shop and get ready for my grand opening," I said. "Are you finished with your questions, Detective?"

"Not quite."

I looked out toward our driveway. "Do you want to talk in your car on the way to Vintage Magic?" My face warmed, again, at the thought of being alone with him. "Because I seem to have misplaced my rental."

Werner stood. "You talk. I'll drive. But you can't work in your shop today. It's a crime scene."

"The whole shop!"

Seventeen

The intoxication obtained from wearing certain articles of clothing can be as powerful as that induced by a drug.
—BERNARD RUDOFSKY

"Before you leave, Madeira," Aunt Fiona said, "can we talk for a minute? The subject is important and time sensitive."

I questioned Werner with a look about delaying our departure, since he was driving.

"Go ahead. I have some calls to make," he said. "I'll be outside."

Eve grabbed her keys and followed Werner to the door. "I'll meet you at your shop in about an hour."

My dad went silently up the stairs.

Aunt Fiona and I sat at the keeping room table. "Thanks for the sandwich. I really needed it."

"You shouldn't go so long without eating."

"You sound like Mom when I used to forget to eat because I was too busy dressing my Barbies."

"All twenty of them." Aunt Fiona sat forward and took my hand. "I'm sorry about the delay in preparing for your grand opening, sweetie. I have a timing problem, too, and I'm thinking that maybe we can help each other."

"What is it?"

"I'm the chairman of the White Star Circle of Spirit, Southeast Connecticut Chapter. We sponsor a Halloween costume ball every year, but this year, we've lost our location. We were booked into Sampson's ballroom, but it's gone."

"How can I help?"

"I've been on the phone to our board members all morning, and we were wondering if you'd let us hold our costume ball upstairs at your place? Please. We'll publicize it as your grand opening ball, sponsored by the Circle of Spirit, and invite the general public. That's a huge room you've got."

"Three thousand square feet," I said, but I sat back stunned. "It's got rough-hewn timber beamed ceiling and walls. Never was, never will be, a ballroom."

"All the better for Halloween. Caskets and hearses and spiderwebs. Oh my."

"That's right," I said, picturing it. "We could use the funereal rubble as decorations. Except that we wouldn't be able to see them. There's no electricity up there."

"I thought of that. Our rental fee is enough to pay for you to have electricity and lights put in, as the place stands right now. One of our members is a licensed Connecticut electrician, and he and his crew are prepared to drop everything and wire your upstairs as soon as we give him the go-ahead."

I shook my head. "I wouldn't *charge* you."

"In this case, I insist, because we're forcing you to get

work done before your budget allows. The price is not negotiable."

"I was planning to set up a workspace up there as soon as possible, in the back corner, a sewing room. Would that be a problem?"

"It's a necessity. I've been waiting for you to come home so you could fit me for a costume. Our theme is classic movie characters. A lot of our members were waiting for you to come home, too. They're sure that your vintage treasures will fit their movie character needs."

"I love it. Oh. Can Dolly come to the ball, too? She can wear her Katharine Hepburn as Tracy Lord wedding gown from *The Philadelphia Story*. She has so few chances to wear it."

"You mean the dress she wore to your sister Sherry's wedding?" Aunt Fiona asked. "Dolly told me that she was planning to go and meet Dante in it. I was afraid she'd die right there at the wedding."

"So was I," I admitted. "I was never so happy to see someone leave."

I watched Aunt Fiona go to the kitchen and her offer registered. "You'd be bringing me customers! I'm as thrilled about that as I am about helping you and having lights upstairs."

"The place is huge," she said, putting a cinnamon bun down in front of me. "Your sewing corner won't bother us. And if you're worried about us touching anything, we could put up screens."

I inhaled the bun. "We'll have to move fast. As soon as the police clear out?"

"The circle is ready if you are."

I applauded. "As for the ball, I'm more excited for Dolly

than I am for myself, even though it'll be a great opportunity to show off my shop. I'd love to get some of my outfits on mannequins, however bare the downstairs might still be at that point, so people who come to the ball can get an idea of what I plan for Vintage Magic. And I'd like to furnish the lounge area leading to the dressing rooms before then, too. Come shopping with me this week?"

"Sure. Can we rent your ballroom?"

"Of course. Call me superwoman. I can get it done. Have you already advertised the ball?"

"Yes, so we have to do a big media splash and fast to tell everyone that we're having it at Vintage Magic now, instead, as part of your grand opening."

I shot to my feet. "My grand opening. However the downstairs looks, I'll actually have one because of you." I hugged her. "You're a godsend."

"A Goddess-send. And don't celebrate too soon. You have a lot of work to do."

"Starting with returning my rental and buying a new car, and in between, I have to set up shop and clear Tunney's name. Two murders in such a short time. What is this world coming to?"

"Two?" she asked.

"Sure. Sampson and the bones."

"The bones, of course," Aunt Fiona said. "A young woman, according to Detective Werner."

"I don't know enough about her yet to talk about it, even to you, Aunt Fiona"—except *maybe* her name, I thought—"but I intend to start looking."

"You know that you can talk it through with me when you get some vibes, right?"

I found myself pacing again. "I have to find the last person who saw Tunney at the market last night and anybody who might have seen him run over to the playhouse. Obviously the time each event occurred is key—Sampson's death, the fire, and my burglary. What time does Tunney close on Fridays?"

"Around the time the fire started."

Eighteen

I design to hit people at a gut level; to capture the soul and
raw beauty of people and nature.   —LINDA LOUDERMILK

❧

"Can you stand it?" I asked Werner as we stood in the
parking lot of Vintage Magic. "Twelve days before my
grand opening and there's yellow crime scene tape across
my front door? And look, more donation boxes from our
neighbors."

"Our neighbors are well-intentioned," Werner said.
"And the crime scene crew will be out of here before the
day is over."

"The day nearly is over. I slept through most of it. Hey,
aren't you tired?"

"I got a few hours," he said. "Not as many as you—"

"I'll stop whining. I'm being selfish. Look at our beautiful old playhouse. What a loss to the community and its
historic profile."

Werner and I crossed my parking lot to take a closer look.

Sampson's building smoldered still, half a wall standing, firefighters sifting through the rubble.

Councilman McDowell, the publicity hound, was giving a TV news interview, using the grisly scene as a backdrop.

"He'd hang around at the dump," I muttered, "if a reporter and camera crew were due to show up. Leave it to him to cash in on a tragedy. Was the fire set?"

Werner jiggled the change in his pocket. "We found accelerant on the curtains the first time, and on the bones the second time."

My stomach lurched again. Why did I believe the bones belonged to Isobel? I didn't know any Isobel. "What about Tunney?"

"Prime suspect. I questioned him last night and let him go, so no arrest. Yet."

"Thank you."

"Don't. I do my job, whatever it calls for."

I nodded. "Have you seen any sign of Vinney Carnevale since all this happened?"

"We're checking trains, buses, planes."

"This is the first time you've answered my questions about a case without biting my head off."

"Let's call it a trade for your hypothetical scenario."

"What scenario did I hypothesize?"

"In a roundabout way, you said that the first fire might have been set as a diversion to get you out of your building so someone could get into your storage room."

"If I said that, I didn't hear myself."

He shrugged. "Good detective work, Ms. Cutler."

Ms. Cutler. "About last night—"

"Never happened," he said. "I'm a gentleman, believe it or not, and gentlemen don't tell."

I certainly wished he'd tell *me*, so I'd know what did happen, precisely. "I appreciate that, Lytton. Your questions back at the house, did I answer them to your satisfaction? If you want more answers, ask away."

"I might be back for more."

Whoa. Was that a double entendre on his part? Or wishful thinking on mine?

Neither. Definitely. "I'm a phone call away."

"Have a good day." He left with a wave and didn't look back.

"Have a good day yourself, Detective." I watched him go, freaked out because I remembered the sound of his heartbeat accelerating beneath my ear, and relieved because we were back to formality, if not impolite indifference.

While I waited for Eve, I opened some new boxes of clothing at my door, being careful not to touch any, especially after last night. To my surprise, I found that a set of pristine double-wide, white file boxes held a vintage treasure trove. Designer clothes, half of them couture, mostly from the seventies to mid-eighties, though a few might be older.

Who in the world could have left me such treasures? Who around here could have afforded to buy them new or vintage?

I'd wear most of them, especially the buff-colored suede fringed wrap skirt, and the white–and-beige, leather horizontal-banded three-quarter coat. I moved corners aside with box covers. I adored the ivory beaded silk faille floor-length cape, reversible to black sequined faille. Evening wear at its finest. I resisted the urge to hold it up to search for a label because I didn't want it dragging in the parking lot or taking me back in time.

A poodle skirt topped one box, an aqua silk beaded cocktail dress with a petaled skirt, another. I found a beige shift dress that I believe went with the leather dress coat. My favorite was a Cardin burgundy minidress with a pocket high on the chest, which I just might keep for myself.

"Hello," a woman called from across the street as she ran my way. "I'm Fiona's next in charge for the Halloween Ball," she said, out of breath as she reached me. "Are you Maddie Cutler?"

She had the most beautiful head of long red curls I'd ever seen. "I am, yes."

"Thank you so much for letting us hold our ball here. Oh, I'm Virginia Statler, and I need a costume today, because I'm on my way out of town first thing in the morning, and I won't be back before Halloween."

"Oh, but my stock isn't here yet."

"What about this stuff?" She started rifling through the white boxes and opened the last two.

I was a little taken aback. I didn't even know what to charge for these things. Normally, I'd research them before putting them out for sale.

"Oh, this is it," she said. "I'll be the heroine, whoever she is, from *Flower Drum Song*. I'm sure I can find a Japanese fan to go with it." She held up a rare Japanese wedding kimono. Uber valuable. In Japan, it would cost at least five thousand dollars new. I'd priced them when my old boss Faline held a fashion show there.

"I have at least two if not three Japanese fans in my vintage stock in storage," I said, "but as for the kimono, I'd have to look it over for flaws, but it's worth at *least* three thousand."

The woman didn't blink. "I've always wanted one. I know that's a fair price for vintage, even if it costs more, unless it has a cigarette hole in it or something. I've wanted one for years to mount in Plexiglas on the wall in my living room, which I'll do with this one, after the ball. Do you want a deposit so you can hold it for me?" She took out her checkbook. "Will five hundred dollars do?"

Who knew that I'd find vintage collectors with money to burn right here in Mystic? Normally, I wouldn't take a check from a stranger if I couldn't immediately verify it with her bank, but if I was keeping it for her, I'd have time to do that.

She handed me the check, and before I knew what she was doing, she tried on the kimono, right there in the parking lot. I squeaked and ran behind her to grab the fabric and keep it from trailing in the leafy lot. Virginia talked nonstop the whole time, as if a parking lot sale were normal for something this pricey.

In a dizzying blink, I saw a young man in a white tux walking into a country club. "I certainly hope this is worth the expense," he said to his companion, a young man similarly dressed.

"Think of it as an investment, old boy," his friend said with an English accent. "She's worth a bloody fortune, and she's gorgeous besides. You'll have everything you ever wanted, and it'll hardly be a sacrifice to put your shoes under *her* bed."

She, it turned out, was wearing the kimono with a Japanese wig, and she was having a conversation with Marie Antoinette and Cleopatra.

A moneyed costume ball, no doubt about it.

When I dizzied my way back to the present, I was carrying Virginia Statler's "train" as she walked around my parking lot, still talking about the Circle of Spirit and her friendship with Fiona. No, she hadn't seen me zone. I'd evidently been sleepwalking while keeping up with her. Good thing she was one of those women who didn't need a second person to take part in her conversation.

In the vision, I'd seen a man who appeared to be looking to marry for money. Why else would his presence there be considered an investment? But I knew better than to jump to conclusions. Whatever happened to the "investor" and the woman in the kimono, I might never know.

One thing I'd learned from Aunt Fiona, who understood these things as only a witch and an empath could, was that I usually got these visions from particular vintage clothing items when the universe wanted them known. "Usually" being a relative term, because the one time I'd read vintage clothing in the past, the items involved a murder.

On this particular day—after one murder took place and one was discovered—my question to the universe would be: which murder do my recent visions involve? Sampson's or the bones? Or were they leading me elsewhere?

I couldn't see Isobel or the kimono having anything to do with Sampson's death. Unless Sampson had been the money-grubber investor at the expensive costume party, and the woman in the kimono killed him and set the fire? Random thought. Wild conjecture.

Someone besides Vinney setting the fire? Gut wise, I didn't think so.

Virginia took off the kimono, folded it, and tried to hand it to me. "Can you just set it back in the box?" I asked, afraid to touch it again for fear I'd "see" something more.

"Too bad about the playhouse and poor Tunney," Virginia said, closing her Chanel purse, "but he certainly had motive."

"He did?" I asked. "What kind of motive?"

"I don't subscribe to gossip," she said as she left. "Have a good day."

Nineteen

Well, damn, Aunt Fiona's chatty friend subscribed to just enough gossip to whet the appetite. I only hoped that Virginia Statler didn't know any more than the Sweets did. As for Tunney's motive, maybe I should ask Tunney and Suzanne Sampson about that. Separately, of course.

Turning back to the kimono, I realized something about the woman who probably once owned the clothes in the pristine white file boxes—matching boxes giving the impression they came from the same person. The original owner liked vintage, yet followed fashion trends, and she could afford to do both with panache.

As I put covers back on boxes I noticed that Virginia hadn't put the kimono in its original box, giving me the opportunity to see what other clothes had been packed beneath it. What I saw made my fashionista's heart skip. A cape to die for—capes being my weakness. Beneath it, I could also see a slim black sheath dress to match.

Without thinking, I threw the cape over my shoulders and fastened buttons, hidden beneath a slimming black placket. In rust linen with black piping along each vertical seam from neck to hem, I adored the padded shoulders, a la Yves Saint Laurent. The cape had no collar and its zippered pockets were aligned with and hidden in its side seams.

I loved the outfit so much I might keep it for myself. I was wishing I had a mirror when dizziness overtook me, and I barely had time to acknowledge my rash action before I was forced to sit on one of the boxes as my world darkened to match my unfamiliar surroundings.

A man in a pricey gray pinstripe suit slipped a legal-sized set of old green-and-brown ledger books into a home safe.

"What are you doing?" a woman asked from behind him.

At the sound of her voice, his body went rigid. His jaw stiffened, and the tic in his cheek became pronounced.

Belligerence transformed his movements from furtive to contentious. "I'm doing my job," he said, his voice as familiar as a newscaster or a weatherman. "Short service today?" he asked.

"I think Father had a golf game."

"Your father or the priest?"

"Both."

The couple spoke with polite indifference, or dislike, either because of a quarrel or out of habit.

Mr. Incongeniality slammed the safe door, twisted the dial with a nervous move, and let a painting slip into place, possibly a Monet, though it could be in that style by a lesser-known artist. A good one.

"I wish you would trust me," he said.

"I might say the same. Why do you bring the books home, slave over them when you have a bookkeeper to do that, and lock them away from me? Or are they a second set of books that no one else knows about? The *real* story?"

"Nice talk."

They stood in a room paneled in dark walnut. An old-fashioned male-only study with an antique Tiffany lamp in greens and golds.

From a round, gaudy-legged marble-topped table, he took an etched, square decanter from its brass carrier and poured himself a snifter of brandy.

"Isn't it a bit early for that?" she sniped.

Still keeping his back to her, he shrugged. "Whatever it takes."

"To drown out my voice?"

"Those are *your* words." He hadn't once looked at her.

The glass-fronted bookshelves lining the room revealed pricey leather-bound books. I couldn't read titles but I suspected vintage from their muted colors and gold leaf. Autographed pictures of men shaking hands dotted the walls between, and there was no mistaking the White House in the background on at least one.

The place reeked of money and good taste, but not class, given the fact that Mr. Hostile needed an attitude adjustment. He slipped behind a huge desk, putting even more distance between him and the woman, a body-language slap in the face. I nearly saw his face then, but he bent to look through a drawer, avoiding eye contact, insulting her further.

His ebony hair curled in waves that he tried but failed to tame. He wore a scent I knew well, because my grandfather had worn it, which wasn't enough to make me like him.

"I have work to do," he said in dismissal.

The woman stepped boldly forward, close enough to touch his desk, so close Old Spice mingled with Chanel No. 5. Her hands were milky smooth, long fingered with perfect, clear-glossed oval nails. Her engagement ring in platinum, like her wedding ring, had an emerald-cut diamond the size of Texas.

She leaned forward, an aggressive move, and as she did, a rust linen garment with black piping rested diagonally against her forearm. A cape. "You work," she said with sarcasm. "I'll go to the fair by myself."

"That quilt will never win," he said, without looking up.

She gave a bitter laugh. "Neither will you. I'm meeting Daddy at the club for drinks at six. I'll make your excuses. He and I have a lot to talk about. In case you care."

"I don't."

"I know."

I opened my eyes and looked into Eve's.

She'd parked her car to shield me from the police going in and out of my shop's front door.

I blinked against the glare of the sun. "When did you get here?"

Twenty

I have no desire to give lectures on the subject of fashion. I put my money on feelings: Wear it and enjoy it.

—GIANNI VERSACE

"That was a long zone out," Eve said with concern as she sat beside me.

"My second since I got here, and frustrating. The woman in my vision was wearing this, but I never saw her face." I touched the cape, shivered despite the sun, and stuck my icy hands in its unzipped pockets. "I might have seen the same couple in my first vision. I'm not sure."

Eve held up a caramel latte to tempt me.

I shook my head. "Not right now. Thanks." I was still too connected to my vision to cut the psychic cord.

"By the way," she said, "you just put period to any doubts I might have harbored about your psychometric ability."

"But you're a scientist."

"Yes, well, I'm a scientist who believes in *you*."

"Thanks, sweetie." My warming fingers closed on a

sharp-edged piece of plastic in one of the pockets, so I took it out and held it in my palm for both of us to see.

"A leopard fingernail," Eve said. "It's awfully long."

"Takes a certain kind of woman to wear fingernails like this," I said. "Were animal-print fingernails in vogue at the same time as this cape? I'll have to ask Aunt Fiona."

With fear still wrapped around me, and a strange fingernail in my hand, Eve put the latte's sippy slot to my mouth and about poured it down my throat.

Her action made me want to chuckle, but I didn't dare, because I didn't want to spill coffee on the cape. However, my sweet friend and her sweet, life-giving shot of inner warmth made me feel like myself again. Alive. Happy and in control. No, I didn't know who killed who, but Eve put things into perspective for me.

All in good time. I had to live my own life while I worked to make the puzzle pieces of other people's lives and deaths fall into place. Prepared to do just that, I slipped the fingernail into the cape pocket, zipped it, took the cup from Eve's hands, and let it warm my own.

She nodded. "Glad you're coming out of it."

"Thanks to you."

"Do you think the fingernail belonged to the woman who owned the clothes?"

I shrugged. "Note to me: check local nail salons to see who does nails like this and how long they've been in style."

"You're smart to look for the 'artist,' rather than the canvas. You could find out who has them done that way with some small talk while you're getting your own nails done." Eve smirked. "You'd look great with pumpkins on black for Halloween."

"Don't put it past me. I had ladybug fingernails one of the times Nick came to New York. That's how I got my nickname."

"I can't stand it anymore," Eve shouted, as if she'd snapped. "I have to ask. What and who did you see in your vision?"

I sighed. "The back of a man's head, the top of it, though I think his actions mattered more."

She finished her coffee. "So what were his actions?"

"I believe that the woman suspected him of cooking the books, by his reaction to getting caught putting ledgers in a home safe. She practically accused him of it."

"An embezzler? Who caught him? Who is the woman?"

"His wife, I think. Lots of animosity between them. She was going to a fair where, I believe, she had a quilt entered into some type of craft contest. Can we search for award-winning quilts on the internet?"

"A contest like at a country fair? Sure, but I'm not sure we'll find anything from that far back. Do you know what it won? And, hey, I'm no fashion expert but those clothes are here because they're vintage, right? How long ago was this contest?"

I slipped from the cape and remembered how long Dante said the bones had been here. "Try late seventies, early eighties."

Eve scoffed at the outfit. "She wore *that* to a fair?"

"Fashion snark from the woman in black?"

She chuckled. "*You're* wearing black."

"Sure. A Mary Quant mini tent dress, black-and-tan Lagerfeld pumps, and a matching two-tone Chanel bag. I have a look. You have a color. Mine is one choice in an un-ending palette."

Eve wrinkled her nose like a kid. "Mine is my favorite."
Nobody could make me laugh like Eve.

"The woman could have changed for the fair." Whatever
clothes she was wearing likely went the way of the meat on
her bones. I shivered. I was making myself nauseous with
speculation.

"Okay," Eve said. "I'm ignoring the *was*, because you
think she was killed, right? Never mind. Don't answer.
Names to plug into the search?"

"Mr. Hostile and Mrs. Courageous, though I fear her
courage was misplaced." I sighed. "What if she's Isobel," I
said, "and that's her quilt upstairs?"

Eve crushed her coffee cup and tossed it in the backseat
of her top-down convertible. "It's upstairs, if the cops
didn't take it as evidence."

"Right," I said, clenching my fists at the thought of not
getting another shot at it. "I'm beginning to believe Aunt
Fiona. There *is* a reason I get signs from the universe."

"Two people have died. Sounds like two reasons."

"But none of my visions seem related to a specific murder." Why?

My cell phone rang. "Nick! How's it going? Are you all
right? How's Alex?"

"Your brother's fine," he said. "But I checked the Mystick Falls paper on the net this morning. You had quite the
night last night."

I wondered if *my* ears were red after having Werner
carry me out of there. "How do you know?"

"Front page, the two fires, the charred body, you trying
to rescue Sampson; you staying with your building to protect it."

"Oh, for the love of Gucci. They put that in the paper? I don't suppose they mentioned my near arrest?"

"What?"

"Yeah. Half the story. Don't believe everything you read in the papers. Can you access FBI files from where you are?"

"What's it to you?"

"Missing persons case, probably this area, late seventies, early eighties."

"Who am I looking for?"

"Isobel. Approximately thirty years old." In the event those were Isobel's bones. "No last name."

"Is that a positive on the Isobel?"

I hesitated.

"Madeira? Not another vision?" Most people had one conscience, I had three, my own plus Nick and Eve, the two who annoyed, mocked, and sometimes saved me.

"Please, Nicky," I said in my most seductive tone.

Eve faked a gag.

Nick sighed. "No fair. No phone seductions in the middle of a . . . phone call. And most people don't get to request random FBI searches, you know, so keep this query to yourself, would you?"

"Always."

"You're a pest, but you're my pest. I'll give the search a shot. Let me know if you get a vibe on any other details."

"She was rich," I added, ignoring the warm fuzzies from Nick's claim, likewise my guilt over Werner's early-morning rescue. "An heiress, maybe." One who could make talking to her father sound like a threat.

"A kidnapping?" Nick asked, his computer keys clicking in the background as he took my information. "Might there have been a ransom note?"

"I never thought of that."

"That's why I'm the professional, ladybug. I'll narrow it down to a missing person, possible name Isobel, possible age twenty to thirty, in southeastern Connecticut, that time frame."

I bit my lip. "And see if there are any abandoned wells around here that have been dry for like half a century."

"Hunch or vintage outfit?" Nick asked.

"Both?"

"Ah, ladybug, sometimes you scare me."

"I hope I do more than that to you."

Eve rolled her eyes and started looking through some other boxes.

"Oh, if I could get my hands on you now," Nick threatened.

"What would you do if you could?"

"Don't talk so loud!" Eve yelled, fingers in her ears.

Nick growled. "Use your imagination."

"Can I call you?" I asked.

"About what your imagination comes up with?" He was using his bedroom voice. "Please do."

"Nick. Be serious."

"Call, but I turn off the phone when I don't want to give away my location, so I might not answer."

"Are you and Alex in danger?"

"Gotta go, ladybug."

My phone went dead. "He hung up on me!"

Eve headed back my way. "A missing person?" she asked.

"A hunch based on the well. I didn't tell you, but I've seen it more than once."

"So," she said, thoughtfully. "Not a 'wishing' well. A nightmare well?"

"Deep. Dry. Isolated."

Twenty-one

I am always returning to one piece of cloth—a rectangle—
because it is the elementary form in clothing.

—ISSEY MIYAKE

❧

A couple of Werner's officers took the new boxes of clothing donations inside and left them in a hearse stall. I mean,
a designer nook. So I wouldn't have to touch the cape and
dress again, I had Eve put them in her backseat before I got
in. "I'll try the dress on later and see if I can get anything
more on the couple."

Eve looked in her backseat. "You shouldn't do that
alone."

"Are you volunteering to be there, or should I ask Aunt
Fiona? I do need to talk to her."

With a finger to her chin, Eve pretended she had a di-
lemma. "Oh, I think Fee should have a turn."

I needed Eve's humor. "Chicken."

"Cluck. Don't we have a car to return? What time does
the rental place close?"

"Oy. Let's go. I don't want to pay for another week."

Two seconds before the rental place closed, Eve waited while I turned in my car. "I'm beat," I said, getting into her passenger seat.

"You've only been up for a few hours."

"I have two night's sleep to make up for. Take me back to the shop to see if the cops are gone."

She turned her car in that direction. "Do you know what kind of car you want?" she asked.

There was only one car dealership in Mystick Falls, and I liked to support the locals. "Tomorrow, after school, you can drive me to Goodwin's. I want an Element."

"You just returned an Element."

"I know and I loved it."

"It's a big rectangle."

"Basic structure. I've heard it called an Amish buggy and a four-slice toaster. I don't care what anybody else thinks. The design is brilliant and I love the way it drives. Easy on gas, big enough to haul clothes, backseats that disappear to make like a truck bed. I'm in business. It's perfect. I need one. I want one."

"Do me a favor," Eve said. "Tomorrow, when we get to Goodwin's, pretend you're not jonesing, so you don't pay too much. And be prepared to follow my lead and walk."

"You like playing the money game, don't you? You're such a Connecticut Yankee."

She buffed her nails on her vest then pretended to admire their black sheen. "I *have* been known to make car salesmen cry."

I chuckled. "Fine. I choose; you negotiate, genius."

"I am a genius. I wrote you a sweet computer program to run the shop. Keeps track of stock, designers, vintage year, provenance, flaws, every thingamabobbin you can imagine. I designed a bookkeeping module that works with it: quarterly tax reports, the works. Bodacious program, if I do say so myself. It'll work with a tax program, too, so I can file your quarterlies and such."

"Eve, that's such an enormous gift."

"You're worth it. Are you all right?"

I rubbed my temple. "I'm not sure." I grabbed the cape and dress off her backseat and set them in my lap.

Eve did a double take. "Oh, please don't do that in my car."

"Why? I don't pee my pants when I have a vision."

"No, *I* do!"

Nobody could match my skewed sense of humor as well as Eve. Except maybe Nick, in bed.

When we drove by my shop, the crime scene tape was gone. "Yay. Pull in so I can run up and see what they took. Don't even stop the engine. I'll be back in two minutes."

It didn't look as if they'd taken anything. Not even the quilt I found folded on the fainting couch, back side up, also quilted but with a different palette of colors, this side as dusty-clean as the other.

No body grunge. Dante was right. What a relief.

I was guessing the police hadn't figured out that the bones had been wrapped in it. I was of two minds: Don't tell. And don't tell until *after* I spent more quality time with the quilt.

I went with: don't tell, yet.

I wanted to take it home, but I didn't want to touch it, so I emptied the drawer from the cabinet and sat the folded quilt on top so I only touched wood. Last time I checked, I couldn't read old furniture. On the stairs, I screamed when Dante materialized in front of me.

"See?" he said. "You always scream, no matter where I appear around you."

"I have to run, but I'll be back tomorrow."

His disappointment gave me a little heart twitch, but I kept going. I locked up, opened Eve's back door, and set my package inside.

Eve about fainted when she saw the quilt. "We're now carrying two, no, three psychic firecrackers? In *my* car. Don't take this wrong, but I want you and your vision makers the hell out of here."

"Take me home, then."

"I'll do the computer search on the quilt tonight." She smacked her head. "Bizarro! Do you think that's the prize quilt we're looking for?"

"If I'm taking my clues from the universe, I think it's possible, though I won't say I'm thinking straight. I'm weeks behind in getting the shop ready and twelve days away from my grand opening, which won't be half bad now that the White Star Circle of Spirit witches are having their Halloween costume ball at my place."

"Say again?"

I told her about Fiona's request.

"Can I come?" Eve asked.

"Sure, and bring a date."

"You're on."

When we got to my house, she ran my psychic firecrackers up to my room for me, she *so* didn't want to be around when I touched them.

"I have an idea," I said when she came back down. I

handed her a cinnamon bun. "Want to go and talk to Sampson's sister?"

Eve checked her watch. "It might be a bit late for a social call by the time we get there. It's a heck of a haul around the river along those winding roads."

"Not by rowboat, it isn't."

"You're right. We could be there by seven forty-five as the fish swims."

"The Sweets hinted that Suzanne was dating Tunney, which would only give him motive for killing Sampson if he planned to marry her *and* if she's Sampson's heir *and* if he's greedy, which he most certainly is not."

"On the other hand," Eve said, "maybe she seduced him into it and she's the greedy one. Men have been known to do stupid things in the name of love."

"So true. I'd like to think Tunney's above that, but— Let's tell her we need her help to get Tunney off the suspect list and gauge her reaction."

"Makes sense," Eve said. "Want to change clothes?"

"Of course!" I ran upstairs.

"Can I borrow a spare Windbreaker or something?" Eve asked behind me. "That's the beauty of wearing casual all the time. I'm up for anything."

"Except formal," I said, donning a cashmere cowl-neck top, jeans, matching jacket, a Hermès scarf, and least-favorite boots, in case we had to get out in the mud.

From my closet, I tossed Eve an orange variegated knit poncho.

She squeaked and dropped it as if it would bite. "Get out of my way, you wackadoodle. What do you have that's black, or at least dark?"

She pulled out the same poncho in browns and blacks. "Brat," she said, sliding it over her head.

I laughed. "You can't blame a girl for trying."

We knew our rowboat and had long ago mastered the art of cutting swiftly through the water, the two of us in sync. Soon, we were pulling up to the Sampson dock.

One problem. Sampson's sister wasn't alone, but sitting on the patio kissing a man in a wheelchair. Flirting and foreplay, definitely, when she was supposed to be dating Tunney, or so the Sweets implied, as Virginia Statler nearly did when she bought the parking lot kimono.

"I don't think it's a good time," Eve whispered.

"No kidding. She's cheating on Tunney."

"Nah. They're . . . exploring new territory."

"Is that man-magnet speak?"

"Yes, we rule mere mortals."

I started rowing. "Let's hope Tunney agrees."

"You're not going to tell him?"

"Of course not, but he's bound to find out."

Sampson's sister stood. "Is someone in the water?"

"There's no one there," the man said. "Stop being so easily spooked. You'll give us away."

"Row faster," I whispered.

"She didn't see us," Eve said, out of earshot.

"I'm having heart palpitations, anyway."

"Did you expect us to get into, and out of, more trouble at home than we did in New York?"

"Out of? Don't count your chickens. Werner could be waiting at the boathouse when we get back."

"So let's put the boat in the Sweets' boathouse and walk home."

"Eve Meyers, you wicked little devil. Speaking of which, what do you think that conglomerate was going to pay Sampson for his corner lot?"

"Why does it matter now?"

"I think knowing would give us an idea of how badly someone might want Sampson dead."

"Unless you go through Sampson's papers, I don't see how you can find out."

"I own the corner lot that mirrors Sampson's. I'll give the company a call and see if they make an offer."

"You wouldn't sell. Would you?"

"Of course not. But they wouldn't know that. I want a jumping-off figure."

"You mean a going-up-in-flames figure?"

"Ouch, but yes." After Eve left, I went up to soak in a hot tub and try to put my random puzzle pieces together, but nothing fit—yet.

By the time I climbed in bed, nothing made sense. I dreamed of dead neighbors and bags of bones. Once, I called my knowledge "synchronicity." Consoling word.

Aunt Fiona would call it "universal intervention" *if* I believed in Fee's "pay attention to the signs" theory.

By six A.M., only "lunacy" made sense. My own. Dad would agree. Aunt Fiona would have a different take. I couldn't wait to see her. I showered and chose a seventies, front-zip Lolita minidress—easy off when trying on clothes—Belgian loafers in lizard calf, and a Vuitton bag.

I grabbed the garment bag I'd dropped over the cape and dress set last night and the white plastic garbage bag I dropped the quilt in from the drawer. I couldn't find my father, but his car sat in the drive so I left a note. "Borrowing your car. Call if you need it."

I rang Aunt Fiona's doorbell at seven but she answered in her robe. Very unusual. "Madeira," she said, looking rather like a deer in headlights.

"You're having a sleep in, aren't you? I'm sorry. I'll come back later."

"No. No, I'm up. Come in."

"Fee, I can't find that spare toothbrush." My father came into the living room wearing nothing but his pajama bottoms, the towel he was using to dry his hair temporarily covering his eyes.

"Harry," Aunt Fiona said. "We have company."

Twenty-two

Fashion is the science of appearance, and it inspires one
with the desire to seem rather than to be.

—HENRY FIELDING

❧

"Madeira!" My father's ears positively glowed. How cute
and guilty did he look with his salt-and-pepper hair spiked
in all directions and his towel now unnecessarily covering
him like a loincloth? "I slept on the sofa," he said. "See the
blank—" His gaze whipped to Fiona.

"I like a neat house." She shrugged. "I put the bedding
away."

I turned back to my dad. For the second time that I could
recall, he shocked me. "Dad, you have a tattoo." Harry Cutler with a pentagram tat on his shoulder. No wonder he
wore undershirts summer and winter.

"Your mother made me do it. We'd been touring the Finger Lakes wineries. Had a bit too much Madeira at one. That
was the n—I didn't know what it meant. You don't, do you?"

"Sure," I said. "It's a star." A pentacle he'd gotten nine

months before my birth. He could have said wine instead of Madeira and I wouldn't know, but that was Harry. "You are such a lousy liar," I said.

"No, it's true."

"I know it is, Dad." Which meant that he had, indeed, slept on the sofa. "So, what's up with you two?"

"I took Fee to a psychologist friend yesterday," my father said, "because of the casket thing. He talked to her and said she shouldn't be alone for a while, so I stayed here so she could sleep better in her own bed."

I looked between him and Aunt Fiona. "I see."

"Your father's only helping me out of guilt," she said. "Because he mocked me."

"Yes, and the ogre needs to get dressed," my father snapped, disappearing.

"The spare toothbrushes are in the top drawer of the vanity. In the back," Aunt Fiona yelled.

"I need to talk to you," I whispered as I dragged her toward her sunroom.

"We'll have breakfast together, the three of us," she said, smile forced. "We can talk after your father goes."

"The three of us for breakfast? After that scene? Just shoot me now."

"I'm going home for breakfast," my father said, making us both jump. He looked sloppier than I'd ever seen. Wet hair, barely combed, button-down shirt unbuttoned, one shirt tail in, one out.

Aunt Fiona giggled.

"What?" my father barked.

She winked. "That's a great look on you. Fetching."

"Hey," my father snapped. "I'm trying to convince the kid of our innocence, here."

"I'm not a kid, and *I'm* not innocent. I don't know why *you* should be. I'll just stay the hell away from the two of you first thing in the morning."

My father growled, a bit like a pirate. "You stay with her tonight, Madeira."

"How about she stays with us tonight?"

"Her name is Fiona," she said, hands on hips.

My father shook his head and opened her front door. "How did my car get here?"

"I borrowed it. Care to drive it home so the neighbors don't call the men in white to come pick up the hobo impersonating the fanatically tidy Professor Cutler?"

He sighed, turned, held out a hand, ears red as Rudolph's nose, and caught his keys midair. Then he slammed the front door behind him without saying good-bye.

Fiona and I fell into a puddle of hilarity on her sofa. We'd no sooner catch our breaths than we'd start again. Reliving my dad's look and reactions took us right through breakfast, a break I needed from the death, bones, and fiery chaos of the past two days.

We talked only about my father until the last dish had been put away. Then Fiona went into the living room and took out the cape, dress, and quilt.

She examined them, touched each one, then she lit candles. "This for harmony, for courage," she said, continuing with positivity, vision, and protection.

I'd always experienced peace here in her earth-toned Celtic-decorated home, which I knew nowhere else. Right now, even my psychic firecrackers fizzled as I calmed.

Aunt Fiona sat on the edge of her butterscotch leather recliner. "I know you came to talk," she said, "but I have a proposition. Can I go first?"

"Anything to put off vision chasing."

"I'd like to do a sweeping ritual at your shop before you start moving in, get rid of the negative vibes. And I'm not just talking about the bones, but the residual energy from so many people over the years who might, or might not, have moved on from there."

"Right, those who were embalmed or cremated. I hadn't thought. My shop could be riddled with negative energy."

"I'm sure it has positive energy, too, but that isn't the problem. Negative is. If you'd like, you can join me in the ritual sweeping?"

The invitation threw me. I'd hardly gotten used to being psychometric. I wasn't ready to wear my mother's magic cloak. "Maybe I'll just watch this time."

Aunt Fiona patted my knee. "That's fine, sweetie. Whatever makes you comfortable. How's your schedule?"

"With eleven days to prepare for my grand opening without having started?" I took a calming breath. "Eve's taking me to buy a car after she gets home from school today. Can we sweep negative energy tomorrow?"

"Oh, the electrician is coming tomorrow. I nearly forgot to tell you."

"After the electricians are finished, then," I said. "We can sweep away their negative energy, too."

Aunt Fiona smiled. "You said *we*."

"Did I? Slip of the tongue?"

"Now, what did you want to talk to me about?"

I told her about my visions and tried on the cape's matching dress, walked around in it, but— "Nothing."

She nodded. "Change and we can spread the quilt on the rug to see if we can learn anything more."

After I did, the quilt was ready. "It's beautiful with that

huge heart at its center formed by the way the fabric is pieced. I'd never have known, if you hadn't spread it out."

"I'm anxious to get my hands on it," Aunt Fiona said. "But I wanted to wait for you. Are you ready?"

I got on my knees across from her, beside the quilt. "Let's do it."

Palms down, I got a picture of skillful hands wearing a big diamond embroidering one of the quilt squares and sensed the quilter's love and sadness.

Moving my hands, I saw through her eyes the memory of her husband dancing with someone else and felt her hurt, but still didn't see his face.

I found a bump in the quilt near a zipper. "I found another pocket." I opened my eyes, unzipped it, and slid my hand inside.

Aunt Fiona watched as I pulled my clutched fist from the pocket and opened it.

In my palm sat a platinum wedding ring and an emerald-cut diamond the size of Texas.

Twenty-three

Fashion, even anti-fashion, is forever. It's the only way we can become the characters we wish to be.

—CHRISTIAN LACROIX

❧

I wanted to cry, but I firmed my lips against the emotion overwhelming me at the sight of that ring.

Aunt Fiona rubbed my arm. "Tell me."

I had to swallow before I could. "They belong to the woman who wore the cape. I'm afraid the bones the police found must be hers, too. They were wrapped in the quilt. No, wait. I only saw the well when I touched the quilt. Oh! The diamond is what connects the woman who wore the cape to the quilt *and* to my visions of the well."

"Maybe," Aunt Fiona said, "she slipped her rings in the quilt pocket when she was wrapped in it, so somebody would find it and look for her."

That made sense. "Yes. Her quilt—this quilt, I believe— was entered into some kind of county fair–type competition. Did you get anything from touching it?"

Aunt Fiona shivered. "A dark place. Tire tracks. I'm not as good at this as you are."

I hugged her. "There has to be *something* you're not aces at," I said. "Let's turn it over."

We did and stood back. "Tire tracks," I said. "Just there." I pointed. "Very light. Barely visible."

Aunt Fiona had trouble finding them. "Oh, now I see. It wasn't run over or they'd be darker, so it must have pressed up against a tire."

"A *spare*?"

"In a dark trunk." Aunt Fiona completed my unwanted thought.

"On her one-way trip to the well?" I suggested. "I have to take the quilt and rings to the police. Too bad I can't pass along my visions."

"I'll take you to get your dad's car, but give me your shop key, and I'll fill my car with some of your vintage stash and bring it over, help you start moving in. Meet me there, after. I have some ideas to run by you."

I hugged her. "If Isobel had someone like you, she might have been missed, and found, before she died."

"I love you, too, sweetie."

I called the station from Aunt Fiona's car and made sure Werner would be waiting. My father came out as we pulled into the drive. "I need your car again, Dad. Aunt Fee will explain." She'd know what *not* to say. Dad wasn't ready to know how many of my mother's gifts I inherited. If he ever was, we'd tell him in small doses.

"Madeira, my keys are in the ignition."

"Harry Cutler!" Aunt Fiona was still scolding him as I drove away. Bickering or not, they made me smile, a release valve considering my destination and why.

Halfway there, it occurred to me that the wedding rings might be engraved and that I might be wise to try them on, in case. I parked on a side road facing the river and tried one, then the other, then both.

The rings gave me nothing. Probably what the marriage was worth. *Or*, I couldn't read vintage jewelry.

Whatever was engraved in the wedding ring was so small I stopped at a drugstore for a magnifying glass. I copied the initials into a small notebook I carried for design ideas. The initials were G. I. L. to E. E. M., 7-7-77. The information told me nothing and pretty much put period to the name Isobel.

When I stepped into Werner's office, he came around his desk and shut the door behind me. "To what do I owe the honor? Is that the quilt from your storage room?"

"It is." I placed it on his desk. "You said details were important. I wasn't there when your men searched my storage room, so it didn't occur to me to explain, but the foot bones were wrapped in it. I found a light tire mark on one side and these in a zip pocket on one of the squares." I showed him the rings.

"Is that rock real?" Werner took it between his fingers to hold up to the light.

"It is. Jewelry is fashion, after all. It's vintage and flawless, so it might be thirty to fifty grand worth of real. Maybe more. Initials and dates are engraved in the wedding band. Might help you ID the bones. Or not."

I also had a leopard fingernail, but since it belonged to the outfit that gave me a psychic lead, I'd follow up on it myself.

"Thank you, Madeira. I appreciate the new evidence."

"Happy to help." I was jumping-out-of-my-skin prickly

with the memories of us in my storage room. His hands in my hair, heartbeat beneath my ear. Tenderness. Caring? I wanted to gnaw off my lipstick like in junior high when I faced a boy I had a crush on. Not that I had a crush on Werner. Far from it. But with our guards down, our connection *had* been intense.

Werner wasn't too comfortable, either. His erratic moves and inability to look me in the eye gave him away.

He opened his door but I shut it, both of us still on the inside. "Listen, so we can get back to our old, deep dislike, and away from this nerve-wracking awareness, should I just call you Wiener, again?"

Laughter erupted in the squad room.

I stepped back and followed Werner's gaze to the open transom above his door. "Well, guess I took care of that. Have a nice day, Detective."

I left, wincing at the round of applause I got, which would help ice over our residual tension. Werner should pretty much hate me again. Good thing he couldn't fire every cop who applauded. He wouldn't have a force.

On my way to Vintage Magic, I stopped at Yolanda's, Mystic's most trendy nail salon. I used to babysit her kids.

"Maddie, so glad to have you home to stay," Yolanda said. "Come to get your nails done, I hope?"

"I had them done in New York a few days ago. I'll be due soon. Can I make an appointment?"

After I did, I took out the leopard fingernail. "Do any of your customers have their nails done this way?"

"I have a couple. Leopard and Lace, closer to the highway, probably does more. Why are you carrying a gaudy old fingernail?"

"Somebody left me some primo vintage clothes. One of

the outfits had this in the pocket. Can you mention to your leopard nail customers that if they left me the pricey clothes to come by so I can thank them in person? Unless they'd rather remain anonymous, of course."

She shrugged. "Sure. See you next week."

I stopped by Leopard and Lace as well, made the same request, and though I didn't know the owner, she gave me customer names and directed me to their houses. Bad business, that, with all this right of privacy stuff. I could grind the Mystick Falls gossip mill with this one, but I'd already given it a great big grind at the station.

I stopped at my favorite gift shop and bought a silk wreath and had the owner add some sprigs of dried heather and myrtle, which would afford my shop some protection, according to Aunt Fiona. Something about myrtle at your front door and heather at your garden gate. Or was that lavender at the gate? Anyway, the trim with the aubergine roses, dark green leaves, and a pale sage bow would look amazing on my lavender door.

Then I stopped to see Tunney, who seemed to be getting ready to leave his meat market. "Can I help you, Suzy Q?"

"Maybe. What's the name of the company that Sampson was trying to sell his property to?"

He took a folder from a file drawer behind the meat counter and handed it to me. "This is all I have on the company, my research as a council member. Eventually, they'll damage the economy, though they promised to make it better. The environment and our ecological structure could suffer as well. Main Street, our historic provenance, would eventually disappear—it's happened in other small towns the company 'took over'—but they always flourish. You can have it, but why?"

"Part of my plan to get you off the suspect list."

"Maddie girl, you're the best."

"Well, I haven't done anything yet. I'm just nosing around. And don't you tell anybody."

Afterward, I sat in Tunney's parking lot for nearly an hour reading all the information Tunney had gathered, calling company phone numbers and leaving mine, then I turned Dad's car toward Vintage Magic.

Traffic slowed near Bank Street because my parking lot overflowed with cars. My father directed traffic outside, while Fiona stood at the door as if directing people inside.

Gee, was I having a sale?

Twenty-four

What do I think about the way most people dress? Most people are not something one thinks about.

—DIANA VREELAND

I had to park behind Mystic Pizza, rarely easy, and crossed the street. My father saw me and shouted, "Surprise!" the word suddenly echoed by everyone. I got hugged, kissed, and congratulated to within an inch of my life. "What's going on?" I asked Fiona. "I mean, I love the attention, but why?"

"It's a big day. You moved into your shop."

"I did? Holy Harrods, they brought my stock?"

"They're *not* unpacking boxes," Fiona said, which allowed me to breathe. "They've just moved them from above my garage. Preservation boxes are in the last stall, the way you left them. Anything in a garment bag is on a rack. Tunney is assembling racks. The mannequins you had shipped to my place are in the second-to-the-last stall."

"The second to the last *nook*," I said. "I'm trying to say nooks instead of stalls."

Fiona chuckled. "Best to remove hearse images as soon as possible."

I went to thank Tunney, feeling bad about finding Suzanne kissing someone else. I guess what really bothered me about her was how she enjoyed herself so easily days after her brother's murder.

"Did I hold you up, Tunney, by stopping in to see you a while ago?"

He laughed. "You surely did, Maddie girl."

"Thanks for the folder. I made a good start on my project."

He kissed my cheek. "I'm indebted."

"Looks like it's a wash. There are thirty racks to be built."

He groaned to amuse me and got back to it.

I tried to talk to everyone and couldn't believe how much I'd missed my neighbors. None of them cared about fashion like I did. Some always thought I was a bit nuts. Others considered this a thrift shop and expected me to go broke the first week. Many had left clothes best suited to a scarecrow. One old dear even left me a box of socks to darn. I intended to replace them with new ones.

Our neighbors were used to helping. Since my mother died when I was ten, my siblings all younger, they had been there for the Cutler kids, to fix a skinned knee, attend a hockey game or a school play, or help one of us go into business.

"This is unbelievable," I shouted above the hum of voices. "You're wonderful. Friends and neighbors working together like bees building a hive. My hive. I love you all!" I sent them a double-handed kiss.

Twice I'd gotten applauded today, but this time, I felt a rush of pride and gratitude, in counterpoint to my embarrassment at the police station.

"You can thank them individually tonight," my father said. "Welcome-home party at our place, six o'clock. Don't be late. You're the guest of honor."

"Dad!" I was welling up big time, here. In a minute, I'd be blubbering.

Eve walked in, hands on hips. "Cutler, you started without me, again. You know how I like to be first on the scene. And after I got color for your coming-home party."

I looked her up and down. "What color?"

She held up a pinkie. She might still have nine black fingernails but one bore a tiny little ladybug.

"Red! You got red? For me? Now I *am* going to cry."

"It gets better," she whispered. "I found leopard nails. We're having drinks with her tomorrow night."

Werner walked in, boxes stacked to cover his face.

"Thank you, Detective," I said, though he grunted and kept walking.

I followed, and after he put down the boxes, he wasn't happy to find me behind him. "You didn't fire anybody because of me, did you?"

He pulled me into the deep end of the nook. "No, but if you worked for me, I'd fire *you*."

"That would be fair."

"You're the hero of the entire squad room."

"Your men lack taste in who they look up to. I'm surprised you helped me move in, considering."

"I keep my promises, Madeira."

"I admire your integrity."

"Don't do nice; it doesn't suit." He stepped around me. "Continue to be a brat. Makes life easier."

How cryptic of him.

He hesitated and turned back to me. "And stop trying to solve crimes that are none of your business."

"Big leap from 'thanks for the evidence.'"

"So was your public offer to brand me again."

"Wait," I said, stopping him by catching *his* sleeve. "Which murder isn't my business? The one that took me from my shop so it could get burglarized, or the one where the body was found in my storage room?"

"What makes you think the bones from your storage room were the result of a murder?" Werner asked before walking away.

Twenty-five

It's all about proportion, shape, line, finish, fabric, balance.
—TOM FORD

Among the movers, I spotted my sister, Sherry, and her new husband, Justin Vancortland V.

Aunt Fiona saw them, too. "That's it," she said. "They're carrying the last of your stock. You're all moved in."

Sherry put her boxes on my counter and threw herself into my arms. I hadn't yet seen my favorite baby sister, between her job as a kindergarten teacher and all the excitement since I got home. "I missed you, Cherry Pie. Isn't this great? The whole town pitched in."

"We'd do anything for you, Sis," Justin said, giving my shoulders a squeeze.

I honestly liked my new brother-in-law and I was grateful Sherry hadn't gone to jail for murder instead of marrying him. "Who's idea was this barn raising?"

"Dad's," Sherry said. "He's out there bragging about 'his' construction work."

"Well, he should." She and I walked arm in arm to the front of the shop. "He did a brilliant job. Aunt Fee, did you put this idea into Dad's head?"

"I'd like to say yes, but Harry Cutler showed me up is what he did, and he's going to pay."

Sherry winked at me.

It didn't take long for the place to clear. I waved from the door as cars left. I'd get a chance to thank everyone personally in a couple of hours, anyway.

After Justin and Sherry left, I turned to Eve. "Do we have time to go car shopping between now and six?"

"Sure. You know what you want. Let's go. Goodwin's, here we come."

"Give me a minute to lock up."

"I'll do it," Aunt Fiona said. "Go. Enjoy."

"I can't believe the whole of Mystick Falls moved me in," I said, as we drove away.

"You spent too much time in New York where you don't talk to your neighbors without a weapon in your purse."

I shrugged. "It wasn't that bad."

Eve chuckled. "The worms in the apple? Remember?"

"True, but there are worms around here, too, judging by the body count."

"And the wildcat piece of work we're having drinks with." Eve rolled her eyes.

I turned in my seat. "How did you find her?"

"She found me and invited us for drinks."

"Sounds a bit like an agenda."

"Ya think?"

Eve glanced at me. "You didn't ask me who she is."

"I already had a mental picture of Leopard Nails. Who is she?"

"Lolique LaFleur, Councilman McDowell's trophy wife."

"You jest. The town gossip columnist is married to the publicity hound from hell? Her name sure doesn't give away her courage," I said. "I look forward to meeting the woman who can stand to live with that man. It's a wonder he never broke his arm patting himself on the back."

"I think he did once," Eve said.

"Stop the car and back up a bit."

Eve hit the brakes, looking like I was nuts, but she put the car in reverse so I could see the two women sparring beside their cars on the overlook.

"That's Sampson's sister. She just left the shop," I said, "but I don't know who she's with."

"Lolique," Eve said. "Leopard Nails herself."

"How do they know each other? Why would they argue?"

"Everybody knows everybody around here. Besides, people stop Lolique on the street for her autograph. You know what their stances remind me of? Me and my mother when we disagree on something we've never agreed on. That's a 'here we go again' discussion, if ever I've seen one. The way their arms are moving takes practice."

"I never knew you to be so observant and so *wrong*. Sheesh, drive, will you, before they see us."

Eve hit the gas and we glided away.

I shook my head. "It doesn't add up. For somebody who hasn't been in Mystick Falls long, Sampson's sister knows a lot of people, consorting with the local butcher, Lolique, a local celebrity, and a man in a wheelchair."

"Consorting?" Eve asked.

We made up outlandish "consorting" scenarios until we pulled into the car lot. "You look at Elements, let me do the talking, and don't drool in front of a salesman."

I saluted. "Gotcha."

Inside, Eve interviewed salesmen and I admired a painting of an auburn-haired woman, front and center on an upper-floor wall, pose regal, features delicate, a sweet expression as she looked down on everyone.

"Who is she?" I asked a woman behind a counter.

"Madeira? Maddie Cutler, star pupil, is that you?"

I knew the face but it took a minute to get a name. "Natalie Hayward? How are you?" I'd once taken an advanced sewing course from her, a rare adult who let you call them by their first name. She must be in her early fifties, by now. "You look great," I said.

"I am and so glad that you're back to stay."

"Me, too. Do you work here? No more sewing lessons?"

Her eyes crinkled with her smile. "Administrative assistant to the owner pays better."

So why sit in an information booth? I wondered.

"I'm filling in during the floor manager's break," she said. "I like to get out of the office once in a while. What did you want to know?"

"The name of the woman in that painting?"

"Oh, she's the last of Zachary Goodwin's direct line, his daughter, Gwendolyn. Zachary's great-great-grandfather started the dealership and swore it would stay in the family, though an in-law owns the place now. Gwendolyn's painting has to stay up, or her second cousin inherits. He's the dark-haired man having coffee over there."

"The one in the wheelchair?" The man Eve and I might

have seen kissing Suzanne Sampson in her backyard. How many men in wheelchairs could there be in Mystick Falls?

"Yep. Gary Goodwin. Comes in every day to be sure her picture's still there. God forbid we should have an earthquake and it falls. Gary will take right over." She laughed as if she made a joke, but it seemed forced.

"Would it be a disaster if he took over?"

"No, everyone likes Gary, but he doesn't have what it takes to make Goodwin's flourish."

"Why do you say that?"

"He votes against dealership needs at board meetings, because he hates the owner. Gary should have inherited. Zachary Goodwin's will was a surprise." Natalie caught someone's eye and stiffened.

I looked behind me but saw only the man in question looking the other way.

"Sorry," she said. "I'm talking out of turn."

"It's okay. I like local history. One more thing. Has Goodwin needed that chair his whole life?"

"No, it was a car accident before they opened this place. His physical injuries healed to the extent they could, but that's old news."

"Excuse us," Eve said, pulling me well away from the central counter. "No paying cash, Mad, which I know is your preference," she whispered. "You want a payment plan to give you wiggle room, money wise. You can always pay it off early, if Vintage Magic is hopping. What color?"

I love Eve. She'd jump into the ocean to save me. I knew, because she'd done that when we were five.

I patted the loaded Element in the showroom. "I want this one. It's cinnamon. Isn't it beautiful? The way its color flows from light to dark reminds me of a shiny bolt of sateen that changes color depending on how you move it in the light. See how the color graduates from brown to a dark antique bronze."

"Get real. That's the lighting in the showroom. You need me, Cutler, so go look at a brochure or something while I talk money."

I felt as if I should salute, but I wouldn't mock the hand that saved me a buck. Besides, I *was* used to premium Big Apple prices. Things were different in Connecticut, and Eve was certainly making it easy. No zip, no fuss.

I read a history of the Goodwin dealerships on the wall while I waited. This was the second of two locations. The first, in Groton, had been started a century before. This one was practically a new baby at nearly thirty years.

Later, while I perused the brochures, I spotted Councilman McDowell behind a desk. Our eyes met, so I had no choice but to say hello. "Councilman."

"Welcome back to Mystick Falls, Ms. Cutler."

"You know who I am?"

"From the picture in my wife's column that I get force-fed to me at breakfast."

Right. Lolique, the *Entertainment Tonight* of Mystick Falls. Surprise; the publicity hound made me smile. "I didn't know you worked here."

He stood as I approached. "It's worse than that. I own the place." He indicated the chair across from his desk.

I shook my head and remained standing. "Guess you're the in-law who has to keep the portrait of the Goodwin daughter front and center so her cousin won't inherit."

His expression darkened like a thundercloud. Talk about black looks. "Said cousin once spent months on the psych ward and would run this place into the ground if given half a chance."

I stepped back from Councilman McNasty. "I didn't mean to broach a touchy subject."

He masked his expression like a good little politician. "The Goodwin daughter is my dead wife."

Remove foot from mouth. Proceed carefully. "Forgive me. I had no idea."

He nodded to someone across the room. "Your friend's looking for you. Ms. Cutler," he added, as I turned to go, "I'm glad your building escaped the fire."

Unexpected nicety. "Thank you. I am, too."

As I completed the paperwork for the car, I thought I did see our salesman's eyes fill. Eve had used math and logic to shoot down every deal, forcing him to cut his own profit to make the sale. She *could* make car salesmen cry.

"That was an awesome deal, Meyers. I owe you."

"You sure do. It's root beer by the way."

I gave her a blank look as we got in her car.

"The paint job on your Element; it's root beer."

"Bummer," I said. "Cinnamon's an earth element that inspires wealth. Root beer probably inspires ice cream floats." I faced her. "I hope the robbery and fire weren't signs, though moving in today seemed to turn my luck. An honest to grand opening almost seems possible."

"Forget the opening and tell me about these earth elements and signs. Are you playing witch with Fiona?"

"Don't pop a stitch. It's just a little folklore, which hasn't done me any good." I sighed and bit my lip. "You know, there's something about Goodwin's that bothers me, but I can't figure out what it is."

Twenty-six

To be carried by shoes, winged by them. To wear dreams on one's feet is to begin to give reality to one's dreams.

—ROGER VIVIER

❧

As I got ready for my welcome-home party, Sampson's conglomerate buyer called, and I hoped to get the details I'd been waiting for. By the time we finished talking money, he told me something about Broderick Sampson that I was so happy to learn, I let down my guard and admitted—maybe too soon for more information—that I'd decided not to sell.

The buyer about cried. I, on the other hand, held another puzzle piece. It didn't answer specifics about Sampson's death, but it might help me clear Tunney of the motive people were so willing to pin on him.

I still needed to solve the puzzle of the bones and find out who killed Sampson, so I intended to question everyone tonight. Was it gauche, I wondered, to use one's own coming-home party for unabashed yet clandestine sleuthing? No one would call me on it, except maybe for Werner, but he wouldn't show, not after today.

I chose squashed-heel Mary Janes upholstered in bold pink-on-black chintz, a cheeky shoe by Bennis/Edwards, and paired them with a sixties pink Betsey Johnson minidress, its long sleeves, shirred with elastic in three places, ending with a wrist-flare, an at-home party dress.

The muggy air curled my hair, giving it a bouncy life of its own, so I left it down. After so much time in Eve's convertible, the sun had pulled out the hint of paprika that I liked because it reminded me of my mother.

Cars arrived while I dressed, and I couldn't wait to go down. Chakra hurried me along with her meows.

The Sweets were waiting at the bottom of the back stairs, the ones closest to my bedroom.

"I'm so glad you're here," I said as I hugged them. "I've been dying to invite you to my grand opening ball on Halloween night."

Chakra jumped into my arms to be dutifully petted by them.

As I related details, the younger Sweet's expression soured. "I'm too old for that nonsense," Ethel said.

"Well, I'm not," Dolly, the centenarian, countered. "I'll wear Tracy Lord's wedding dress from *The Philadelphia Story*." She didn't need to say she was more than ready to see Dante again, but I noticed a new twinkle in her eyes.

I took the ladies, one on each arm, and walked them to a sofa. "Can you do me a favor, starting tonight?" I whispered. "Pay close attention to any gossip about Suzanne Sampson and anybody named Isobel."

Dolly trembled in excitement as she agreed, while Ethel shook her head at us. I got them each a plate from the buffet before I went to meet the rest of my guests.

"Aunt Fiona," I said. "Thank you, again, for today. I already thanked Dad, but I know you must have worked hard coordinating."

"Sherry and Justin stayed in the apartment above my garage and handed out boxes to move. That's why I knew when they arrived that they had the last of it. Frankly," Aunt Fiona added, "it's given your father and I something to talk about."

"Are you going to invite him to the Circle of Spirit ball?"

"Invite Harry to a witch ball? I'd rather chew glass."

"I'll invite him, though I might not mention the Circle of Spirit. It's my grand opening, and he's my business partner, of sorts, so he won't say no to me. He might even dance with you."

"Don't bet on it."

"Whatever." I shrugged, but knew how to handle my dad.

I mingled and talked, filled with angst over Suzanne cheating on Tunney. Even my sister-in-law, Tricia, and my six-month-old niece, Kelsey, were here to welcome me home.

Kelsey replaced me as Chakra's new favorite person, so wherever the baby went after that, so did Chakra.

After dinner, Dad asked me to cut the cake. Cameras flashed and everyone called for a speech.

I stood on a chair in the keeping room to be seen from other rooms. "I hope I've thanked you personally," I said, "but if I haven't, thank you from the bottom of my heart. Not only for moving me in but for the clothes you left at my door. I have vintage treasures that will sell. If you see any that you donated for sale, tell me, so I can give you a discount on your first purchase."

I cleared my throat. "Among the donations, however—and I think you know this—are some items not quite designer vintage."

Several people chuckled.

"Not to worry. I'm going to make them work like magic, anyway. Just not *Vintage* Magic. I'll use them to advertise the shop, so everything you've given me is made of gold, like your hearts."

"How can you advertise with nonvintage?" Tunney, a late arrival, asked.

"Tunney! So glad to see you." I blew him a kiss, then I noticed Suzanne beside him, and beside her, Werner.

Scrap. I couldn't ignore Werner after sending Tunney a kiss, but we had a whole different relationship. "Detective," I said. "Whatever it is, I *didn't* do it!"

Kinky retro, I saw his rare smile. Oh! I got a flashback: Werner laughing in the upstairs hall, me in his arms. "Can somebody open a door? It's hot in here."

"What *are* you going to do with the non-designer vintage?" Aunt Fiona asked, repeating Tunney's question.

"I'm having a scarecrow contest, and you're all invited to enter. The day after tomorrow, I'll have a table of freebie clothes to dress your scarecrows."

Light chatter broke out.

"Think theme. You have days to put Mr. or Mrs. Scarecrow together. Judging will take place Sunday at two. Set up your scarecrows from nine to noon, and use the crossed wooden stands that you use on Christmas trees to hold them up. No pole holes in my new parking lot."

Familiar laughter.

"Hang around or come back and look at everyone's scarecrows between twelve and two, have refreshments, stay for the judging, let the tourists enjoy them for the rest of the day, then pick yours up around dusk for your front yard. I'll publicize the event *and* the shop."

"You're a smart girl, Miss Mad," Tunney said.

I saluted. "First prize, second prize, third prize"—I counted on my fingers—"are certificates to my shop. Three hundred, two hundred, and one hundred dollars."

A cheer went up.

"So the old golf shirt with the bleach stain, the dress with blueberry jam are going to help me advertise."

I could *not* look at Werner as people applauded. Too reminiscent of the police station fiasco.

"Who are the judges?" Sherry asked.

"That's a secret, or they'll gain twenty pounds from eating your bribery. You're the best. I am, in fact, supremely happy to be home among you, again. Thank you."

I stepped down and the room buzzed. I went to Tunney as he introduced Werner to Suzanne Sampson.

Werner's stance became rigid as he greeted her, then he turned to me. "I donated the bleached golf shirt."

A joke after today? I never figured Werner for a good sport. "I'll make good use of it."

Tunney nodded. "I wore the dress with the blueberry stain to my senior prom."

Suzanne and I chuckled on cue.

Werner didn't. He watched the two uniformed policemen headed our way.

Twenty-seven

I'm not just selling clothes. I'm offering a world, a philosophy of life.
                                        —RALPH LAUREN

❧

Werner rerouted the officers to the front door as if they shouldn't be there. And well they shouldn't. I'd rather not have my coming-home party ruined, thank you very much. If all our parties ended in some kind of police matter, as my sister's engagement party had, we'd get paranoid and stop partying.

As I released a breath because Werner opened the door to go, he stood aside for more guests to enter.

"Alex! Nick!" I shouted, and Tricia and I ran.

Nick hauled me up and into his arms, my feet not touching the floor. I'd never felt such elation. I hadn't realized I'd missed him so much. Lost in lust, nobody else existed. Nick walked us into an empty back den, pulled me close, hands on my bottom, and pinned me to the wall. I laughed and wrapped my legs around him.

"I've lived for that laugh," he said with a cocky grin. He was safe. He and Alex were safe.

He gave me a welcome-home kiss to die for, all tongue and no breath. And I welcomed him home the same way.

"Ah, ladybug, if we're not on-again, I'm in a lot of trouble, here."

I didn't have a chance to answer because Tunney shouted my name, and Nick swore beneath his breath.

When we got to Tunney, Werner was urging him and Suzanne outside.

Chakra jumped in my arms while I gave Nick an abbreviated explanation, and Nick came outside with me.

Werner stood by a squad car. "I'm sorry about your party. I waited until we got outside."

"You do have probable cause?" Nick asked.

"This is not an FBI matter."

"Probable cause?" I repeated.

Werner sighed. "Conspiracy to commit murder, for a start."

"You think Suzanne and I conspired to kill Sampson?" Tunney asked. "Why would we?"

"Miss Sampson is Broderick's sister," Werner said. "Consequently, he must have left everything to her."

"So you don't have a will," I asked.

Werner ignored me and focused on Tunney. "Since you're dating Suzanne seriously, it follows that the two of you could have killed Broderick to get rich."

Tunney chuckled. "Suzanne and I are not dating at all. We've been over for some time. You're a little mixed up there, Detective."

"Detective," I said. "Since I own the piece of real estate that matches Sampson's, I called the chain store and let them make me an offer. In doing so, I learned, right before the party, that Sampson had no choice but to sell. The IRS was breathing down his neck for tax evasion, and he didn't want to go to jail. Sampson died broke."

Suzanne shrieked.

Werner regarded Tunney, who grinned, but he put Tunney and Suzanne in the squad car anyway.

Werner looked back at me. "Stop sleuthing, Madeira. First chance you get, call the station with the seller's phone number for police follow-up. Now go away."

My jaw dropped. "Talk about gratitude."

"Ladybug, let's go, before he arrests *you*."

"This isn't an arrest," Werner called after us. "I'm taking them in for questioning."

He'd ruined my party, even if he did wait until he got outside. The windows were filled with the faces of curious partygoers.

Our guests speculated that Werner had been waiting to catch Tunney and Suzanne together, a theory that didn't hold water. Whatever his reason, why did he have to take them in at my party? Celebrating ended abruptly after that, and though I hated to see everyone go, an empty house meant more time alone with Nick.

Eventually, only Fiona and the family were left.

"Tricia said she'd planned to stay the night, Dad," Alex said. "And since Nick and I have to fly out early in the morning, is it okay if we stick with the plan?"

"Of course. Fiona's staying as well."

I sighed. Nobody had invited Nick. I walked him outside. On the front step, we resumed where we'd left off, his lips cool and hungry against mine, my fingers in the hair at his nape, my spirits lifting, my problems dissolving, until

Aunt Fiona opened the front door, and we nearly fell into the front hall.

"I've been sent," she whispered with a wink, "though I'm not supposed to admit it. Use the keeping room stairs while your father's locking the back doors. He says Nick will ruin his suit climbing up the getaway tree."

"Yes!" I grabbed Nick's hand, and we ran. Let the spontaneous combustion begin!

Too soon, dawn arrived, and Tricia and I were waving Nick and Alex off. "Same assignment, new location," was all they said before they left. As the waiting limo disappeared, Tricia and I commiserated, compared notes, and she giggled.

"I guess you had a good night," I said.

"Excellent and unplanned. Kelsey might be getting a new brother or sister. Don't worry," she said. "We discussed it first and decided it was a good idea."

"I'll bet you did." We went in arm in arm and met Fiona coming down beside Dad carrying Chakra and Kelsey.

"Oh, so now I know where you were all night, deserter cat."

"Sleeping at the foot of Kelsey's crib," Tricia said.

"Did they leave on time?" my father asked. "I mean, did Alex leave—"

I kissed his cheek. "Thank you, Dad."

"Well," he blustered, "as Fiona said, your mother and I had been married for years by the time we were your age."

"Hey, way to make a girl feel old."

"Not old," Aunt Fiona said. "Grown up and able to make her own decisions."

I checked the time. "With only ten days till my grand

opening, this grown-up has to open her shop by seven for the electricians, not to mention setting out stock."

And I had to make sure that my resident ghost didn't materialize, speak up, and give the guy, or any of his men a stroke.

Twenty-eight

The only way to get forward in fashion is to return to construction.
                                        —JOHN GALLIANO

❧

"Dante," I called when I got to the shop. He appeared, and Chakra and I screamed.

He shook his head. "I rest my case."

"Well, if *I* do that, think of the people who don't expect you to appear."

"Like who?"

"The electricians who'll be here any minute. Do me a favor and stay invisible? I can't afford to repeat the plumber incident. There've been too many weird happenings here already. Before I know it, the place will have a bad rep, and business will suffer. Don't appear, okay?"

He disappeared.

"Dante, I didn't mean to hurt your feelings. You can stay while I'm alone." But he didn't reappear, and that concerned me. "We're friends," I yelled, worried I'd seen the last of him.

With the electricians upstairs, I set up tables and sorted donation boxes into two types, the scarecrow and the vintage. Vintage went on hangers, the rest on tables.

To my surprise, Aunt Fiona and Eve's mother came to lend a hand. "Mrs. Meyers, thank you so much for coming."

Lovable, petite, and soft-spoken, Olga Meyers twisted sentences like she thought in German and translated to English. She wore matronly cotton print housedresses and devoted herself to being a wife and mother. Except for the lovable part, she was the anti-Eve. I'd slept at her house so often after losing my mother, I remembered Mrs. Meyers's good-night kisses better than my mom's.

"Aunt Fiona?" I asked. "Don't you have any clients or court cases this week? You've been around a lot."

"I took vacation time when I knew you were coming home. I figured you could use an extra hand."

"Two hands, extra," Mrs. Meyers said, "with Eve and your dad, for the semester, back to college."

"Well, I certainly can use every hand." I gave Aunt Fiona a steamer to smooth out vintage wrinkles, because I knew she'd use a light hand, and asked Mrs. Meyers to fold scarecrow donations while I continued sorting. By ten, my second floor had working fluorescents, the electricians on their way out the door.

"Olga," Aunt Fiona said. "You needed to start baking by mid-morning for the church bazaar."

"Oh, yes." She kissed my cheek. "Anytime, I'll come and help, Madeira. You call."

Aunt Fiona and I stood alone. "Time for the ritual

sweeping?" I asked. "If you still want to, I mean. If you think we need—"

She chuckled. "No reason to be nervous. You won't break into witch speak or get an uncontrollable urge to circle Mystick Falls on a broom."

I'm not nervous, I'm out of my mind, I thought. Once doors were locked, Aunt Fiona's two big needleworked bags of supplies yielded candles, stones, essential oils, herbs, and sea salt. She had also brought in two, count them, *two* well-used round-bottomed brooms. "Let's get started," she said. "Goddess forbid your father should come by."

"Dad *does* have a key."

"But he also has class this morning. The black and gray candles banish negativity, as does everything I've brought. I chose votives for fire safety and put the black on the floor in corners, not too close to the walls. We'll bless one room at a time and use the same candles in each. Between corners, place one gray candle with a selenite stone, and sprinkle rosemary and pine needles on the floor around them."

She touched my hand. "Okay so far? Not spooked?"

"I'm not," I said, surprised.

"Good. Now, it's important to imagine the negative energy swirling up and away from us as we work."

"What does negative energy look like? Green slime? Jelly shoes? Polyester?"

"Any shape that works for you. Try picturing a spiral of ugly rising through the rooms here and upstairs, then through the roof to disperse into the air. Make it a color you hate and send it flying."

"Smoky folds of chartreuse polyester. I can do that."

"But can you believe it?"

I didn't know I could buy into a "magical" sweeping

away of negativity. I mean, given the building's history, recent and past, it couldn't hurt, yet I wasn't sure I could honestly *believe.* "I don't want to disappoint you, but it's not easy to believe in something that seems like a fairy tale."

"Then picture your mother as she looks in your dream of us dancing beneath the full moon. Imagine her guiding an ugly chartreuse spiral up and out of your building. She'll get rid of the negative energy for you. She'd fight a dragon for you."

Chakra jumped into my arms, and between her soothing presence and the image of my mother, anything seemed possible. "I trust you, Aunt Fee, and I trust my mother's beliefs and magical gifts. I just don't know if I'm ready to make them mine. But you and my mother can rid my building of negative energy, and I can help."

"Thank you, sweetie. Now, light the candles."

She took out the sea salt. "Normally," she said, "I'd use salt water, but I didn't want to stain your newly-finished wood floors, so last night I sprinkled water into the salt and let it dry on a cookie sheet in my oven, though I'll use it like salt water." At the threshold of the people door, she sprinkled it and raised her head as if in prayer.

> Gray Goddess, in your name,
> We neutralize and banish the negative
> From this place where death came.
> Every inch, pediment to peak,
> Negativity depart and nevermore seek.

With Chakra in my arms, both of us calm, I took it all in while I saw my mother whisking negativity up and away from here with the same love she gave to everything.

Aunt Fiona repeated the door blessing—negativity leave but never enter—at the huge unsealed side doors. I still owned two hearses that would need to be wheeled out, after all, so I needed a set of usable barn doors, which also might work for a large display or shipment.

Aunt Fiona neutralized dressing rooms, bathroom, stairs, and the top floor, with door blessings at windows.

The longer she worked her magic, the friskier Chakra became, bouncing off of us, howling as if she were chanting her own call for shelter from harm. And through it, I thought I heard my mother laugh, faint but true.

When Chakra jumped back in my arms, I felt calmer, less skeptical, more hopeful about my spiritual beliefs and the possibility of aligning them with nature. An earth-based belief system made sudden sense. Time to open my mind about my heritage.

After the blessing, Aunt Fee lit two protective smudge sticks—bound, dried white sage leaves—one for each of us, which we held as we circled each room, up and down, the pungent, not unpleasant scent following us, banishing negativity as we went. Aunt Fiona chanted:

> Purify this place with peace and grace.
> Every floor, room, nook, and stair,
> Protection, love, and joy ensnare.
> With harm to none, hear our prayer.

Finally, she offered me a broom so we could sweep our way upstairs. "Only if you want to," she said.

Magic or not. Did I have it in me? More to the point, if I did, was I ready to accept it?

Maybe, maybe not. As my mother's daughter, I answered the question. "I'll accept the broom on the condition that I sweep in Mom's place."

"How appropriate." Aunt Fiona squeezed my hand. "Kathleen cherished this broom. I didn't want the knowledge to color your decision, but your reaction reveals your natural talents coming through."

"I don't mind them coming through on their own," I said, "but I'm not ready to force them."

"I respect that, sweetie, and I'd never have suggested this ritual, if I didn't consider it imperative to your well-being. When you want to read beginner's books on the craft, let me know. For now imagine your mother's hands on the broom, as they so often were, but over yours, guiding you and walking beside you."

"If only I could see her like I can see *him*."

"My name is Dante," our watcher said, uncrossing his arms and uncoiling his lanky body to straighten and approach us. Not hard to look at. Not hard at all.

He examined our brooms, with doubt yet with curiosity and respect for our purpose. "By now, I guess you've figured out that *I'm* not negative."

Fiona chuckled. "I knew that."

"So did I."

Dante's face relaxed. "Then you aren't trying to get rid of me?"

Who wouldn't want a hunk like him around? "Never."

He smiled, chin dimple deep. "Thank you. Proceed," he said. "I'll picture the negative energy here—and there's been plenty—going up in that ugly-colored smoke spiral with you, basement to chimney."

"Concentrate hard on the basement, Dante," Aunt Fiona said. "Neither of us can picture it."

"Happy to," he said.

My confidence grew in our task. Funny how spirit confirmation helped, when so few of us saw spirits at all.

Us? I questioned. Those of us connected to more than one plane. Those of us with a gift. Hmm. I'd included myself in "us" without hesitation. Imagine that.

I followed Aunt Fiona's lead and swept in a circular motion almost feeling the weight of dark energy flying from the ends of our brooms like sparks that burned themselves out. Negativity disappearing, leaving in its place a clean, pure energy that evoked peace and hope.

Funny, Aunt Fiona hadn't *told* me to feel such strong emotions, this certain belief. She hadn't said this time to picture it happening. The act simply slipped into my being on the dawning wings of a natural cognition and spiritual awakening.

As if sensing my newborn yet tentative spiritual harmony, Aunt Fiona hesitated, nodded, and continued. "Sweeping is our last step." She began her final chant:

> Kathleen, raise our quest,
> As we sweep from east to west,
> Neutralize, purify, cleanse, and bless.
> Protect this place with Goddess grace.
> Your daughter's dream from bud to flower
> To grow and prosper by the hour,
> With joy, luck, love, and laughter won.
> Harm it none, we declare it done.

"Oh," I said. "You invited Mom in. I feel her, Aunt Fee, as if I'm six, again, standing beside her in Stroud's candy store. Chocolate. Smell the chocolate? That's Mom."

Aunt Fiona's eyes grew bright. "I smell the chocolate, sweetie. We miss you, Kathleen."

Oh, we do, but I was too choked up to say so.

We ended our sweep in the storage room, where we'd left the candles to burn out after the blessing, because this room, more than any, needed uber-positive energy.

"Madeira? Fiona?" my father called as he entered the first floor of the shop and came up the stairs.

In this crowded room, we hadn't been able to place the candles *against* walls, so Fiona kicked one of the more obvious votives from sight.

My father stopped in the doorway with the two of us holding oddly shaped brooms, ones he probably recognized.

"What the hell is going on here?"

Twenty-nine

I have a kind of in-built clock which always reacts against
anything Orthodox.   —VIVIENNE WESTWOOD

❧

I felt a need to defend my beliefs, a surprising turn I'd have
to reflect on later. "Bad day, Dad?"

He clenched and opened his fists at his side, as if fighting something within himself.

Certain he meant to blast Aunt Fiona, or both of us, for
the ritual brooms, I thanked the Goddess, or my mother,
for the scent of chocolate growing stronger and overshad-
owing that of burning smudge sticks.

Or, chocolate is how my nostrils interpreted the scent.
Goddess knew what my father thought.

He took a deep breath, hands relaxing at his sides, and
breathed easier, as if overcoming his inner turmoil. "You
locked the door in the middle of the day," he said, less hard,
more in sync with the peace of our ritual.

"Dad, this is a business. We're not open till noon tomorrow. The locals are eager. When this was a crime scene, I sold an outfit, outside, from one of the boxes in the parking lot."

His shoulders also relaxed. "To be truthful," he said, as if he couldn't believe himself, "as I cleared the stairs, I got a flash of your mother in labor eating a candy bar on our way to the hospital."

Holy thingamabobbin, he smelled the chocolate, too.

"That shouldn't make you cranky, Harry," Aunt Fiona said. "It should make you smile."

"She's right, Dad."

Welcoming peace, he gave a serene sigh, and his lips curved up, almost involuntarily. "Other men griped about crumbs in their beds. For me, it was chocolate wrappers." He chuckled, surprising us all, even himself.

I dropped my broom to throw myself in his arms. "That's the most open you've ever been about Mom. I've ached to know that kind of silly little detail about her."

He held me tight for a minute, really tight, until he cleared his throat and pushed away as if seeing me for the first time. "Look in the mirror, Madeira. She's right there." He touched my cheek. "That's her dimple."

Like Fiona, I swallowed. "I've been known to eat chocolate in bed, too. Didn't know it was hereditary."

"Poor Nick." My father hesitated, the puritanical professor tripping over unacceptable knowledge about his daughter. "So," he said, changing the subject and rubbing his hands together. "You already made a few bucks?"

"If you want to call three thousand dollars a few."

That got his attention. "How many outfits?"

"One."

"You got me," he said. "You *do* know what you're doing."

It was pure luck that somebody donated a treasure trove of rare vintage and that the White Star Circle harbored a true collector, but I wasn't admitting that to the man who once predicted my failure.

Dad watched while Fiona and I swept up the debris left by the electricians.

"Harry," Fiona said, as we were finishing up. "We need to move some furniture down to Maddie's sitting room area, so the shop will look good for her grand opening."

"Not a bad idea." He looked over the possibilities in the storage room. "It'd save you money, Madeira, if you didn't buy new."

"I know, Dad. I may as well go vintage all the way."

"I can get a few locals to help move you after work hours," he said. "What did you want downstairs?"

"The fainting couch." I ran my hand over it. "The jade-ite lamps, this side table, that desk. I'd use the cabinet if it were enamel black, not hospital white. I'd display my fashion dolls in the glass-front top." And relegate the tools of the mortuary trade to a body drawer.

"I can spray paint the cabinet," Dad said. "Won't take much sanding. Time has taken care of that, but there's a drawer missing."

"It's in my bedroom. I took stuff home in it." A quilt and outfit that Eve feared I'd *read* in front of her, but Dad knew nothing of my psychometric ability, and I prayed he never would.

He nodded. "I'll paint it in the basement at home, happy I'm not teaching as many courses this semester."

"Now if we could figure out a way to shed some light on the collection I put inside."

"Madeira," my father warned.

"I'm thinking out loud."

"You could paint the inside a lighter color," Aunt Fiona suggested, "to give the fashion dolls prominence."

"Pale yellow inside," I said, "and after the outside dries, I'll paint funky fashion designs on it. Maybe make the bottom cupboards look like they have frog closures. I'll see where my muse takes me. Let me know when it's dry, and I'll decorate it before we bring it back."

The scent of chocolate got stronger and sweeter, swirling around us like ribbons of fudge bringing the three of us closer, tying us with a chocolate bow.

"Your mother," my father said, startling me, "inherited furniture from her parents that she loved. In the, uh, early days, after we lost her, I relegated them to the basement beneath a tarp. Take what you want for the sitting area. She'd be pleased."

My mother knew how much I adored those pieces, my first introduction to art deco. The designs fascinated me. I remember tracing them with a tiny finger. I wonder if Mom had just nudged Dad's memory.

Scary stuff, straddling the veil between the planes. Or comforting? Or all in my mind?

My father headed for the stairs. "I'm off to buy black enamel and pale matte yellow paint."

"Thanks, Dad."

He waved. "Madeira, you might want to get that black candle away from your cat. And Fee, don't forget to sweep up the salt by the windows and doors."

He knew!

Thirty

I grabbed Chakra so she'd stop gnawing on the candle and I gave her some of the kitty treats I kept in my pocket. "You gave us away, you."

"She only confirmed our activity," Aunt Fiona said. "Your father probably saw the salt at the front door. He always had a way of ferreting out spells, but I must say, he's mellowed in his old age."

"Old? Dad's a *young* fifty-two."

Fiona grinned. "So am I."

I chuckled as my watch alarm rang. "Time got away from us. I have an hour before Eve and I leave to pick up my car, and another before we have drinks with Lolique."

"Lolique? Councilman McDowell's midlife crisis?"

"You mean his late-in-life crisis. How long have they been married?"

"No more than a year. He had to have his first wife declared dead before he could marry her."

My head came up. "Why? What happened to her?"

"Nobody knows. She went missing years ago, and they say he did everything possible to find her. Him and the Groton police."

Groton? "I saw her picture but didn't know her history. Speaking of whom, come see this." I brought Aunt Fee to the stacked white boxes. "This is where I found the cape and dress. Look, these are priceless." I took out several outfits to show her.

"I might buy this." She held up a patchwork skirt and vest set, slipping her hand in the skirt pocket. "Look, a broken fingernail."

I reminded her about how we found Lolique. "If these *are* from Lolique," I said.

"It's weird that she should break two nails packing clothes," Aunt Fiona said.

"And that they should all end up in pockets? Seems practically premeditated to me." I pulled out a silk draped evening dress by Lucien Lelong in a translucent aqua coloration. A one-of-a-kind masterpiece. "This looks so familiar. I must have seen a picture of it when I studied fashion design. It's decades older than the rest, and I *hate* the way it's been treated. Who would put such treasures in boxes? Help me get them on hangers and into garment bags, will you?"

I rolled a rack over. "I'll send some of them to an artisan friend in New York to be cleaned and restored."

Before Aunt Fiona hung each piece, she searched their pockets and found four more leopard fingernails.

I scoffed. "Nobody breaks that many by accident."

"Maybe Lolique didn't care about her nails or the clothes. They surely belonged to McDowell's first wife."

"I thought that, but they keep leading me to an Isobel when the councilman's first wife was named Gwendolyn." But I'd flashed to Isobel wearing the cape with the diamond on her finger, the diamond from the quilt. "When exactly did his first wife disappear?" I asked.

Aunt Fiona slipped a garment bag over an early Versace. "McDowell didn't live in Mystick Falls back then, so nobody knows the details."

Right. Groton, I remembered. But unfortunately, the only connection I had between the woman in the cape from these boxes and McDowell's first wife was psychic and worthless at best. I wondered what Natalie knew.

When Eve and I left to pick up my car, Aunt Fiona stayed to finish hanging the clothes from the white boxes.

"You're quiet," Eve said. "I thought you'd be chatty after spending the night with Nick."

"You're fishing, Meyers."

"No, you're too quiet. You and Nick didn't break up or anything, did you?"

"You wish."

She gave me an innocent look. Not.

"It's just that we're on our way back to the dealership and whatever was bothering me when we left there is bothering me again, but I still can't put my finger on it."

"I'll tell you what I remember from the last time we were there: that portrait of the councilman's late wife. Was that a rock on her hand or what?"

I looked sharply over at her. "Was it an emerald-cut diamond?"

"I'm not the fashionista here, but it was the focus of the entire portrait. How could you not notice it?"

How could I not be sick at the thought of it? But if the ring in the portrait matched the one I found in the quilt, that would *tangibly* connect Gwendolyn McDowell to the quilt and cape set. Who the heck was Isobel?

"Sorry I have to drop you and leave," Eve said. "But I have a ton of schoolwork."

"No problem. I'm driving that beauty out of here." My Element sat in the parking lot, shiny clean and registered. I needed to go in for keys, warranties, and registration, but I wanted a better look at the portrait, so after the car became mine, I went to the ladies' room.

On my way back, I stopped to examine the picture, and my knees nearly buckled. Gwendolyn McDowell sat for that portrait wearing the Lucien Lelong gown.

Lolique had *definitely* given me the first Mrs. McDowell's clothes, the gown in the portrait being a tangible connection. Now if I found that same ring in the quilt, we'd have a second connection. I wished I could reveal my psychic visions to Werner, especially of the well, but I'd take what I could get . . . for now.

I wanted to match the ring in the portrait to the ring I found in the quilt, but I needed to see it up close.

At nearly closing time, with the place quiet, McDowell did not sit behind his desk. I ran up the employee stairs and down the upper hall beneath which the portrait hung. From there, I leaned over the balcony, as far as I could, to see the ring.

Yes! Emerald cut and twice the size of Texas. Definitely the ring I found in the quilt. I wanted to scream with elation, but euphoria turned to panic when I got bumped from behind with enough force to keep from calling it an accident. I hung forward too far over the rail to be safe.

I lost my grasp for a flailing minute and my bag slid off my arm and hit the floor, pieces flying everywhere.

Broken, as I knew I would soon be.

Someone screamed. Maybe me, then someone pulled me safely back from the precipice.

"Natalie! Thank you," I gasped, heart racing. "I think someone pushed me. Did you see what happened?"

"What were you doing up here?" McDowell came from a nearby office. "Are you all right, Ms. Cutler?"

Natalie looked startled, shook her head, and left.

"Thank you," I called, but she didn't look back.

"I wanted to see your wife's ring up close," I told McDowell. "It's the most beautiful thing I've ever seen. I'm kind of a fashion nut, you probably know. Do you still have the ring? Is it for sale?"

"No," McDowell said, his face suddenly devoid of expression and color. "It disappeared with my wife, a tragedy you keep bringing to my attention."

"My apologies. I'll get my bag and my car."

The minute I got into my Element, I felt safe but needed to hear Nick's voice.

McDowell watched me from the showroom. I shivered, turned my back on him, and called Nick.

"Hey, ladybug. Are you wearing your lucky panties?"

"I must be. I just *didn't* get killed," I explained.

"I should be there to keep you out of trouble," Nick said, "but I can't, so stop taking chances! Is Werner on the case?"

"He is. I may have underestimated him in the past."

"You may have. When is your grand opening?"

"Halloween. Can you be there even if it's late? We're having a costume ball upstairs from eight till dawn. No costume necessary. Try to come, will you?"

"Don't count on it, okay?"

I sighed inwardly. No sense in making him feel worse. "Okay. I'll just hope." Good thing he couldn't see my eyes fill up or he'd know what a real scare I'd had. "Nick, did you find anything on that missing persons search I asked you to do?"

"Nothing. Sorry I didn't get back to you. It's wild here."

"Wild like in the jungle?"

Nick sighed heavily.

"Never mind. Listen, it turns out that the owner of the bones didn't live in Mystic when she went missing. Try Groton"—site of the first Goodwin dealership—"and plug in Gwendolyn Goodwin McDowell this time. Oh, and look up Suzanne Sampson, too."

"Gotta go, ladybug."

"Did you get that?" I asked, but he'd hung up.

Thirty-one

My vision: A nymph who, in her heart of hearts, is a leop-
ardess.
                                              —JOHN GALLIANO

❧

Still shaking inside, I chose my sixties Pucci "waterfall"
handbag with its bold geometric design as a palette to dress
for drinks with Eve and Lolique. I paired a purple V-necked
sheath of my own design with a wide aqua cinch belt and
teal cork sandals.

Eve, in black, wore bell-bottoms, a belted safari jacket
top loosely laced up the front over a white shell, and over
that, the sweater we'd confiscated from Vinney's. "Nice
outfit," I said when she picked me up. I'd been too shaky to
drive when we talked on the phone, so when she offered, I
agreed. "Where'd you get the awesome boots?"

"You mean my Fendi platform, lace-up boots?"

"With heels. Go you!"

"See, I have this friend in fashion who's been a good
influence on me." Eve wiggled her ladybug pinky.

"I'm so proud." I hadn't told her about my close call that afternoon, but I couldn't talk about it yet. "I forgot to try and get a vision from that sweater," I said.

"I know. That's why I grabbed it, then I thought it might add to my layered look."

"I'll take it home with me later. I read Lolique's newspaper column today," I said. "I think she's hiding a brain behind that big hair, voluptuous figure, animal prints, publicity stunts, and celebrity."

"I'm not so sure about that."

"Eve, she planted so many fingernails in those outfits, she would have thought I was a moron if I didn't go looking for her."

"Why would she do that? She found us."

"Impatient? I don't know, but she must have a reason, and I'm going to find out what. Listen hard with that uberbrain of yours, tonight, will you? Watch her body language. Memorize every bit of the conversation."

"I always do."

"You know, for a second, I thought she gave me the clothes because she *wanted* me to read them, but that's impossible. Only you, Sherry, Nick, and Aunt Fiona know that I'm psychometric."

"Maybe she did give them to you for a *reason*. That might be right."

I shrugged because I couldn't imagine what the reason would be. "Where are we meeting her?"

"At Cubby's."

"A sports bar? Why didn't you tell me? I would have dressed down."

"Don't toy with me," Eve said. "You don't know how to dress down, but I'd pay good money to see you try."

At the bar, we were escorted to a table on the deck overlooking Mystic River where Lolique waited.

Was she for real? Between her fluffy name and leopard nails, I half expected her to be wearing a midriff-baring leopard corset and mini skirt with fishnets and thigh-high boots, though I mentally conceded that she wouldn't bring a whip to a restaurant.

I was almost wrong. She wore a yummy, uber-expensive butterscotch leather skirt, a black cashmere top with an "oops, my boobs fell out" V, and a politically incorrect genuine leopard jacket. She also wore a loose chain twenty-four-karat gold belt—or so it appeared—with a Prada bag and matching shoes I'd die for.

Despite her lack of concern for animal rights, she signed autographs with flair and enthusiasm, her rings, all four, gleaming like they'd come off a pirate ship.

Once we sat at her table, the celebrity hounds backed off. Eve introduced us before we gave our drink orders.

Never having been one for equivocation, subtlety, or small talk, I let Eve take the lead with what Lolique seemed to like most: fan worship, however fake.

Me? I needed to chill before I put the knot in my knickers on the table, metaphorically speaking, of course.

"I must say, Madeira," Lolique purred, "I didn't figure you for a margarita girl but a fine white wine."

"And I spotted you correctly as the dirty Manhattan type."

Lolique raised a brow. "I'm a 'what you see is what you get' kinda girl."

How scary was that, considering what we could see? "Lay it on the table, do you?" I asked.

She winked and called for another, dirtier Manhattan.

"Whether people want me to lay it out or not, that's how I made my rep."

"Mind if I lay it on the table, then?"

She nailed a cherry. "I'd find that refreshing."

I leaned forward. "Good. Why did you leave me a fingernail trail, like bread crumbs, to make me come looking for you?"

She chuckled and raised her glass. "You're a smart one!" She sipped her drink. Slowly. Like she needed time to compose an answer. She set down her glass. "I wanted to sweet-talk you into letting me do a story about Vintage Magic."

"I was under the impression that you never ask permission, and you already did a column about me."

"Not a gossip column, a real story. We have a lot in common, you and I."

I so did not think so. "Like what?"

"A love for vintage and couture fashion, a love for this town—"

She was a good little liar. Eve bumped my knee with hers. She thought so, too.

"You could have waited to drop off those boxes until I was there so you could ask me straight out. And while we're speaking of vintage couture, the clothes you left are amazing. Thank you doesn't begin to cover it."

"Well, the drinks are on you, then."

I raised my glass. "On me." I'd have to read between the lines to figure out what the town's biggest celebrity *really* wanted. "You can do a story about Vintage Magic, right before my grand opening to plug the event."

"Deal." She shook my hand. "When would be a good time for me to come by the shop and talk to you? I don't feel like working tonight. Do you?"

I shook my head, agreeing with her and wondering what her real goal for tonight was. "Tomorrow at noon," I said. "You can pick up some scarecrow clothes."

While checking her vibrating BlackBerry, she looked curiously up at me, so I told her about the contest.

Eve got another beer and I got another margarita.

"I'm jonesing for a cigarette," Lolique said, "because I know I can smoke out here, but I also know how bad secondhand smoke can be, so I won't. I usually only smoke around my husband so I can inherit sooner." She laughed at her own joke.

Eve and I about choked on our drinks.

"I tell him that all the time. He doesn't laugh like he used to." She shrugged.

I recovered first. "How did you and Councilman McDowell meet?"

"We met accidentally on purpose lots of times over the course of a few months before he finally smartened up and decided to rescue me."

"How lucky is he?" I raised my margarita to soften my snark.

"You're right. I'm a catch." She ordered a third and told the waiter to keep 'em coming. "Saw him on TV again tonight, the blowhard. He practiced his playhouse fire speech the night *before* it burned, you know?"

I set down my drink. Was she trying to frame her husband, or was she planting seeds like a good little gossip columnist? I did not know if I should take this woman seriously or not. "Lolique," I said, "that sounds a bit like an accusation."

"Not really. He's ready for any disaster. Hell, he's ready to be president of these United States. I just thought the fire speech trumped his usual weird. He didn't like that I caught him at it, either."

I shook my head. "Is this something you should be telling the police?"

"Oh, Lordy, no. If I do that, I'll never inherit the old goat's money. Eve, why are you wearin' the goat's sweater?" Lolique fingered the wrist of Vinney's cardigan.

Eve straightened. "This is my boyfriend's sweater."

"Not if it has a little bitty cigarette burn under the left arm." She accepted a fresh drink.

Eve raised her left arm, and there it was, a little bitty cigarette burn.

"Is he doin' you, too?" Lolique asked, clearly having at least one Manhattan too many.

"Councilman McDowell?" Eve looked both shocked and nauseous. "I don't think so!"

Lolique waved away her protest. "I don't even care."

"Here," Eve said, "you want it?" She started to shed the sweater, but I kicked her, because now I really wanted to try and get a visual from it. *Why would McDowell's sweater be at Vinney Carnevale's house on the night Vinney robbed my shop?*

"You keep it," Lolique said. "He's been bellyachin' about losin' it for days. He loves the damned thing because *she* gave it to him. He only wears it in his sanctum sanctorum, anyway. That means his office. Now I'll get some kicks knowing where it is while I'm forced to listen to him whine."

"You don't seriously think your husband and I . . . ?" Eve sipped her beer, because she couldn't finish her sentence.

Lolique chuckled. "Honey, I'd sell you the schlub if I could keep his money and get away with it."

"I. Don't. Want. Him," Eve said. "Never did. Never would."

Lolique looked puzzled. Bad for wrinkles. "Who *is* your boyfriend?"

Eve hesitated. "Vinney Carnevale."

Lolique slapped the table. "You are *so* screwed." She chuckled. "I didn't know," she said. "I did *not* know." She got up fast and without grace. "Potty break or I'll pee my pants."

The flamboyant columnist waved to her adoring public as she crossed the bar. I turned to Eve. "You and the councilman?"

She returned my skepticism. "You and Jaconetti?"

"Seriously," I said. "Is she trying to pin the fire on Mc-Dowell?"

"She seriously is, but what did she mean by saying I was screwed? For dating Vinney? I figured that out, but she meant something entirely different, in a nasty way. Mad, why did we find the councilman's sweater at Vinney's the night of the fires? What can that mean?"

"That means," I said, "I can't wait to get my hands on it to see if Sampson's death was in any way connected to . . . Gwendolyn's."

Eve frowned. "Who the hell is Gwendolyn?"

Thirty-two

The only real elegance is in the mind; if you've got that, the rest really comes from it. —DIANA VREELAND

❧

"I suspect that Isobel is Gwendolyn," I whispered. "Shh. Here comes trouble with a capital L."

After a few more Manhattans, Lolique listed like a sailboat in a high wind, and though she wanted to drive her Beemer when we left, I took her keys from her. "We're taking you home. No arguments."

"Where to?" Eve asked.

"To my castle, Jeeves," the six-foot sexpot said as we folded her into Eve's little sports car.

"The name is Eve and where may we *find* your castle?"

Lolique ticked off a set of convoluted and confusing twists and turns. "If you drive off a cliff into Mystic River," she said when she finished, "you've gone too far."

"Great," Eve mumbled as she started her car. "Directions from an inebriated bimbette."

"I wasn't with the Bimbettes, I was one of the Florettes, a troupe of world-class exotic dancers. That's where I got my stage name, LaFleur—that's French for the flower. And that's where the old goat rescued me. He said I made him laugh, so he pried me off my pole and carried me to his castle, like a rich prince in an antique Jag. Then he took off his hair. Rude awakening."

I snorted.

Eve grinned, reached over, and gave me a playful shove.

As we drove through the farthest reaches of the Mystick Falls woods, Lolique was lying on the tiny backseat of Eve's Mini Cooper, her legs in the air, walking her spikes across Eve's closed convertible top.

Eve looked in her rearview mirror. "You put a hole in my roof, you'll pay for it."

"I can afford it. I'm *rich*!"

Lolique said the word "rich" the way Tony the Tiger says "great." But it was obvious that flaunting her money was part of her celebrity persona. Still, you'd think she'd be herself once in a while. Though she did say that she was "what you see is what you get."

After an aborted rendition of "We're in the Money," she laughed. "We've got his money, and *her* money, even her *father's* money."

"Who is the *her*, in '*her* money'?" I asked.

"Saint Belle, the perfect."

Belle? Isobel? I turned in my seat to look back at Lolique. "I thought your husband's first wife was named Gwendolyn?"

"Gwen-do-lyn," Lolique said with snark, like the drunk she was. "No wonder she hated her first name."

My heart raced to the point that I had to hold my chest

to keep it in there. Gwendolyn Isobel. G. I., the first two initials in the ring. Except that Lolique had said Belle, not Isobel.

Heck, I thought I might have spoken the name of the person whose dresses were cut into quilt squares. Isobel could have been Belle's mother for all I knew. True, the man the woman spoke to in my vision had hair, which time could surely erase, but he'd seemed to dislike the woman so much, he'd never call her a saint.

According to the portrait at the dealership, the ring definitely belonged to McDowell's wife, and since I found the ring in the quilt, that could have been the quilt that Gwendolyn Isobel and the man whose face I never saw were talking about. But the bones, who knew?

"Lolique, were those *her* clothes you gave me? Isobel's, I mean?"

"Screw the goat!" Lolique said with a military raise of her fist. "He wanted them locked in the attic forever, but I picked the lock on the wardrobe and gave them to you. Expensive. Couldn't bring myself to . . . burn—"

Silence.

"Did she pass out in the middle of a sentence?" Eve asked.

I looked in the back. "Yep."

"With her legs in the air?"

That turned my attention. We burst into stifled laughter.

"Stop it," she said, "or I'll have to—"

"Pee your pants?" That was a long-standing joke of ours. I'd done exactly that once on Halloween when we'd sneaked out after dark, peeked in a window, and came face-to-face with a witch, Aunt Fiona to be exact.

"No, smarty. Pull over until I can drive again."

"I'll drive," Lolique said, punctuating her offer with a snort and a snore.

Following her pre-coma directions, we found ourselves on a narrowing, sandy lane lined with bushes, ripe with rose hips. "We're lost," Eve said.

"No, look, there's a house on the hill, lit up like a twenty-four-karat gold Christmas tree. The perfect castle for a greedy old goat." I rubbed my arms against the chill the sight evoked. "It's forbidding enough to house vampires."

"Too much Buffy or too much Sookie?"

"Barnaby Collins on DVD, if you must know. And that's who McDowell reminds me of, minus the hair. I wonder when he stopped wearing the rug."

"Sweetie here probably burned his rug."

I looked in the back. "I wouldn't put it past her."

As we pulled up the drive toward the house, Lolique had not changed positions. "I think rigor mortis has set in."

"We'll have to help her to the door."

"Yay. I want to see if I recognize anything inside from my vision, you know to match it with McDowell and his dead wife. Take off the old goat's sentimental old sweater first. I don't want him to claim it."

"Right."

Carved of cold gray stone, the Gothic, towered mansion overlooked a steep cliff-side drop to the Mystic River.

"Should we take her to the front door or the back?" Eve asked as we drove closer.

I looked in the backseat. "Lolique?"

"You want a lap dance, honey?" She opened her eyes and looked surprised to see me.

"Uh, no, thanks. Where's the old goat's office? In the front or the back of the house?"

"Front."

"Drive up to the front," I told Eve.

She gave me a double take but said nothing and followed my directions.

It took both of us to get Lolique standing, more or less. "Man, she can snore," Eve said.

I hit the doorbell. "You bet your French knickers she can."

The councilman let us in. "I've got her." He took Lolique in his arms. "Ms. Cutler?" he said, as if asking for an explanation.

"She invited us for drinks. She's doing a story on my new shop, and we partied a bit."

"But *she* partied heartier than both of you?"

I shrugged. "She ate the salty nuts. They made her thirsty."

"How kind. Thank you for bringing her home."

Eve and I got back into the car and Eve backed her Mini Cooper down the drive. It was so narrow I was glad I wasn't driving my new Element.

"Why didn't you turn around on the landing field up front?" I asked her.

"I wanted outta there. Fast."

"Too bad. Turn the corner, back into the woods, and stop beneath that tree."

"What?"

"I wanna look around a little bit."

Eve hit the brakes and gave me a look of pure shock.

I took advantage of the moment, threw open my door, and ran.

"Madeira Cutler! You come back here."

I turned to her, spotted a huge white owl watching me, and took his look for approving wisdom, so I crossed my lips toward Eve and turned to sprint through the woods. The underbrush was wild with bittersweet and Chinese Lanterns, which I might have appreciated at a different time.

It wasn't long before I heard Eve's door shut. She could run faster than me any day, but her Fendis should slow her down some. She was *not* used to running in heels. Still, she grabbed my arm sooner than I expected, and I screamed.

"What the hell are you doing?" she snapped.

"Shush. I'm going to peek into a few windows to see if I recognize anything."

"Like the room from your vision?"

"No. That didn't take place here. Aunt Fee said McDowell moved here from Groton after he lost his wife. I was hoping his office furniture might be the same, though."

"You'd go to jail on a long shot? Besides, Councilman McDowell is hardly likely to have been in that vision."

"Lolique said 'Saint Belle,' which *could* stand for 'Isobel.' *Her* money referred to his first wife's money and *his* money referred to the councilman's. I need to look. If you don't want to come, go home. I'll walk."

"If I go, I'll call Werner is what I'll do."

"Go ahead. He might like a look around."

"I'm not leaving you."

"Well, duh. I knew that."

She elbowed me.

We sneaked up beneath a lit window. Eve's teeth began to chatter, though she stopped them quickly enough. "Déjà vu all over again," she said. "Halloween at Fee's, except that we could get arrested for peeking in these windows, and we won't find a friendly witch staring back at us, either. Good thing you used the bathroom before we left the bar."

"Brat. You're more afraid than I am and you *didn't* use the bathroom. This is the kitchen. Are we in the back or in the front of the house? We cut through the woods and I lost my bearings."

"I think we're on the side. This way," Eve said, so I followed, but she got turned around, too, because we ended up in the backyard.

The estate had an ultramodern guest or pool house, on the opposite side of the pool, with walls of windows and light peeking out between the drapery panels. I wanted to check that out after the main house, but I wasn't ready to give Eve my itinerary.

I peeked in a window of a parlor full of marble-topped tables, the kind I was looking for but none that matched my vision.

Eve grabbed my belt, yanked me to my knees, and pointed to Lolique running across the yard and around the pool, toward the guesthouse.

"She doesn't look as drunk as she did a few minutes ago," I whispered. "Let's go."

I followed Lolique, Eve two steps behind me, mumbling her bald refusal to follow.

We crouched in the bushes outside the guesthouse and looked through one of the slits in the drapes. I couldn't believe my eyes. The Goodwin cousin sat in his wheelchair, his back to us, facing the sofa.

In the kitchen area, open to the living room, Lolique took a beer from the refrigerator and drank from the bottle. Not quite as flamboyant as she pretends to be.

"How did it go?" Goodwin asked.

Lolique laughed and danced without a pole. "I did it, I did it. The dopes are dupes, and the old goat's on his way up the river. No paddle."

"Exactly what McDowell deserves," Gary Goodwin said, "the way he blatantly manipulated a dying old man into leaving him the Goodwin dealership."

Lolique shrugged. "Zachary Goodwin was the old goat's father-in-law."

Goodwin slammed his hand on the arm of his wheel-chair. "Zachary was my uncle, dammit. Blood is thicker! That dealership should be mine."

"And it will be," Lolique said, though she fluffed her hair in the way she did when she said McDowell had prepped his fire speech before the fire. Was she lying this time, too? Did she want the dealership and McDowell's money? I couldn't believe Goodwin hadn't caught on to the woman's mean-spirited greed.

"What are you two up to?" asked a man standing in shadow, who surprised both Lolique and Goodwin.

"Stupid ass," Lolique said. "You screwed me out of my inheritance with your spur-of-the-moment fix the other night. What are you doing here? You know the schlub doesn't want you anywhere near here."

"He doesn't want *him* here, either." Shadowman pointed to Goodwin. "Good thing you use this as your home office, Lol, or the light in here might make the old goat suspicious." Shadowman chuckled.

Lol. The man knew Lolique well enough to use a nick-name. "As for your inheritance," he continued, still in shadow, "you've got more money than God. I did what I had to do to get the job done."

"Except leave the schlub's sweater behind," Lolique snapped.

I saw the man's hand as he snapped his fingers. "Oh yeah. Whatever happened to that thing?"

"You gave it to your twit of a girlfriend."

"Hey, she's no twit. She's freakin' brilliant. Hardest con I ever pulled, pretending to date her."

I felt fury radiating off Eve in hot waves.

Lolique turned to Goodwin and pointed toward the guy in the shadows. "I thought you said he was out of this for good."

"For good?" Shadowman said. "Nobody offs me. I'm too smart."

Lolique laughed. "Why the hell are you here, then, Lazarus?"

"Sanctuary," Shadowman wailed. "Sanctuary," he moaned like a ghoul as he stepped into the light for a split second, but that was all we needed.

I looked at Eve and mouthed, "Vinney?" which she confirmed with a nod as he disappeared back into the shadows.

Lolique flopped down on the sofa and gave Goodwin the evil eye. "Sometimes I wonder whether *you're* worth keeping around."

"Don't get smart with me," Goodwin said. "I know who you really are."

I turned to Eve to speculate on that one, but she must have moved to another window to get a visual on Vinney. "Hey?" I whispered, and she put her hand over my mouth, presumably to shut me up—except when I looked up at my silencer, Eve didn't look down at me, Vinney did.

I'd lost sight of him inside. Now, he had me crushed in a

headlock, one hand over my mouth, the other closing around my throat.

I saw stars, and beyond them, a cold-blooded look in my captor's eyes.

Not only could he have murdered Sampson. He could have enjoyed it.

My killer's face blurred and darkened.

Thirty-three

1972: The first woman falls off her cork sandals. Millions follow.
—VOGUE

❧

As if through a tunnel, I heard a whomp, and then I was sucking air into my lungs in greedy gulps while my captor went down like cement shoes in deep water.

Eve grabbed my hand and dragged me toward the woods.

"My shoe," I whispered. "I fell off my shoe."

"Lose the other one."

"They cost—"

She jerked on my arm so hard I fell off the other. "Ouch, ouch, ouch," I whispered as she dragged me through the woods, me in bare feet, her walking like Peg-Leg Pete without the peg.

"My stockings are torn and my feet are cut," I whined.

"You're not the only one."

"You are *not* wearing stockings."

"Yeah, that's the crucial point, here."

I looked back. Vinney was still down. My throat hurt remembering. "Are you packing a sledgehammer? What did you hit him with?"

"The heel of a boot."

"Thick and lethal."

She scoffed. "I aimed at his head stitches. Pulled a con on *me*, did he? I don't think so."

Ouch. "Remind me not to cross you."

She stopped and ducked, but she forgot to warn me, so I tripped over her and went flying. Now my hands were scraped, too. I understood her reasoning, however, when I saw Councilman McDowell heading for the guesthouse looking fit to kill. He growled when he saw Vinney's prone body, stepped over him, and walked faster, if that were possible.

From the woods, we could hear McDowell shouting—the man had lungs, I'd give him that. He'd seen Eve's car in the woods from an upstairs window, started to investigate, and found what he called "felon cars" in his garage. He didn't want Gary or Vinney anywhere near his place and wanted to know what the hell was going on.

After a tirade and a half, McDowell came slamming out of the guesthouse, shouting for them to "Get out!" He grumbled about being mad as he hotfooted it up the hill and disappeared around the house. Two seconds later, he burned rubber as he sped down the drive. Man, he couldn't get away fast enough. He truly did "not want to be connected to the law-breaking scum" in his guesthouse.

Because he too was guilty?

Vinney groaned and grabbed his head, and the sound seemed to alert Lolique. She and Goodwin came out, and when she got to Vinney, she straightened and looked around, as if she could smell the fear rolling off me and Eve.

We ducked neck-deep into the overgrowth.

Lolique pulled Vinney to his feet, none too gently, and shoulder-shoved him toward the big house, which she wouldn't have gotten away with if Vinney wasn't sporting a head bleed. Silently, she pushed Goodwin's chair up behind Vinney. Along the way, she grabbed one of my shoes and stuck it in her pocket, her grin malevolent.

My gasp made Eve put her hand over my mouth. I jerked it away. I'd had enough of that for a lifetime.

The "felons," all three, skirted the house, then one by one, three more cars sped down the drive, Goodwin's bringing up the rear.

"That bimbette stole my shoe!"

"She called us duped dopes." Eve took a twig out of my hair. "Mad, this is one time that acting first could have finished you. And I mean that literally."

I grabbed my throat. "I'm thinking that at least one of them must be the killer."

Eve shuddered. "Of Sampson or Isobel?"

"Yes."

"Shouldn't we get the hell out of here?" Eve whispered furiously.

"I'm thinking about it."

Eve sucked in a breath. "Those words *always* send prickles of fear down my spine."

"I have to get my other shoe."

"You *are* a nutcase."

"You've known that since we were five when you jumped into the Mystic River to save me."

"More fool me."

"The guesthouse is wide open. Let's go look around."

"You are certifiable," Eve said. "I'm leaving."

"Don't worry. I won't leave fingerprints on anything, and after we're finished, we'll call Werner and tell him we saw Vinney here."

"I thought you wanted to look inside the *main* house."

I snapped my fingers and changed directions. "Smart girl."

"Dumb, dumb, dumb," she said, smacking her temple with the flat of her hand while trying to keep up with me. "You've finally sucked the genius right out of me," she said. "Though I must say, I'm proud that you left your other shoe behind."

"Oy!" I ran back for it. "Thanks," I said catching up to her. "Here, I got your boot, too. They must have cost you—"

"Three hundred and seventy-five dollars."

"I *am* a bad influence on you. Is that why you deserted me?"

"Deserted? Vinney disappeared and I heard footsteps, so I hid in the bushes to unlace one of my lethal boots."

"My hero."

"Damned straight."

The back door of the mansion stood ajar. We went in and tried to head straight for the front of the huge edifice, but the place was like a dark maze and we didn't dare use lights. Bad enough we could hear a dog barking somewhere in the house.

Each room was a dead end. "Where the Hermès is the hallway?" I whispered, the barking coming closer.

"This place might be old enough to be laid out like your father's house, Mad. You have to go through rooms to get to others. Wait. I found a bathroom. Too much beer."

"Leave the door ajar," I said, "in case they come back, so I can warn you."

Eve the Bold whimpered, but she did as I asked.

"Don't touch anything but the paper," I said, "and flush with your elbow."

"Wait for me."

"Don't worry. My turn next."

"Mad," Eve said a few minutes later, as I washed my hands. "The dog is here."

"I can hear it growling," I said, peeking out. "Wow. He sure is a big one." The dog backed up to growl at both of us. "Hey, cutie," I said to the miniature dachshund as I took kitty treats from my pocket and dropped some on the floor at my feet.

After he ate them, he wagged his tail, so I bent down to feed him a few from my hand. Then I picked him up. "What a good doggie."

"Are you holding him for ransom?" Eve asked.

"No. Insurance. If he likes us, he'll be quiet."

Dog in hand, we backtracked to the back door, then we walked through the rooms and managed to reach the front hall.

I peered in one of the doors leading off of it.

"This is it. McDowell's office." By then my eyes had adjusted to the darkness. "Nothing's the same in this room compared to the one in my vision," I whispered. "Except, maybe—" I used my shoe to move a big painting aside, which action called for a few more kitty treats on the dog's part, and sure enough, there was the safe. "Those ledgers might still be in there," I said.

"*If* it was the councilman you saw, he *owns* Goodwin's now. No need to cook the books."

"*If* he embezzled from family, can Uncle Sam be far behind?"

"A cape, Mad. All you have is a cape."

The light went on, and I whipped around to scold Eve for hitting the switch.

Werner's hand fell from the switch, his gaze locked on mine.

Thirty-four

I like fashion to go down to the street, but I can't accept
that it should originate there. —COCO CHANEL

"Mad and Eve strike again," Werner said. "Safecracking
and dognapping, this time?"

I lowered the painting. "Sure, I always open safes with
a shoe. This is McDowell's watchdog. See?" I put the little
guy down and he began a growling approach until he cor-
nered Werner. Then the dog lifted a leg and tinkled on the
detective's shoe.

Werner jumped aside, making the dog growl the more,
and gave me a look that I'd come to interpret as his "I could
beat you" look. "You gonna call him off?"

I bit my lip to hold in my amusement at both the dog's
antics and at Eve, bent over double, out of Werner's range of
vision.

I cleared my throat. "Here, boy." I put the last of my kitty
treats on the floor and McDowell's dog came galloping back

as only a wiener dog could gallop. Oh, I'd thought a pun. Good thing I hadn't called him a wiener dog in front of the Wiener.

Werner looked me up and down and shook his head.

Because of it, I took stock of my appearance. Torn stockings, mud on my knees and, ugh, sore, muddy feet. They'd be able to track my bloody muddy footprints right through the house. Eve, too, since she wore only one shoe and one foot was as bare and bad as mine.

Werner shook his head. "You're a blight on the pride of the fashion industry, Madeira. Shame on you. You look like a frostbitten flower bed."

"I match my bag. My bag! I lost my Pucci bag!"

"You left it in the car," Eve said.

I relaxed. "Whew!"

Eve chuckled. "Funny you should mention flowers, Detective. Because I *was* gonna make Mad lie down in a flower bed to hide in plain sight, if they—"

"They?" Werner raised his brows.

"Vinney was here," I said. "We were gonna call you."

"Too bad you forgot."

"We didn't get away from them until they left."

"At which point, you decided to ransack the house?"

"No. Vinney robbed me, remember? And he probably put the bones he stole from my place into the playhouse fire." I raised my arms. "Look at me. I'm not hiding an old mailbag of anything."

"Does anybody have a house key to show me this time? Officer," Werner said, indicating Eve, "take that shoe from Ms. Meyers, will you? It seems to have blood on the heel."

Eve sighed and handed over the boot in her hand.

"Looks like," the officer said, bagging it.

"It's Vinney's blood," Eve explained. "He had Maddie by the throat. I hit him in the head, exactly where he got those stitches the other night."

"The stitches you took him to get?"

"Well, yes, but tonight my best friend's life was in danger. I wrote off Vinney the minute he tried to kill Mad."

"Madeira, you said 'they.' Who else was here, besides Vinney?" Werner asked.

"Detective, did you hear Eve? I nearly died. Strangled. Literally. Could we have a moment of acknowledgment and maybe a 'so glad you're alive, Mad'?"

"Strangled, eh?" Werner nodded thoughtfully. "For the first time, I understand the mind of a perp."

I stamped my sore foot and regretted it.

Werner eyed me with a thimbleful of concern. "How's your throat?"

"A little *sore*," I snapped.

He took a box from his inside jacket pocket. "Here's a cough drop. Now, who else was here?"

I was underwhelmed by his concern, but the cough drop felt good.

"Councilman McDowell," Eve told him. "He let us in when we brought Lolique home drunk."

Werner shook his head in denial. "No. The councilman is working late, tonight. He called from his office to tell us that the silent alarm on this place went off. So, here we are."

"The rat!" I said. "They're all rats. He probably called from his cell phone as he drove away from here."

"Save it for the station. Put them in my car," Werner told the officer, "and make sure forensics goes over this place after they're finished in the guesthouse. Ms. Meyers, give your keys to the officer and tell him where to find your car."

"In the woods off the drive. I left the keys in the ignition."

We sat for a long time in the backseat of Werner's car waiting for him. I sighed. "I'm so glad we stopped to pee. Too bad the doggie didn't."

"Highlight of my night," Eve said. "You think we can borrow that dog sometime. I'd like to introduce him to Nick."

"Nice."

"Jokes aside, this time, they're gonna book us, Mad."

"Maybe not, if we give them the facts. All of them. Everything we know." I pointed to my head and shook it, to remind her that my visions were off-limits for sharing with cops.

She nodded her understanding. "You think they bug a detective's car?"

"Shut up."

Werner opened the door and got into the driver's seat. "You're lucky you're not in cuffs." He started the engine.

We said nothing.

"Ms. Meyers, the only car we found in the woods belongs to Mrs. McDowell."

"Lolique stole my car!" Eve wailed.

"Worse, she stole my rare Pucci bag. It probably sells for more than your car, because there are less in captivity. Your car you'll get back, but my bag won't be in it." Neither will the councilman's sweater, dammit.

"I thought the designer was Gucci," Werner said, looking in the rearview mirror. "Not Pucci."

I shook my head. "You need to get your Pucci, your Rucci, and your Gucci straight."

"Not if you set me on fire," Werner said, "but maybe I shouldn't be giving the two of you any ideas."

"We're not criminals!"

"Let's see, I've got you for breaking and entering—"

"Entering," Eve said. "Not breaking. They ran so fast, they left the doors open. Check with the alarm company."

We were under a streetlight when Werner nodded imperceptibly, which I wouldn't have noticed, otherwise. "I found you," he continued, "in front of a safe talking about cheating Uncle Sam, and discussing a cape as if it were evidence."

Holy scrap! "That was pure spec—"

"Save it for the station."

"This is the station," I pointed out.

"So it is."

They questioned us separately.

For my part, it was easy to answer only the questions I was asked with the bits of truth we'd garnered. What Werner didn't ask, I didn't answer. The hard part was explaining why we'd speculated about embezzling and a cape.

"I can always tell," Werner said as I tried to talk my way around the vision and all it entailed, "when you're talking straight and when you're giving me the runaround."

"We were only speculating about McDowell cheating the government."

"That I believe. But Ms. Meyers mentioned that you had a cape."

"I have a dozen capes. Eve's talking about the one I found in a donation box in front of my shop. Lolique gave those clothes to me. I think they belonged to the late Mrs.

McDowell. I liked the cape and I was thinking about keeping it for myself, but I changed my mind. It's at my shop. Do you want it? Really, it isn't evidence. I brought you the quilt and rings, both solid evidence."

Werner relaxed and steepled his hands. "We know who the rings belonged to."

I stilled. "Good. Any leads on the case?"

"What makes you think they had to do with the case?"

"The unidentified bones that were in my storage room were wrapped in the quilt where I found the rings."

His face a bit red, he did relax. Whew. He trusted me again. Maybe. "We're going to get you and Ms. Meyers some first aid for your bloody feet."

"Do you treat all your perps this well?"

"You're bleeding all over the place. The upholstery in my car will never be the same. And we're not *too* nice, because we're going to keep you here until we can talk with McDowell's alarm company. Unfortunately, we couldn't find any sign of an alarm system, and we don't want him to know we're checking up on him. Our clerk is calling a long list of area alarm companies as we speak. You might be here a while. Do you want to make a phone call?"

"No, thanks. I'm a big girl. My father won't worry. He'll think I'm at Eve's."

"And her parents will think she's at your place. How long have you two been playing that card?"

"Pretty much since we were five."

"Well, Ms. Meyers forgot. She made a phone call to her mother, who kindly delivered these." Werner set my embarrassingly dorky alligator slippers on his desk in front of me. "For after your feet are bandaged."

"I left these at Eve's years ago," I said, picking them up. "I designed them in fashion school. Our assignment was to make something creative with an *alligator* zipper." I unzipped my alligators' mouths so their teeth would show.

Werner chuckled.

"I got the highest grade."

"Mrs. Meyers also left you each a pimento cream cheese sandwich."

"Yuck! Eve and I hate those. Just the smell tests our gag reflexes, and she knows it. The woman's diabolical."

"She did seem to think you deserved whatever I had in mind." His eyes twinkled as he stood and took my arm. "Lean on me if it hurts you to walk."

I carried my slippers and I leaned, while my stomach growled but I ignored it. It hurt worse on the hard floor than in the grass or on the rug in the McDowell house.

Werner saw that my eyes were tearing up and he slipped an arm around me.

"You're not going to carry me again, are you?"

"Not through the squad room, I'm not."

"Good." I tried footwork variations and found it easiest to walk on tiptoe. In the squad room, the eleven o'clock news was on. We stopped to watch McDowell shouting his outrage over his home being broken into.

"He'll do anything to get on the news," I said, glad he wasn't using any names. Then again, he couldn't know whether Eve and I were still at his house when the police arrived. "He's trying to plug his dike," I said, "in case Vinney might be thinking of using him, or his guesthouse, as an alibi or hiding place sanctioned by McDowell— which the old goat most assuredly did not."

Werner nodded and I got the urge to tell him about McDowell practicing his fire speech the night *before* the playhouse fire, but I was pretty sure that was Lolique using us as dupes. Maybe. "The councilman isn't honest," I said. "I'm sure of that, because he's lying about what happened tonight. But I think he might be worse than a liar."

Werner looked at me with speculation. "Does McDowell know that's how you feel?"

Possibly, I thought, since he saw Eve's car in the woods by his house tonight, so he must know we were nosing around. He'd also learned that I'd been "hanging" around at his dealership—upside down, mind you—to examine his dead wife's picture, and yet . . . "I don't think so."

"Keep it that way."

Thirty-five

Sometimes there are two very opposite directions, and we go
with the stronger one at the end. It's an impulse thing, like
'Oh, I love both so much, but it's got to be one or the other
because the two don't work together.' —MARC JACOBS

❧

Eve and I appeared doomed to spending the night at the
station, but where?

I had to perform some Mad—as in Madeira—Magic,
and fast, like charming my way out of a paper bag, also
known as: a jail cell.

We found Eve getting her foot bandaged in first aid.

"I'm hungry," I said as we finished. "How about you,
Eve?"

"Not enough to eat the sandwiches my mother brought.
Is she a trip or what?"

"A trip through the scary house," I said, "unless she's
helping, which she does so well."

"Mothers," Werner chuckled, escorting us, one on each
arm, across the squad room, but not in the direction of his

office. Scrap! "Detective, could you go for some Mexican food?"

He slowed. "I'm going off shift in a few minutes."

"Good, you can get it, and when you get back, between the three of us, we can put together the pieces of the murder puzzle while we eat. No sense in you eating alone." I know, low blow, but for a worthy cause.

He hesitated.

"My treat," I said.

Clearly, he was torn. "I'll have to put you in a cell while I get the food," he said, almost to himself.

"Don't forget the Mexican beer," Eve said. "I could go for some cold Cerveza Dos Equis. Sound good to you, Mad?"

I wanted to elbow her for missing the point. "We can wait in your office."

"So you can look though my files and talk my men into helping you?" But he'd stopped walking.

I guessed that my charm would no longer serve where the Wiener was concerned. "Dos Equis, yes," I said.

"But what do you want to eat?" Werner asked.

"Enchiladas, chimichangas, burritos, chile rellenos. We like to mix it up and share. What about you?"

He rolled his eyes, took some bills from his pocket, and tossed them on a desk. "Jimmy, did you get that?"

"Yes, sir."

"Go as soon as you're off shift and get some for yourself. Get a couple of six-packs of Dos Equis. I'll be off shift by the time you get back and I'll need self-medicating." He looked us over, head to foot. "It's gonna be a looong night." He then steered us toward his office.

Whew! "Thank you for not putting us in a cell."

"I should have my head examined. You're a manipulative perp, you know that?"

I tried to look innocent. "That's us, scheming perps wearing the lamest slippers on the planet."

"She does have a sadistic streak, my mother," Eve muttered. "When I called, she didn't ask *why* we're here but said we probably deserved it."

"She's a smart one," Werner said, rolling two comfortable executive-type office chairs up to his desk.

Eve sighed, wiggling a plush pink foot from which a dimpled face with yellow yarn hair smiled—her old Cabbage Patch doll slippers. "Though my feet do feel better. Even the one that's not cut hurts from wearing heels. How do you do it, Mad?"

"Sore is better than ugly. I'm a vain fashionista."

Eve barked a laugh. "And a stupid one."

Werner cleared his desk, shaking his head the whole time, probably as much at himself as Eve, for getting sucked in.

"My feet are wrapped in a cloud," I said. "I padded the soles of my chubby gators with three inches of foam at a time when platforms were making a comeback."

Werner stopped procrastinating and sat behind his desk.

I sat forward. "I'd like to speculate about the two murders given the latest information we've garnered. Okay with the two of you?"

Werner gave me a pointed look. "You're playing sleuth again."

"I'd be stupid not to. If a metaphorical fireball lands in your lap, you get the hell out of the way, and you find out where it came from so you can keep it from happening again. I'll bet you've got questions up the wazoo that you'd like to toss out. Heck, Eve and I might know some 'details' that verify your speculation and vice versa."

Werner shrugged as if he could care less. "I'm in it for the beer."

"Fine, but you're missing a primo brainstorm. Eve, let's talk about McDowell's first wife."

"Gwendolyn Isobel," Eve said, "known by Councilman McDowell as Saint Belle."

Werner sat straighter.

"Right." I eyed Werner. "That was her quilt, her diamond, and her wedding band I gave you. She died around thirty years ago, right?"

He gave a grudging nod. "An heiress. Thirty-three years ago. Cold case. Ice cold."

"Did you get an ID back on the bones from the FBI lab yet?" I asked.

Werner crossed his arms and shook his head in the negative.

"Tonight Lolique admitted to us that she gave me Isobel's old clothes for my shop. I say Isobel because Gwendolyn didn't like her first name so she used her middle name."

Werner grabbed a notebook. "A hot lead for a cold case."

"See, wasn't this better than locking us up?"

"I'm reserving judgment."

"So the bones might be Isobel's, because they were wrapped in a quilt she'd taken to a fair. Her rings were in the quilt, so maybe she slipped them in a pocket while locked in a trunk, hence the tire tracks. Now, the bones left in my building were clean."

Werner's jaw dropped for half a beat. "How do you know they were clean?"

"Simple deduction, my dear Watson. No body grunge on the quilt."

Werner's head came up before he went back to his notes. "What happened to her between the trunk and the body drawer?" he asked.

"Hey, you have to throw something into the pot," I said as our food arrived.

Before I opened containers, he grabbed a beer and swigged it from the bottle. "Her bones would have been clean if left unburied," he muttered. "It takes maybe three to five years in the open air," Werner said, "for them to get . . . clean."

I was glad he didn't give us details for a visual. I watch *Bones*. I know the drill. Yuck. "Did anybody ever demand a ransom?" I asked.

"McDowell said no."

I tasted a forkful of enchilada. "Oh, this is orgasmic."

Werner's elbow slipped off the desk so he ended up juggling his fork like a hot potato while I caught his beer bottle before it tipped.

Eve and I drank our beer the way he did. Good and cold. "So, motive: greed, envy, lust? Or Isobel pissed someone off, got in their way . . ."

Werner chewed thoughtfully. "Her body was exposed to the elements but out of sight. She could have been left—"

"In the bottom of a well," Eve said, taking the heat away from my vision.

"In a heavily wooded area," Werner added.

I nodded. "In a cave or a quarry?"

"So if it was so well hidden, why move it to Mad's place?" Eve asked.

"Construction?" Werner and I hypothesized in sync.

"Nearly the same reason the bones were moved this second time, because I was moving in."

"I'd like to know," Eve said, "if Suzanne and Tunney are off the hook for Sampson's death."

"Suzanne's done a runner," Werner said, "but we know where she is. They're barely suspects now that I verified Sampson's status. Mad, I owe you an apology for that night."

"Accepted." I waved my bottle his way. "You have a job to do. Just, please, try not to do it at another Cutler family party in future. What about McDowell?"

Eve waved her fork. "Oh, oh. We heard Goodwin say tonight that he thinks McDowell manipulated Isobel's father, also Goodwin's uncle, into leaving McDowell the dealership."

More notes. "I'll look into it."

"And Mad and I think McDowell killed Isobel."

"Guesswork," Werner said.

I tilted my head. "We know McDowell can't be trusted. The question is whether he wanted the dealership enough to kill for it. Isobel would have inherited if she hadn't died. She would have become her husband's boss. Maybe she was planning to divorce him."

For half a beat, we sat back to digest the information and sip our beer.

One six-pack down, one to go, and I was starting to feel it.

"Okay, Detective," I said sitting forward. "Chew on this. Eve and I saw Gary Goodwin and Suzanne Sampson kissing, outside at her place."

"From a boat," Eve said. "No entering involved."

Werner grinned. "Suzanne Sampson divorced both Gary

Goodwin and Broderick Sampson. The gossips decided she was Sampson's sister, and Suzanne didn't bother to correct the misconception. She wasn't faithful to either husband and she has the occasional fling with both, not necessarily at the same time. Lolique is Suzanne's daughter by Sampson."

"Ah, so they both started hanging around when they thought Sampson was going to make a fortune. Lolique still thinks her father was rich, by the way." I told Werner what a mean-spirited stitch Lolique was tonight.

"Then the two murders are connected," Eve added.

I inhaled my beer and coughed a minute. "Connected by Vinney!"

"Vincent Carnevale," Werner said. "Another of Goodwin's stepchildren."

"You've been doing your homework," I said.

"I should hope so."

"So Lolique and Vinney are step-siblings?" I moved my jalapenos to the side of my plate.

Werner speared one for himself. "Yup. Same mother, different fathers."

"To me, Vinney had less motive than any of them," Eve said, "Yet I practically saw him steal the bones."

"Mad?" Werner asked, "how did you know how long Isobel had been dead?"

"Easy. I have some of her clothes. She followed fashion trends and liked vintage, but I have nothing newer in style than the mid-eighties."

Eve conveniently dropped a few details of my visions into the pot as speculation, but she also threw in a brilliant question, like could Vinney have been hired? I hadn't thought of that. Werner had.

We were still at it, our minds on overload, when an officer came in. "I found McDowell's alarm company—he's had several plus some outside contractors. His current company said his alarm did *not* go off last night. And it isn't silent. We couldn't find the alarm at the house because the remote keypad's in a box disguised as artwork in the front hall. The company rep said that was McDowell's idea, like it was stupid."

"All part of the lie to cover his ascot," I said, "in the event neighbors or passersby said they *didn't* hear an alarm. Which they wouldn't have because the door was open, and he didn't take the time to set it before he left. I think McDowell acts first, then he thinks."

"You should know," Eve said.

Werner opened his mouth and closed it again.

But if McDowell acted on impulse, which he had tonight, maybe Isobel's disappearance was too well planned for him to be her killer. But I did not want to give that man an out, even in speculation.

An officer returned Eve's personal possessions, and I used her cell phone to call my father, since my phone had gone the way of my Pucci bag, credit cards, and license.

Aunt Fiona came with Dad, wearing his sour expression.

"We weren't charged," I said, before he could say anything.

"But you spent the night in jail," Fiona said. "Why didn't you call me?"

"Us." My father corrected her. "Why didn't you call us?"

Whoa, scary statement there. Were they an "us"? Dad

hadn't tripped over the words at all, which didn't mean he wouldn't tomorrow.

"I didn't call because we only had to stay until our story could be verified."

Eve nodded. "A couple of hours, a few beers, some Mexican food, and good company. The detective didn't pick us up until well after midnight."

"Picked up by the police," my father said.

"I like to live on the edge." I laid my head on his shoulder. "Can we go home now, Daddy? I'm tired."

Aunt Fiona winked at my "Daddy's little girl" ploy.

"Thank you both for an excellent chat," Werner said as we headed for the car, and that was the last I remembered until Aunt Fiona woke me when we got home.

"I'll tell you about it in the morning," I said, going inside. "I mean, when I wake up."

"Which has to be around eleven," she reminded me. "You're giving away scarecrow clothes today."

I whimpered. "I'll set my alarm."

Not nearly enough sleep later, I got to the shop, where people lined up around the building. Parked cars slowed traffic. Potential contest entrants and a few unknowns, who, I think, needed free clothes, swarmed the tables.

That's when I heard the news from Eve. Her car had been found beside the river with a hole in the convertible top. A hole the size of a spiked heel.

Later, Werner told me that my Pucci bag was neither inside nor out of the car, and I hoped it hadn't ended up in the river. Baste it, I hoped *I* didn't end up in the river.

Vinney's, I mean the councilman's sweater had gone missing, as well.

I couldn't drive my car until I got a new license. A few days ago, I thought that once I had my car and my stock had been moved in, I'd be home free. So not.

I watched my back that day, but uniformed officers came for scarecrow clothes, so Werner watched it, too.

McDowell wasn't the first enemy I'd ever made. He wouldn't be the last.

But he might be the deadliest.

Thirty-six

Choose your corner, pick away at it carefully, intensely and
to the best of your ability and that way you might change
the world.   —CHARLES EAMES

❧

I had plenty of reason to fear McDowell, I thought as I closed
up shop, my father waiting in the parking lot, but what about
the self-effacing man who wanted a dealership so badly
he went there every day, hoping a portrait might fall?

I knew anyone who got in Lolique's greedy, spiteful
way should fear her. She'd implicate her husband to get her
hands on his money.

Vinney I had reason to fear, his eyes so filled with
bloodlust when he tried to choke me they haunted me.

The following morning, Eve called as I got ready for
Halloween Ball fittings. "I got the news from Tunney—he
who knows everything," she said. "Vinney skipped town."

I grabbed my throat. "Must have happened during the
night, but skipped or not, I don't like Vinney on the loose
now that he tried to kill me."

217

"I don't like it now that *I* tried to kill him."

"We'll both take care. Eve, can you surf the net and find out what Zachary Goodwin, Isobel's father, died of?"

"I'll try," she said before she hung up.

I was so jumpy after Eve's call I decided that the best way to watch my back was to keep my enemies close, the ones I could find. I called Natalie at the car dealership, ostensibly to thank her for saving my life the other day, but I knew she kept McDowell's schedule. A bit of chitchat netted me the time and location of his lunch date with his wife. Natalie admitted, however, that McDowell liked to have his schedule leaked for publicity purposes. Big surprise.

That noon, at a local restaurant, I pretended to run into Lolique and the councilman, where I asked them to judge the scarecrow competition.

The councilman seemed delighted by the prospect, and I knew he'd bring television coverage, because he never left home without it.

Lolique's reaction to my invitation was tepid, at best, until I mentioned giving her an exclusive on the Vintage Magic article. Not that she'd really wanted to write that story. She'd just wanted to dupe us dopes, which was beside the point.

"You know, Lolique, I lost the Pucci bag I carried when we had drinks the other night. I wondered if I'd dropped it in your front hall when we went in with you." *When you were hammered,* I wanted to say but didn't. Yes, I was giving her an opportunity to return my bag with dignity.

She raised her chin. "I'll ask Maid if she found an old handbag."

"I'd appreciate it. Have you seen Vinney lately?"

McDowell stiffened. "I don't care if he is half related to

her, if he comes near either of us, again, I'll have him arrested for trespassing."

Was the old goat clueless or what? Vinney was a burglar suspected of arson and murder. He wouldn't stop at trespassing.

"We haven't seen him," Lolique said, eyeing her husband with such disdain I almost felt sorry for him. Almost.

After I left the restaurant, I went to see Werner.

"You're gonna think I'm crazy," I said as I sat down across from him.

He leaned back in his chair and crossed his arms, looking almost comfortable in my presence. "Madeira, I already do."

I rather enjoyed sparring with him but shocking him was more fun. "I asked Councilman and Mrs. McDowell to judge the scarecrow competition."

Werner sat forward so fast, it was a wonder he didn't snap his spine. "He's nobody to mess with, Madeira."

"I know. That's why I want you to judge, too. And I won't accept 'not if you stick a fork in my eye' as an answer."

He nearly smiled. "At least we'll know where they are."

"Exactly. Is that a yes?"

"Under the circumstances, I'd consider it my civic duty."

"You believe me about them, now, don't you?"

"Let's say that the quilt, the rings, and the Mexican beer chat helped."

He had to know that I'd done some primo sleuthing while we were at it, but if he wasn't saying, then neither was I.

For the next couple of days, along with everything else I did, I catered to Fiona's fellow witches looking for outfits for the Halloween Ball and to our neighbors still hunting for scarecrow clothes.

Fiona put out plenty of stock for both events.

I named my nooks—*not* hearse stalls—which Eve printed on her laser printer. I slipped each "address" into street name–type frames and hung them at the entry to each nook: Shoe Heaven, Bag Lady, Vive la Paris—for haute couture—Eternals, Little Black Dress Lane, Very Vintage, Unique Street, Around the World, and Mad as a Hatter.

For a while I'd toyed with naming the nooks after designers, but there were too many, and this way, I could mix it up and seduce my customers into looking through everything.

One of Aunt Fiona's witch friends, Rebecca Engle, asked to try on the buff suede wraparound fringed skirt that belonged to McDowell's first wife.

"I'll turn it into a Native American costume for the ball," she said, "and I can wear it as it is afterward."

I'd avoided touching it up until now, so I waited with dread for her to exit the dressing room.

"It fits like a dream," she said, still wearing it.

I released a breath, glad I didn't have to touch it.

"Can you sew another button on it while I'm wearing it?" she asked.

"Of course." I looked around for Aunt Fiona, thinking maybe she could sew it on, but she'd gone to bring some sewing upstairs. A minute; I would only have to touch it for a minute.

I found a small clear button and thread and stood Rebecca on the riser facing the triple mirrors. "I need the skirt tighter," she said, "but I'd like to keep the original button, in the event of too much dessert."

I tried hard to concentrate on nothing but my sewing;

nevertheless, carnival sounds filled my ears, while into my dizzy view came a man's hand, wearing a big tigereye ring, offering a glass of what looked like lemonade.

The woman who accepted the glass wore the suede fringed skirt and sported an emerald-cut diamond. Isobel's diamond.

"I hope it wins," he said—not the voice of the man she'd argued with over the ledgers.

"Mom would be so proud, if it won," Isobel replied. She knew him well enough to say "Mom"?

"You did a great job on it."

A merry-go-round whirled beyond them. I heard a public announcement for a pie contest as a half-empty glass of lemonade hit the dirt, then so did the woman. Unconscious. The man reached for her. "Let's go," he said.

"She'll be fine," Aunt Fiona said. "She didn't get a lot of sleep last night."

I focused on Aunt Fiona and Rebecca looking down at me. Did I wig out? I found myself still kneeling on the floor, sitting back against my legs, a needle in my hand, Rebecca's new button in place. "Did I take a catnap?" I asked. "I've got to stop reading all night."

"If you go and change, Rebecca," Aunt Fiona said, "I'll ring that up."

"Have I priced it?"

"Yes, two hundred dollars."

"It's a steal. How bad *did* I zone?" I whispered.

"Not bad, though it was the first time you had a vision in front of me and a customer. It's a good thing you don't twitch and drool when you do."

"Gee, thanks, something else to worry about."

We got Rebecca square and out the door.

"What did you see?" Aunt Fiona asked pushing a folding chair against the back of my legs.

"That maybe Isobel was drugged or poisoned at the fair? There must have been something in that glass of lemonade. The man didn't seem at all surprised that she lost consciousness."

Another customer approached us, and several more costumes went out, all from my original stock, thank the Goddess, because that vision had drained me. I couldn't touch any more of Isobel's clothes today.

While I was prepping for another afternoon of giving away scarecrow clothes, my cell phone rang.

"Nick, are you okay?"

"I am, and I've got a couple of minutes to talk for a change. First, I was able to access the local forensics report on Sampson. He was struck in the gut, fell, and cracked his skull on the corner of a cabinet. *That's* what ultimately killed him. Time of death was shortly before the fire. The only fingerprints on the scene considered suspicious belonged to a Vincent Carnevale."

Who was on the loose. I sighed. "Looks like Sampson might have gotten in the way of Vinney starting the first fire, which seems more and more like a ruse to empty my building, so he could grab the bones. Maybe that's why I'm not getting visions about Sampson, though I am getting them about the bones. Any ID on the bones? The FBI lab got those, right?"

"We got them, but identifying a set of charred bones will take a while. They also have to wait their turn." Nick sighed. "Whoever you're dealing with, on either case, doesn't play nice. Watch your back, ladybug."

"Believe me, I am." He didn't know the half of it.

"Enough about murder," Nick said. "How are *you* doing? What are you doing?"

"What am I not doing? With only a week left to get ready, I'm setting up shop and filling nooks with vintage clothes, when I'm not fitting witches for movie costumes or chasing murder suspects."

"I'm proud of you."

"Say that after you see the place."

"I might be too busy getting my hands on you then."

"Mmm. Looking forward to it, but since you're there and I'm here—" I cleared my voice. "Let me tell you what else I've done."

"What else?" he asked, and I could sense his smile and his hunger.

I ignored my physical reaction to the timbre of his voice and started to pace. "I got an alarm system. It'll take about two days to install, but it should be ready in time for the opening. An *upscale* system, extra protective and very noisy."

"You should have had that done right away."

"Never mind the 'I told you so.' I *should* have, but break-ins, fire, and murder got the best of me."

"Which is why you should have—"

"Enough with the jabs, already. Trust me, this system will scare the scrap out of anybody who dares to try and break into Vintage Magic."

Thirty-seven

When I put my signature on a dress, I regard myself as the
creator of a work of art. —PAUL POIRET

❧

My shop wasn't open in the evening yet, and I decided to
keep it that way, until the murders were solved and the
killer or killers were put behind bars, or until my alarm
system was finished, whichever came first.

With time running out—six days and counting—until
the grand opening, I took an evening and the better part
of a night in my father's basement, to painstakingly hand-
decorate the white cabinet from my storage room with the
glass-front top. Now a black enamel cabinet, thanks to my
dad.

To marry the boxy utilitarian design to Mom's art deco
pieces and Dante's fainting couch, I chose nature and fashion. On each side of the cabinet, the first angle people
would see, I traced a side profile of my own design—
inspired by a sixties, Yves Saint Laurent wool jersey Pop

Art dress—a naked woman standing on her toes at the bottom back, her head leaning toward the top front, as if peeking at the contents of the cabinet.

Except for the curvaceous profile's blonde locks, black lashes, and red lips, I painted her an all-over flesh pink.

Before I got to the drawers, my father called from upstairs. "Madeira, you have a visitor."

"Who is it?" I wiped my hands with a rag.

"It's me, Mad," Werner said. "I'll come down."

"I'm in a mess," I said. "Can you stand the smell of paint?" I opened another window.

"Sure. No problem." He whistled when he saw the cabinet. "Is there anything you can't do?"

"Yes. I can't keep my opinions to myself."

He smiled with his eyes. "I noticed."

"Do you mind if I paint while we talk?"

"Go ahead. I know you're in a time crunch." He looked around. "What are these?" he asked, hefting a bright red marble egg in one hand, a yellow one in the other.

"Aren't they gorgeous? They were my grandmother's. I forgot they existed until I found that box of them in my mother's art deco sideboard. I just cleaned it, because we're taking it to my shop when this is done."

He tossed an egg in the air. "What are you painting on the bottom, there?"

"This is a picture my mother cut from a magazine." I indicated the framed flower garden shoe propped against a chair. "I'm putting one facing shoe on each door." They were squash-heeled pumps of loosely woven tulip leaves. I'd let the occasional vibrant pink to pale yellow tulip nod from their woven stems.

"The picture is of a daffodil shoe."

"I'm making it my own." On mine, the flowers grew in different directions from each other, which I thought added to the overall character of the piece.

I stood back to examine my work. "As a vintage fashion-plate piece, it fits the bill, and it'll accent the colors in my tapestried couch. What did you want to talk about?"

"I have a source that says Sampson probably died because he got in the way of the arsonist."

I didn't dare tell him that I knew, because I didn't want to screw Nick. Well, I did, actually, but— "You want to bounce some ideas off me?"

His hands in his pockets, Werner rocked on his heels and jiggled his loose change. "Let's call it speculation, part deux." He stopped, reached into his inside jacket pocket, and pulled out a bottle of Mexican beer.

I chuckled as I accepted it and popped the top.

"Why would Suzanne *pretend* to be Sampson's sister when she was his ex? A blood relative is a more likely suspect."

"You said you believe she didn't bother to deny the gossip. Maybe because, as his ex, she could get the house, so she was playing it cool so people wouldn't delve too deeply into her background . . . or into the background of somebody she cares about?"

"Lolique?" he asked.

"According to Lolique herself, she was a pole dancer, which could merely be a part of the colorful persona she gave herself. Frankly, I can't see a politician marrying a pole dancer, myself, especially McDowell. He's too careful of his image. Then again, I think he killed his first wife, so what do I know?" I sighed.

"And another thing. If Vinney took the bones out of

your building, who put them there? Couldn't have been him. He's too young."

A man afraid of a ghost, I thought. "A hired killer? Or even someone hired simply to move her from her cave, quarry, or well. It didn't have to be her killer."

"True. We've started a search for caves, quarries, and wells, but it's not all up to us. McDowell lived in Groton when his wife went missing. Besides, we have to get an ID on the bones before we jump to conclusions anyway."

"Sampson was a victim of circumstance, wasn't he?" I asked. "He died because of the bones. He was in the wrong place at the wrong time."

"Seems like." He indicated my cabinet. "Are you going to put that in your shop? It's a brilliant piece of artwork."

"Thank you. The door opens on the aisle formed at the left by my checkout counter and at the right by my stock nooks. I'm planning a sitting area for the back, between the end of my checkout counter and the behind-the-stairs entry to my fitting rooms where the horse stalls were. People will cut though the area to get to the fitting rooms and friends can relax while they wait for someone being fitted."

"Sounds like a place where women would like to disappear for an afternoon."

"That's what I'm hoping. I'm thinking about serving fine teas, too. Or," I added, "if my shop turns out to be a yawn, I can take a nap on the couch."

Werner shook his head. "Not a chance. You think the pole-dancer celebrity will shop at your place?"

"I hope not. She scares me."

"I always knew you were a smart girl. Blunt, but smart." He turned to go. "Keep working. I'll see myself out."

Early the following evening, my crew—my dad, Tunney, Oscar from the hardware store, my brother-in-law, Justin, and his father, Cort—brought my sewing supplies and several of my old sewing machines—along with my new one—from my house and from above Aunt Fiona's garage, to set up my second-floor work area.

In the far corner, Dad put up about twenty feet of drywall, upon which he attached what I call my "bobbin walls" and the hardware to hang rows of any size spool or bobbin. With only five days to opening day, my nerves were shot, but the small accomplishment calmed me.

In the way Thomas Edison kept every chemical known to man in his workshop, I'd dreamed of having threads, ribbons, trims, laces, and fringes of every kind.

In New York, I'd bought galloon lace, Venetian lace, ruffled lace, novelty and eyelet lace, diamond braid, beaded trims, looped fringe, metallic trims, sequined trims, and more, in every exotic color imaginable. Maybe I'd gone overboard, but I couldn't wait to get them up.

After the men set up my corner, they carried the fainting couch, tables, lamps, and bric-a-brac downstairs in time for members of the White Star Circle of Spirit to decorate for the ball upstairs.

We left them rearranging caskets, spreading sparkly black draping, stars, and moons from their bags of tricks. Being witches, they had a prickly effect on my father, but he took the men to our house for my mother's furniture and my decorated cabinet.

When they got back, the men polished off Aunt Fiona's red velvet cake, then arranged my sitting room. Often.

"I don't like the fainting couch there," Dante said. "Move it to the other wall."

Aunt Fiona and I glanced at each other. "The couch," I said. "Try it coming out of the right-hand corner."

Good thing Justin and Cort, who'd already moved it twice, didn't know a ghost was directing them. Cort shook his head. "You're just like your sister," he said, speaking of my sister Sherry, his daughter-in-law.

"Thank you for the compliment. Now, where should I put the cabinet?"

"Against the enclosed stairs," Dante said. "Facing the fainting couch in the opposite corner. I love what you did with that cabinet." My ghost bowed with his compliment. "Dolly will be impressed with your renovations and decorating."

I wished I could thank him. The jadeite lamps looked amazing on my mother's tables. I brought an old urn from upstairs to set on my mother's sideboard.

Dante chuckled. "That's—"

"Gorgeous!" I said. I did not want to know if it was meant for ashes.

"The whole sitting area is gorgeous," Aunt Fiona agreed. "But it's missing one special element, which I have in the car."

When she returned, she unrolled the folk art wall hanging that had hung on the wall above her fireplace for as long as I could remember. "Call it a shop-warming gift," she said.

A spiral of stars in bronze, silver, and gold, surrounded by a mating sun and quarter moon centered the multilayered, tapestry-like hanging.

"I remember when your mother made that," my father said. "Fiona, Kathleen would be so pleased."

I hugged it as if I were hugging my mother. "Aunt Fiona,

it's the best gift ever and I can gaze at it every day. It'll be like Mom is looking out for me."

"I always knew the time would come for you to have it. It's time." We hugged.

Cort looked around. "You've made an enticing shop of this place, Madeira. Women will love it."

"Little girls, too," I said. "I can see your little Vanessa dragging you here for a new purse every other week."

"Is she a trip or what?" Cort asked, his pride in his granddaughter abundantly visible.

"I have to agree with him, Suzie Q," Tunney said. "Who knew you could make a class act out of a shack?"

"It's not half ready for my opening, but it's beginning to look like a vintage dress shop to be proud of, isn't it?" Personally, I thought it looked splendid.

If only I had known how soon it would be ruined.

That night my new alarm system got put to the test.

At about four the next morning, the alarm company called, and we were off.

Werner was waiting for us in the parking lot when Dad, Fiona, and I got there. "The alarm scared your intruder away, Mad, but not before he or she did some damage. I can't tell you how sorry I am."

Four days to my opening, and I stood in the doorway of my beautiful shop, dumbstruck.

My enamel cabinet, the one I'd worked so hard painting, had been toppled and it lay facedown on the floor with a small ax embedded in its top.

"If not for the alarm," Werner said, "the ax might have been used for some serious chopping."

"You know how hard I worked on that."

"I do. But our crime scene team thinks your alarm

worked great. Looks like the ax was tossed from the front door and the perp ran."

"Pure spite," I said.

"Who hates you this much?" Werner asked.

"Who stole Eve's car, then put her heel through the roof? Who wants her husband to be blamed for the playhouse fire? Who is royally ticked because Eve and I spied on her and her nefarious relatives?"

Werner was taking notes again. "Do you think McDowell's wife is capable of this?"

"This is chump change, Detective. I think she's out for blood. Lots of it."

"Yours?"

"I may not top her list, but I'm up there."

"Why would you be?" my father asked, his brows deeply furrowed.

"I made a calculated error where she was concerned. I underestimated her. I didn't adore her. I didn't become her dupe. I started by challenging her and ended up mocking her . . . though I did think she was in a drunken stupor at the time. Turns out, she was faking."

"In other words," Werner said, "Lolique hates your guts and she'd stop at nothing—"

"That about sums it up."

Thirty-eight

It's always the badly dressed people who are the most interesting.
— JEAN PAUL GAULTIER

❧

Scarecrows, scarecrows everywhere.

On contest day, three days before my grand opening, I dressed like a cliché: baggy black jeans with a few bright, temporary patches. A white, pirate-type blouse, and a long voluminous, silk scarf in bright Pucci colors. With them, I wore my Jack de La Rose patchwork spikes and, close to my shoulder, the matching bag.

Once people started arriving, I got so busy I had to lock the bag beneath my checkout counter, wrap the scarf around my neck twice, and let the ends riff in the autumn breeze.

For several hours, I couldn't keep track of anyone, while my parking lot bustled with people, not cars, and scarecrows kept multiplying.

"You look like you're freezing," Eve said, as she handed me a hot caramel latte.

"A little bit." I shivered and warmed my hands on the cup. "Your hair is black," I said, "but so is your lipstick. You rarely wear lipstick. And what's with the eye makeup? I like."

"You're dressed as a scarecrow," Eve said. "I'm dressed as a Goth. Costume seemed appropriate."

"You didn't have far to go."

She gave me a hand-on-her-hip pose. "*Neither* did you."

I chuckled and shivered.

Eve wrapped the scarf around my neck one more time. "Would it *kill* the outfit for you to get warm?"

"I'm going in to see if I can find a jacket."

"You will," she called after me. "You have hundreds."

"A *coordinating* jacket," I admitted.

Eve's laughter followed me inside.

"How are you doing, Aunt Fiona?" I asked as I searched the racks and she put more of my vintage collection on hangers.

"Trying to do my bit while guarding the place," she said. "The cabinet looks as good as new. You can't even see the ax slash in the top."

"Dante protected it," I whispered. "He said when the blow from the ax knocked it over, he used his energy to lower it slowly to the floor. That's why not even the glass in the doors or shelves cracked."

"Did he see who threw the ax?"

"Yes, somebody wearing a baggy black leather jump-suit with a skeleton painted on it, mask, toque, and all, except that he saw red curls sticking out the bottom of the hat as she turned and ran."

"She?"

"Since it's a skeleton, I thought for sure it was Vinney, until Dante mentioned the red curls. It was Lolique."

"Did you tell Werner?"

"Sure. I told him my ghost saw her."

"Oh, right."

"Be careful around her," Aunt Fiona said. "I'm glad Dante saved your cabinet."

I put on a red suede peplum jacket, pulled my blouse ruffles out at the sleeves, and checked the look in my three-way mirror. All I need, I thought, is an eye patch.

"Not bad," Aunt Fiona said. "Say 'argh.'"

I grabbed a pair of red leather gloves. "I do look rather piratical, don't I? Though I don't think, strictly speaking, that pirates wore red or colorful patches."

"You look adorable, as always," she said, smoothing the back of my jacket.

Sherry came in and kissed my cheek. "Sorry we're late."

"Only a little. Everyone waited till the last minute to set up, though they should be done by now." I checked my watch. "The judges should be arriving shortly. Dad put two tables outside. All you and Justin have to do is keep them stocked with punch and treats."

Sherry made a face. "I haven't opened the boxes, yet, and the smell of the treats is getting to me."

"Why? Are you sick?"

Justin kissed my sister's cheek. "Only in the mornings." He grinned.

I screamed with delight as Lolique and McDowell walked in trailing a cameraman from the local cable channel, who started filming the hug fest.

I waved my hand in front of the cameras. "No, no, no.

You're filming the flower before it blooms. Come back for my grand opening, all of you, on Halloween."

McDowell leaned close, which the cameras caught. "Guess I'm not the only publicity hound in the area," he whispered, while it looked like he kissed my cheek.

I had to fake a smile to keep from shuddering.

"We got you a local news spot, and I'm your ace reporter for the day," Lolique said. "You can thank us later." Then she threw some probing questions my way. But I had no intention of going live with an interview. "Let's go see the scarecrows," I suggested for the cameras, feeling stupid, like a reality show host with something amazing in store.

Outside, we'd set up a riser with a podium. There, I gave McDowell a microphone, fool that I am, so he could talk about his favorite subject: McDowell.

While my family set up refreshments, Eve and I took a walk through scarecrow heaven. Local shops had entered to advertise. Smart marketing for them. Good publicity for me. We admired angel scarecrows, a pizza man, witches, devils, punk, Goth, and a rock star with a guitar, every kind of scarecrow I never imagined.

"Mr. and Mrs. Councilman are going to have a hard time choosing," I said.

"What the heck is the councilman's first name?" Eve asked. "Besides Schlub and Old Goat?"

I chuckled. "Eric. I saw it on his nameplate at the dealership."

We finished walking the rows of scarecrows, more than fifty, when I saw Werner and took my turn at the microphone to introduce and thank the judges.

"Since, we don't want them consulting with each other," I said, "councilman, could you start at the end of the rows?

Mrs. McDowell, start in the middle, and Detective Werner, start at the beginning?"

The McDowells complied. Werner saluted.

"Entrants and friends," I said, "please wait until the judges are finished before you view your neighbors' works of art. While you wait, you'll find refreshments on the tables behind me."

As soon as I got off the riser, Eve pulled me into the shop and shoved her cell phone into my hand. "I got a message from Vinney."

"Shut. Up! What did he say?"

"You have to listen. I'm not sure, but I think he said, 'You're a bitch.'"

Thirty-nine

I want to invent new ways of making clothes in new materials, with new shapes and fashion accessories that are up-to-date with the changing ways of life.   —MARY QUANT

❧

I listened to Eve's voice mail. "I think he's saying, 'Y'all's a bi—' He doesn't finish the last word, does he? Is he southern?"

"No. Maybe he thinks we're both bitches."

"Can you amplify the sound?" I asked.

"No, that's as loud as it gets."

Each of us listened to it several more times.

"Can you hook it up and amplify it with a computer?"

"Not at home," Eve said. "But I'll try in my computer lab at the university tomorrow."

"Judging is finished," my father said, coming inside.

"My prize certificates?" I asked Eve.

"I put them behind the counter."

I grabbed them. "I'd better get out there."

"Not until the ballots are tabulated. Sherry has the score sheets I made."

"Eve, what would I do without you?"

"You won't have to find out if you don't let Vinney near me. Should I call him back?"

"Not in this crowd. Wait till I'm with you, 'kay? His tone skeeved me out. It's so dramatic then . . . end."

"Mad, we have the winners," Sherry called.

"Go," Eve said. "I'll wait."

Back at the podium I took the mike. "First prize goes to number thirty-three, Vanessa Vancortland, for her bride scarecrow."

The crowd gave an audible "aw" when Cort, her grandfather, held up the three-year-old so she could accept her certificate.

"Vanessa, this is going to buy you a lot of bee-utiful purses." Sherry's flower girl and niece, Vanessa, was a handbag connoisseur who even had a sleep purse in which she kept Duck Duck, her bedtime buddy.

"Second prize goes to number twenty-five: the Oscar Norton family for their baby-rocking granny scarecrow. And last but certainly scariest, number six: our own Tunney Lague for his bloody, meat-cutting vampire scarecrow."

Laughter accompanied the applause.

When Tunney accepted his certificate, he took the mike from me. "Let's give a big round of applause to Maddie and friends, who gave us such a wonderful day."

After the awards, people looked at the scarecrows for a while, but most of the crowd left when the food ran out.

At Sherry's request, Justin went across the street to Mystic Pizza and brought back pizza and sandwiches. The best.

Justin, Eve, and I sat on the steps. Dad, Fiona, and Sherry each got a folding chair from Justin's trunk. The wind had died down and the air warmed a bit as we ate, waved to neighbors as they collected their scarecrows, and generally babysat the dwindling assortment.

"How many do you think are left?" Eve asked.

"Fifteen or twenty," I said.

"If you do this again next year, I might enter. Let's go look at them."

I followed, certain she was antsy. We didn't stop until we stood in the middle of the scattered scarecrows.

"I'm dying to call Vinney," she said. "I'm scared, but I have this gut-instinct need to do it."

"No reason to be afraid. You're surrounded by people who love you."

"Suppose he knows that I was the one who hit him that night outside McDowell's guesthouse, and he *is* saying, 'You're a bitch.' Maybe it's a threat."

"He can't hurt you over the phone."

She hit speed dial and listened, again, but I was distracted by the faint sound of slot machines behind me. "Do you hear a slot machine?" I asked.

"That's not funny!" She snapped her phone shut.

"I didn't mean it to be, but don't worry, it stopped."

Eve got a sick look on her face and hit speed dial again.

I heard the slot machine again. "Can you hear it?"

"That's not a slot machine. It's Vinney's cell phone. Mad, he's here." She dialed again, and in view of my father—I even waved to him—we followed the sound to the first scarecrow in the last row, a crudely painted leather skeleton—like the one worn by Lolique the night she broke into my shop?—from which the sound of slot machines burst forth.

"This one wasn't here before," I said. "People *started* setting up here." With a sick feeling, I put my gloves back on to raise the skeleton mask . . . and saw vacant, staring eyes.

"Vinney!" Eve gasped.

"Don't faint," I said.

Forty

Fashion must be the intoxicating release from the banality
of the world. —DIANA VREELAND

❧

Still wearing my gloves, I touched the scarecrow's bare
hand, stiff and unbending, and if I hadn't been sure before,
I knew now. "It's too late to call an ambulance," I whispered.

Eve just stared at me while more scarecrows were taken
away and people chatted a few feet away from us. Just as
well that she was speechless, under the circumstances. I
took her hand and led her back toward the family. Without
a word, we sat on the steps.

Sherry frowned. "What's up with you two?"

"One of the scarecrows—"

I touched Eve's hand. "Sherry, how's your tummy,
sweetie?"

"It's great now that it's full of pizza."

"Justin, maybe you should take her home."

"What? Has something bad happened? I want to know. I can take it. Finish the sentence, 'one of the scarecrows . . . '"

Eve swallowed. "Has a dead body in it. Vinney Carnevale's body."

Sherry gasped and Justin wrapped a protective arm around her.

I wished I hadn't left Chakra home, because I could use her calming presence, right now. But I'd been afraid she'd be frightened or get stepped on with so many people around. "I don't think any of us should panic right now, especially with so many neighbors nearby."

"I'll go make sure that we don't need to call 911," my father said, and I didn't bother to argue.

The leather skeleton outfit had not been baggy on Vinney's robust build. It had to be the same leather skeleton jumpsuit.

"Let's wait to call Werner until after the other scarecrows are gone," I suggested.

My father heard me as he came back, shaking his head. "A few minutes won't matter to Vinney."

I covered my face with my hands. "I really don't want any more crime scene tape around my shop."

"A man is dead," Eve said. "And you're worried about crime scene tape?"

"The man who nearly strangled me. Who you nearly killed with the heel on your shoe to save my life. Ten minutes ago, his phone message freaked the hell out of you."

"You nearly lost your life?" my father said. "I dearly hope you're exaggerating."

"I am, Dad." Not.

He looked like he didn't believe me. "We need to shield the last of our neighbors from the grisly sight," he said. "It would be too easy, as the scarecrows thin out, for someone to go and check out the skeleton." My father got up. "Let's move the last of them closer to the curb."

Eve and I sat frozen as dad and Justin went to separate the scarecrows from the murder victim. Sherry and Aunt Fiona weren't saying much, either. Two more cars and a van arrived. Dad and Justin helped them load up.

My father came back. "The last of the real scarecrows are on their way."

"Justin, I think you should take Sherry home, now, because I have to call Werner."

Sherry stood. "Please, yes." They left as I dialed the police station and asked for Werner.

"Lytton," I said, when he came on the line, "can you come quietly back to Vintage Magic. No sirens?"

Werner sighed. "What now, Madeira?"

"I can see why our night watchman got the feeling he was annoying you with his calls."

"Low blow."

"Well, try not to place blame before you hear the facts. Somebody stuck an unentered scarecrow in the back row . . . in plain sight of all of us, even you. It's Vinney Carnevale in a skeleton costume. He's dead."

It didn't take Werner five minutes, no sirens. Eventually, however, the ambulance, police cars, and coroner's car sure attracted attention.

I put my hand on Werner's arm. "Please, no more crime scene tape."

"No need to cordon it off," he said. "There were at least

a hundred people here, today. Any stray evidence has been trampled. What happened? Nobody took him home, so you checked him out?"

His cell phone rang.

Eve raised her open phone to show that she'd called him. "He'd left me a cryptic voice mail message so we called him back. That's when we heard what you're hearing."

Werner listened to her call, pointed to her phone, and it got scooped into an evidence bag.

"Hey! I need that."

Werner denied her request with a shake of his head. "You'll get it back as soon as we analyze the message." He looked at his men. "The skeleton's got a phone on him. What are you waiting for? Find it." He signaled for the men with the coroner's stretcher to wait, but his team searched without luck.

"Ms. Meyers," Werner said, "don't open the evidence bag but use your phone to call him again."

When the phone rang, the officers lifted the back of Vinney's black Halloween cape to get at the phone in his back pocket. To do so, they had to lift his leather jacket, and when they did, something fell to the ground.

I grasped Eve's arm. "That's my Pucci bag!"

"Now what would a man want with this?" the officer said, picking it up.

"Maybe, he was trying to name his killer," I said.

"His killer?" the officer said. "Who? You?"

Forty-one

Fashion marks time.
—YOHJI YAMAMOTO

❧

"Bag it," Werner told the officer, "and keep your opinions to yourself."

I turned on my heel. "Eve! His message; I'll bet those were his last words. He called you for help. He wasn't saying 'You're a bitch' or 'Y'all's a bitch' like we were guessing. I'll bet he was saying 'Lol's a bitch.' Lolique. *She* killed him." I turned to Werner. "I *knew* she stole my bag!"

Werner looked at me like I had two heads.

"Oh, for the love of Gucci, it's not like I want the bag back, after this."

"You can't have it, anyway. It's evidence."

"Look, it has tire tracks on it, likely done with the same spite and the same heavy foot as the hole in Eve's convertible top."

"Lolique?"

"Of course, Lolique. What killed him?" I asked.

"Cyanide," the coroner said. "That's not blue face paint."

I put my arm around Eve. "Detective, that outfit is handmade. It might have a tale to tell."

Eve began to tremble. "He called me with his last breath," she whispered as they put Vinney on a stretcher and covered him, his knees still bent.

In all our years as friends the only other time I remember her crying is at my mother's funeral.

"Detective," I said, "I might have some answers inside that you don't have questions for yet."

Werner waved off the coroner and officers and followed us into my shop.

"We'll get coffee," my dad said, taking Aunt Fiona by the arm.

"I don't like that we found something of yours on the body," Werner said.

"I am *not* guilty of anything. You had us in the backseat of your squad car when I realized that purse went missing, remember?"

"I'm worried because it might be a message that *you're* in danger, brat."

"Brat? And yet that's the *nicest* thing you've ever said to me." Then I remembered the night of the fire. "Well, maybe not the—"

"Right," he said to shut me up. "Lolique's car was left parked in place of Ms. Meyers the night I picked you up at McDowell's, I remember, so I'm guessing that she still had the purse?"

"That's what I said." I turned to Eve. "Didn't I just say

that? Anyway, I think the purse was Vinney's way of naming his murderer. So, can you pick up Lolique?"

"Not until we get a time of death, because Lolique was here judging the scarecrow contest all afternoon."

Scrap! "Well, let's get back to Isobel's murder. I have these clothes that Lolique brought me, and I didn't see them as evidence until dead things started pointing toward Lolique."

He nodded, grudgingly.

I thanked my stars and let it go. "This gown," I said, "is the one McDowell's dead wife is wearing in her portrait at the dealership. In it, she's also wearing the diamond I gave you."

Werner gave me a respectful head tilt. "I'll get a warrant and pick up the portrait tomorrow, evidence that the ring is hers."

"If you take it down," I said, "McDowell will lose his dealership, and Gary Goodwin, Isobel's cousin, will get it. I'd pay money to see that portrait come down. What time are you going?"

"Now, Madeira."

"Come on. That's not fair. I just gave you evidence you didn't have before."

"I know you did. But life's not fair."

"You bet it's not," Eve said, wiping her eyes with an embarrassed chuckle. "I'm working tomorrow and I'll have to miss the show."

"Do you have any more of Isobel's clothes?" Werner asked.

"I sold a few pieces." I nearly ducked. "Don't get mad."

He raised a brow. "They were yours to sell. You didn't

sell the quilt or the diamond. I've got your number, Madeira."

I wondered if that was good or bad. "The clothes on these racks all belonged to the first Mrs. McDowell."

Werner seemed to be considering options. "I've got a description of what she was last seen wearing."

"Anything here fit the bill?" I asked.

"Well, that's the problem. The description doesn't tell me anything. It's in fashion speak, as described by Mrs. McDowell's secretary at the time. If I get the description, can you match it to an outfit?"

"If I do, can I go and see you take down that portrait?"

Werner denied my request with a shake of his head as he called the precinct and had someone read the clothing description in his file. "She was last seen wearing 'a rust linen fitted cape—" He listened again. "With black piping over a black linen sheik dress." He looked up at me. "Got that?"

"It's a sheath dress, but yes, I'm afraid I do have it." Except that she was really last seen wearing the suede fringed skirt that Rebecca bought, but I couldn't tell Werner that. My first vision, however, had been correct, and yet my arms and legs felt weighted as I unzipped the garment bag and removed the described outfit, careful only to touch its hanger. I blinked a couple of times as I handed it to him.

He could see that I was shaken. "Is this the cape you were going to keep—Madeira, are you all right?"

"It's silly," I said. "You play with people's clothes and you get attached to their bones." I wiped my cheeks with the back of a hand. Eve wasn't far behind me.

"You two would make terrible cops. Stick with fashion," he said. "You don't get hurt that way."

I so wanted to differ.

"By the way," he said as he left with the cape and dress outfit, "the brakes on your Element are locking. You should get the dealer to look at that tomorrow morning . . . around ten."

Forty-two

I have the reputation of being easygoing. But inside, I'm like nails. I will kill.

—CALVIN KLEIN

❧

Eve was right. I did have a hard time dressing down. Just to take my car in for service and witness the toppling of the McDowell empire, I dressed in a moiré silk plum shirt with Janice Wainwright jodhpurs and a pair of Michael Kors cork wedges in plum with one of his famously massive totes to match.

Call me crazy but I felt the need to pack a gun to go anywhere near McDowell. I settled for a less violent means of self-defense. I filled the well of the oversized tote with some of my grandmother's marble eggs. I wanted the bag uber-heavy in the event I found it necessary to smack the man.

When I picked up the bag to leave, however, the echoing sound of breaking pool balls followed. To muffle them, I found it necessary to wrap each egg in rolls of fabric, lots of it, until I stopped knocking as I walked.

Okay, so it weighed a bit more than my usual purse, like twenty pounds or more, and I had to carry it slung over a shoulder like a farmer carried a sack of potatoes, but the weight of it made me feel secure.

At the last minute, I remembered to take my cell phone from its charger, but I didn't want the slim red miracle of technology to get pulverized by the contents of my purse. So I slipped it in my pocket.

I was forced to leave my car at the end of a long line of cars waiting for repairs at the service center because I didn't have an appointment, a great excuse to linger. I sighed. Two days until my grand opening, and I'm playing hooky. Eve is always right; I must be certifiable.

I found a comfortable sofa, from which I could see both Isobel's portrait and McDowell's desk, because I didn't want to miss the incredulous look on his face at the moment of his karmic fall.

I don't normally wish anyone ill, but the man murdered his wife, a woman with whom I'd formed a bond, probably from experiencing her last moments in my first vision with she/we beginning to fall down that well.

I wished I could see Lolique's face when she learned they were going to be poor. Not that it would matter to her in jail, which is where she belonged.

I'd brought a fashion magazine and got into an article about Marc Jacobs. Next thing I know McDowell is standing in front of me. I questioned his space-invading presence with a look, and he stooped down in front of me while I imagined him wrapping Isobel in a quilt and sticking her in the trunk of his car. Wait? Whose voice had I heard at the fairgrounds?

"You don't like me much, do you?" he asked.

Understatement falling on deaf ears. Look out below. "Call it instinct," I said, wondering if he knew that his stitch of a wife was a killer, too.

"If you've decided that you don't want to give me your business, Madeira, I'll take the car back and send you over the state line to my competition in Rhode Island."

"Is that where the well is? Or is it on your Groton property?"

He stood like *I* was the scary one. "What the hell are you talking about? You need to get a grip, Ms. Cutler."

I did. I got a grip on my shoulder bag, until Gary Goodwin rolled his wheelchair over. "I sense some animosity, here. Let's not make a scene, McDowell. Ms. Cutler, help an old man. Come, push my chair out into the fresh air while you wait for your car."

I'd need two hands to do that, and I didn't want to let go of my purse. When I thought I'd have to say no, Natalie Hayward came over. "Can I help, Ms. Cutler?" she asked as she got behind Goodwin's chair and started pushing him toward the door.

Okay, Goodwin had been in the guesthouse with Vinney and Lolique that night, and what I didn't know about him bothered me more than what I knew. But he didn't have a lot of choices in life, because he was stuck in that chair.

"Coming?" Natalie asked.

I checked the clock on the wall. Ten minutes till Werner arrived.

Since the police were on their way, I figured I could chance it. "A short walk," I said.

"I'm not sure that's a good idea," McDowell called after us.

"You wouldn't think so," I said beneath my breath as I walked beside Goodwin's chair.

He chuckled. "You hate the bastard as much as I do, don't you?"

"That transparent, am I?"

"You're utterly transparent, Ms. Cutler, in a challenging sort of way."

What did that mean?

"We have some wildflowers behind the addition. Natalie, go around by the side of the building. It's gorgeous back there in the fall."

"Mr. Goodwin," I cautioned, "I don't think you want to be gone too long this morning."

"Why's that, eh?"

I smiled. "I know nothing."

"You certainly don't," Lolique said, waiting for us as we rounded the building.

She held a small gun in her hand, and Natalie didn't blink or miss a step when she saw it.

I hesitated. "Mr. Goodwin?"

"Ms. Cutler," he said. "You disappoint me. I thought you were such a quick study. Natalie Hayward has been in my employ since this branch of the dealership opened. She keeps me abreast of current events."

"He pays very well," Natalie said. "Very, very well."

"You're his mole?" I said. "Wait! You pushed me and pretended to save me?"

Their silence spoke volumes. With the gun, Lolique indicated my path toward the woods. "Keep going," she said. "Don't stop now."

That's when I saw it across the field on the outskirts of

the woods: an old-fashioned wishing-type well, where I knew that wishes were useless. "Are you going to throw me in there, too?" I asked, the past becoming clearer when I noticed his tigereye ring.

Lolique had been right. I was a duped dope.

She chuckled. "Don't look at me. I didn't throw Isobel in there. She died before I was born."

"But you're the woman who was seen sneaking in and out of the playhouse, aren't you?"

Lolique scoffed. "No, that was my mother, before the locals caught on to her presence and she accepted the role they handed her as Sampson's sister. She'd moved in with him, again."

"Without bothering to break off her affair with me," Goodwin said.

"Poor you," I said, tongue-in-cheek to Gary. "And what about you, Natalie? Why?"

"True, I hated Isobel," Natalie said. "Daddy's little girl, keeping watch, so no one could get close to him."

I'd taken sewing lessons from this woman! "You had a thing for Isobel's father?"

"What if I did? I didn't kill anyone."

Goodwin chuckled. "Natalie would have helped if she could have cozied up to the old man, but she didn't know what I planned. She's been my most loyal helper."

"Thanks loads, Dad," Lolique snapped.

"Natalie's not as loyal as you think," I told Goodwin. "She's a gossip. Told me the first day about your accident, about how badly you wanted the dealership. She's not loyal at all."

Goodwin whipped around to look at Natalie, now looking daggers at me. If only I could make the three of them duke it out and forget about me.

"And your daughter, Mr. Goodwin. You must be so proud."

"My stepdaughter," he said.

"Thanks again. Okay, so Sampson was my biological father. Rich as God. And my stupid-ass stepbrother goes and kills him before he can change his will in my favor. He paid, though. Keep pushing, Natalie."

"So that's why you killed Vinney, Lolique? Revenge?"

"What an amazing hypothesis," she said.

"*Not* a hypothesis. Vinney ratted you out. He called Eve and gave you up with his last breath." I was lying of course, but she didn't know that. "And as for Sampson's money, you may still get it, now that the truth about his divorce to your mother is out. I'm sure there'll be *something* left after the IRS takes their share. Years' worth of back taxes, I hear."

She stopped walking and stood still as a snake about to strike. I so wish she'd point that gun in another direction.

I had to break her, though. "You see, your father was selling his corner lot because he had to. You and your mother climbed out from beneath your respective rocks to finesse a man headed to prison for tax evasion."

Lolique gave a feral hiss through her teeth, and I felt fear and fury radiating off her in waves, small consolation since we were getting closer to the well, too close. "You killed Vinney for nothing, except, hey, maybe you'll inherit your father's debt, anyway?"

"Vinney was a son of a bitch. He was supposed to pin that second fire, the one we *planned*, on my husband by planting his sweater with the bones. Does he do that? No. He kills my father to start an unplanned fire, sic the law on us, and ruin my chances to inherit Sampson's and McDowell's fortunes. Two fortunes! Vinney deserved to die."

"So you killed him."

She raised her head with pride. "So I killed him."

"Vinney was a good son," Goodwin said almost to himself, and I understood suddenly his stay on the psych ward, as if he lived in a different world than the rest of us. He looked up at me, but I'm not sure he saw me. "Vinney took the bones out of your building for me."

I remembered Dante's story of the night the bones were brought to my building . . . Goodwin brought them. Dante taunted him, and he left so shaken he had a car accident, and ended up in a wheel chair in a psych ward. Puzzle pieces were falling into place like clockwork toys, click, click, click.

Goodwin's face changed and he radiated hate. "Why the hell did you go and buy that old shack?"

My heart beat like a drum, and my hands were so sweaty it was getting hard to keep a grasp on my bag.

My connection to Isobel grew strong, and her fate fell into place. "You put Isobel here when this was an empty lot, didn't you? Before construction here was a glimmer in Zachary Goodwin's eye."

"I should have put her husband here with her," Goodwin said. "While I was dropping her here, McDowell was having drinks with her father, outlining the brilliance of building a second dealership on this very piece of land. I'd thought it was smart to put her on land that her old man owned. But the old man and McDowell, they planned to build here in secret. Kept projected ledgers. No one knew. Not even Isobel. She told me that she thought her husband was embezzling."

Click. Another puzzle piece fell into place.

The closer we got to the well, the harder my heart pumped, the more slippery my hands became. I could barely keep a grasp on my bag. But if I moved it, everyone would know how heavy it was.

I wanted to use it, but I had three targets. One with a gun.

I'd keep Goodwin talking and wait for my best shot, because the more he talked, the slower we walked.

Werner should be at the dealership by now. Would he look for me?

"Why *did* you kill Isobel, Mr. Goodwin?"

"For the dealership, dammit. I'm blood. Her father said it would be mine when he died."

"Why isn't it yours, then?"

Five feet from the well.

"McDowell became his right hand, his expansion idea put him in favor, and his grief at Isobel's loss *appeared* to match her father's. Then, when Isobel goes missing, the old man has a stroke, and who takes him in? McDowell."

Serves you right, I wanted to say. Had McDowell been sincere, at least about Isobel? I wondered way too late.

"Why did you move Isobel's bones in the first place?" I asked him. "Why not leave her in the well?"

"This was about to become a car lot. I couldn't hide a body this close to a construction crew, then the public."

"Why did you bring them to *my* building, then?" I was stalling but he hadn't figured that out yet. I was surprised that he couldn't smell my fear.

"It was a morgue," he shouted, "full of body drawers. I

didn't think I'd live to see the place fall down. You messed with me by buying it. I've killed once, I can kill again." Hate laced his last words.

An icy fear ran down my spine.

"Why did you keep the quilt until you moved Isobel from the well to my place?"

"She made the quilt from my aunt's clothes and my aunt was good to me."

"But you killed her daughter."

"So now they're together." He raised a hand like he'd done them a favor. Psycho.

"The night I brought Isobel to your place—" He shook his head. "I had the accident that put me in this chair."

"I know," I said. "That's called karma."

He tried to backhand me, but I stepped from his reach. "Do you want me to sic my ghost friend on you again?" I asked. "Too bad I can't get him to trip you down the stairs in your chair this time."

Goodwin roared like a wounded bear. It would be to my advantage if he lost it altogether. He might be less careful, though his two bodyguards looked on with quiet amusement. They wouldn't let me get away with anything.

"Lolique, why did you call Isobel 'Saint Belle' the night we had drinks?"

"The old goat worshipped her, and he was guilt ridden because they'd quarreled the day she went missing. He still calls her name in his sleep, the schlub."

Isobel and McDowell had been having a simple quarrel in my cape-wearing vision. I'd called that one wrong.

Two feet from the well.

I did some fancy footwork around the chair to confuse them all, back to front, a not-so-happy dance.

Lolique homed in with her gun, but she was so focused on me, she tripped over a clump of grass, and fell.

I ducked behind Natalie as the gun went off.

Natalie fell. Had she caught the bullet?

Lolique scrambled around in the grass. She must have dropped the gun.

While she looked, I slipped my hand in my pocket and pushed the single-digit speed dial for Werner, covering the sound by shoving Gary's chair into the stone base of the well.

He screamed in pain as Lolique scrabbled to her feet.

As she came our way, her attention on Goodwin screaming, I swung my bag and knocked her down. But the bag was so heavy, it flew from my slippery hands and landed in the well.

Lolique rose and came straight for me, and I realized how strong hate and greed could be.

"Where's the gun?" Goodwin yelled. "Kill her now!"

"You're stupid, Goodwin," I yelled, ducking Lolique's clawing charge. "The police are taking down Isobel's portrait right now. You were home free."

"No!" Gary howled like a madman and caught my attention.

Lolique caught me off guard and tackled me. I ended up balanced on the edge of the well, like I'd seesawed on the edge of the upper-floor railing to see the portrait.

Lolique laughed in my face and shoved me backward with both hands.

Like Isobel, I was falling.

Forty-three

It is the unseen, unforgettable, ultimate accessory of fashion
that heralds your arrival and prolongs your departure.

—COCO CHANEL

❧

I smelled chocolate.

The light was bright, the tunnel narrow, and on the
other side, someone called my name.

I opened my eyes. "Who knew that God would look like
the Wiener."

God growled, and then he got touchy-feely and ran his
hands over my arms and legs, my head and back. "Anything broken?" he asked.

"Everything." It didn't smell like chocolate anymore.
It smelled musty and damp. It smelled of decay. The dirt
around me had bugs in it, lots of them, and . . . bones. Small
bones.

"Can I just say that you took ten years off my life? By
rights, you should be dead," Werner said, and I could feel

his hand trembling against my arm. "Smart of you to throw down a bean bag chair first."

"I landed on my bag?"

"Well, it's not a purple marshmallow."

"You bet it's not. My bruises are probably shaped like eggs." I gasped, remembering. "I hope you didn't take down the portrait."

Werner chuckled. "We're having a conversation in the bottom of a well, Madeira."

"So . . . you're *not* God?"

"I'm not a wiener, either."

"Did I say that out loud?"

"You've probably got a concussion. It doesn't count. McDowell was more concerned about you being out here with Goodwin than about my plan to take down the portrait."

"Goodwin killed Isobel and threw her down here," I said, "not McDowell. Vinney was abetting his handicapped stepfather, the murderer, by removing the evidence of Goodwin's crime from my building."

"I know. And Vinney killed Sampson to set the fire as a diversion, like you said. Goodwin and Lolique are up there confessing."

"Singing like canaries?"

"You watch too many old cop shoes, Mad."

"Enough to know that these small bones might belong to Isobel. Goodwin was sloppy when he moved the bones out of here." I hurt when I moved but I picked up the ones I could reach and slipped them into Werner's shirt pocket. "Take good care of Isobel."

"Leave it to you to keep trying to solve a crime when everything seems hopeless."

"*Me?* Solve a crime? Don't let Tunney hear you say that."

"Don't worry, I won't. We're in a well, Mad. Weren't you dreaming and talking in your sleep about a well the night of the fire?" Werner asked. "You remember, before I took you home?"

"I can never seem to remember my dreams," I said to evade the question.

Werner looked as if he didn't quite believe me.

"What about Natalie?" I asked to change the subject. "She worked for Goodwin and had a thing for Isobel's father, but I don't think she was an accessory to murder."

"We'll talk to her if she survives. She's already on her way to the hospital, which is where you're going." Werner fingered my bag. "What did you put in here?"

"Madeira?" my father called from the top of the well.

"I'm okay, Dad," I called, grabbing my head. "Ouch. I have a really bad headache, though."

I heard sirens. "What'd you do, Lytton, call the cops on me?"

"That's your ride. I'm going to go up now to make room for the rescue team down here."

"Oh good. I don't think I can climb that rickety ladder."

I must have passed out, because the next thing I knew, I was strapped to a kind of cradle while being pulled up the well shaft. I wished that Isobel might have had the same chance.

As I was placed in the ambulance, my father and Aunt Fiona stood beside me. They both had tears in their eyes.

"Don't cry," I said. "We caught Isobel's killer."

That's the last I remembered until I woke in the hospital with Werner standing at the foot of my bed and McDowell standing beside it.

"What day is it?" I asked.

"One day before your opening. And you'll be there," Werner said, "on crutches."

"Figures. A ball, and I won't be able to dance."

"Be positive. You're going to your grand opening, not your funeral."

"I'm positive that you're right."

"I usually am," Werner said with a wink.

McDowell cleared his throat. "Thank you for allowing Isobel to rest, Madeira. I've needed closure for a long time."

"No wonder you got angry every time I mentioned her. But why did you run that night Eve and I took Lolique home, then lie about working?"

"I wasn't calling the police on you. I told you to get out."

I touched my head. "You what?"

"I yelled, 'Get out, Mad!' "

"From our vantage point in the underbrush, Eve and I could hear crickets, crackling leaves, an owl hooting, and you telling your unwanted guests to get out."

"But I said your name."

"Yeah, and I thought you were 'mad' as in furious, but thank you for telling us to get out. Nicest thing you ever said to me."

"I called the police on the people you saw in my guest-house. I couldn't pin anything on them, but I knew they were crooked. Even my so-called wife." He scoffed. "I should never have married her, but she was so full of life, such a great actress—as in she pretended to care for me— Hell, I thought someone young and fun would cheer me up. Help me recover from my grief over losing Isobel. I'm a foolish old man."

I touched his hand. "You loved Isobel. 'Nuff said."

"Sell her clothes, Madeira. It's time for me to let her go."

For the first time ever, I felt sorry for Councilman McDowell.

"What about her quilt?" Werner asked. "It's evidence, but you'll get it back, eventually, or Madeira will, since she gave it to us."

McDowell paled. "I saw Gary in prison last night for the first and last time. He told me more than I wanted to know until I walked. Destroy the quilt."

"But it's a masterpiece that Isobel created," I said. "Let me donate it in her memory, naming her as the artist, to a quilt or textile museum."

"I never want to look at it, again. I don't want to know where it ends up. And its history stays buried."

"Done." I looked at Werner. "I'm thinking that the Pucci bag is going the same route."

When Eve came in, Werner and McDowell left.

"Hey, peg leg," she said. "They're letting you go. Your father and Fiona are in the hall. I've got your clothes." She held up a paper grocery bag. "Don't scream, and I'll help you get dressed."

Everything she'd brought me was black, no purse in sight.

Forty-four

Goddesses live in the heavens. They do not stand, they do not walk, they glide and sway. The goddesses are laughing and balance on heels as slender as the tip of a little finger.

—LOLA PAGOLA

❧

Opening day arrived in a flurry of activity, but I was amazingly ready for it, thanks to my family and friends.

Though I had sent an invitation to my former employer Faline, a world-class designer, I did not expect her to take any part in my grand opening. So, talk about a shock. Not only did she show, she was the first one in the door that morning, and she brought fashion, television, and movie icons, vintage collectors, and with them, the kind of press money could not buy.

Vintage Magic was about to buzz the New York fashion world. Oh, she had an ulterior motive, countering the "feral cat" stories that proliferated about her after I resigned. I'd heard them. But hey, if she wanted to prove we were still friends, fine, as long as she wasn't my boss.

Moneyed vintage clothes hounds and glittering person-alities who brought fame wherever they went were literally shopping in *my* shop because of her.

"Faline, I can't thank you enough for this."

"Thank you for going along with it. I owe you. We'll do lunch the next time you come to New York?"

"Fashion week?"

"I'll get us tickets. First row, beside me?" Faline purred.

I danced a mental jig. "Absolutely." I needed to keep my finger on the pulse of the fashion industry, and she'd just offered me a rare and impressive "in."

The media blitz they brought alerted the locals who loved to rub elbows with the stars. My shop rocked, literally.

Councilman McDowell held an impromptu press con-ference out front—surprise!—but he talked about *me*. Go figure.

Now the last of my customers, the ones who were com-ing to the Circle of Spirit ball in an hour, dressed as film stars, were getting ready in my dressing rooms.

The media went ballistic when Scarlett O'Hara came out wearing a gown made from Tara's drapes. "Fiddle-dee-dee," Aunt Fiona said. "I'm so glad that I came to Vintage Magic."

Under the eye of those cameras, my grand opening re-minded me of a fashion week extravaganza where each gown shone more spectacular than the last and *everyone* looked like a celebrity.

Even some of my old friends from New York attended the grand opening and the ball sponsored by the White Star Circle of Spirit, Southeast Connecticut Chapter. Mock movie stars mingled with the real thing on my crowded second floor before the doors officially opened.

I'd chosen to wear Isobel's Lucien Lelong gown, the one she wore for her portrait, as my way of setting her free, especially here, where positive energy could envelop her spirit. Of course, it had the advantage of covering the cast on my leg, though nothing could hide my crutches, nor my inept use of them. Nevertheless the Schiaparelli pansy evening bag from the thirties hanging from my wrist helped to pretty up the crutches a bit.

When Councilman McDowell arrived, minus his killer wife—awaiting trial in jail, because he'd refused to post bail—I doubted the brilliance of my costume choice. He came toward me as if I were wearing a homing device.

"I'll change," I said when he reached me.

"No, don't." He took my hand. "You look beautiful. I didn't think anyone else could do it justice. I was wrong. Isobel would want you to have and wear it. In a way, you helped me find her. She's at rest now. I am, too. Seeing you in her gown helps. Thank you."

"No press tonight?" I asked.

He shook his head. "I'm not running anymore, not from my past and not for office. Enjoy," he said, kissed my hand and disappeared into the crowd.

Dante appeared. "Did you *have* to sell my extra tuxes? Six other men are dressed like me. Don't I feel special?"

"It's not like anybody can look down their noses at you," I said as I hobbled on my crutches toward the window. "Look. You're about to feel *very* special. My father and Aunt Fiona are bringing Dolly inside."

"Are you sure that's Dolly? Her earth body looks pretty worn out."

"I'm sure she'd agree."

Cleopatra, high priestess of a local coven, stopped beside me. "Madeira, this is wonderful," she said.

"I'm so happy that you're enjoying yourself."

Dante watched her go. "I don't ever remember reading that Cleopatra carried a broom."

I turned to enjoy the colorful display of costumes and decorations. Open wooden caskets on pedestals had pots of bittersweet and Chinese Lanterns, gifts from McDowell, inside. They protected my sewing corner from the dancers, and my walls of colorful trims looked like part of the decorations.

I'd used many of those trims as I improvised on some costumes, like Scarlett's and Cleo's. Others fit the chosen "actresses" beautifully, like Harlow in draped white silk as a fallen angel. Loretta Young draped in forties blue as the bishop's wife.

Audrey Hepburn wore a little black dress, long black gloves, and used a cigarette holder, a la *Breakfast at Tiffany's*. Another Audrey hailed from *My Fair Lady* at Ascot in black and white.

Madonna looked cool in her corset top and pointy boobs. Cher wore a scanty white gown with plenty of cleavage and an elaborate headdress that I made with an old turban covered in rows of new beaded overlong fringe that covered the wearer's brow and touched her shoulders.

Many of the "stars" wore striped stockings, but they weren't the only ones carrying brooms. One called herself Sandra Bullock from *Practical Magic*. Another, Elizabeth Montgomery from *Bewitched*. Glinda the good witch from *The Wizard of Oz* waved.

I'd sold two of the outfits that I'd bought in New York at some point, and one each from Vivienne Westwood's

Witches and Pirate collections, but the movies the owners claimed they belonged to escaped me at the moment.

Of course not everyone wore *my* clothes. Some had created their own costumes. And not everyone carried a broom; mostly the members of the Circle of Spirit did, except for Aunt Fiona.

She and my dad finally got to the top of the stairs with Dolly Sweet in her Katharine Hepburn gown from the wedding in *The Philadelphia Story*.

When Dolly got to me, she put her hand to her heart. "Isn't he beautiful in that tux and top hat?"

"Which one?" my father asked.

Only Fiona and I knew that Dolly was talking about Dante, coming her way.

"She's not too steady tonight," Aunt Fiona said. "I think we should bring the fainting couch back up for her."

I snapped my fingers. "What a great idea."

I signaled for our small band to stop playing, and I took the mike. "Can I ask for a few gentlemen volunteers to bring up the fainting couch from my sitting room downstairs?"

Enough men went down so my father didn't have to let go of Dolly, and just as well.

"Thank you, cupcake," Dolly said. "What an incredible evening. I can't believe that Ethel thinks she's too old to enjoy this. Well, her loss. You've done wonders with this place. How did you get that delicious detective to let his officers guard everything downstairs?"

"The officers are off duty. I'm paying them tonight. And that delicious detective is dancing with Eve. They came together." Eve had warned me that Werner asked her. She wanted to make sure I didn't mind. Why would I?

Dolly giggled. "I think he has a crush on you."

"Dolly Sweet, don't you go starting any of your old rumors," Nick said.

I squealed as he leaned in and kissed me, his hand sliding down my back. "Hi, gorgeous. Nice crutches."

"God bless us, every one!" I quipped, before his lips met mine once more.

I loved the way Nick could eat me up with his gaze and make me promises at the same time. Shiver.

He kissed me a third quick time. "Thank God you're safe. I don't know every detail yet, but I'm shaking in my wingtips."

"Who *are* you?" I asked. "The Clyde half of Bonnie and—?"

"No, silly. I'm a Fed. Same movie."

Dolly laughed harder than any of us. The fainting couch arrived just in time, because the old girl couldn't breathe and laugh at the same time.

"Do you think she's all right?" my father asked as we walked away. "She's talking to herself."

She was talking to Dante, of course, her debonair suitor, sitting at her side, kissing her hand.

"You'll talk to yourself, too," Aunt Fiona said, "when you're a hundred and three."

I urged them toward the dance floor. "Go ahead, you two. Take advantage." I turned away so my father could put his arm around Aunt Fiona without feeling guilty. I wasn't entirely sure how I felt about them as a couple, I just knew that Harry Cutler had seemed more alive lately than he had in years. Mom would surely approve of that.

Nick got an old stuffed chair in good condition from the storage room for me to sit on, while he sat on the arm and knuckled my nape, shivering me to my toes.

Dante stood in the middle of the dance floor and made a sweeping motion with one hand that sent the band's music fluttering as if in a cool breeze.

The bandleader raised his baton, and they played "Hawaiian Wedding Song."

I sat forward. "*That* wasn't on my playlist."

Dante took the hand of a beautiful young woman wearing the wedding gown from *The Philadelphia Story.*

My throat closed, my vision blurred. "Nick, Dolly's not breathing."

He ran. I called 911, my hands shaking, my emotions mixed. I didn't want to lose her, but how could I take her away from her love?

The way she and Dante waltzed and looked into each other's eyes, you'd think this was their wedding day.

Members of the Circle of Spirit moved to the side. Many saw Dante and Dolly as I did. Those who did cheered and raised their broomsticks to stir the air. As they did, my trimmings and laces flew from their bobbins like colorful streamers rushing forth to circle and curl above and around the young lovers.

Dolly laughed up at Dante. Utterly romantic.

He kissed her and kissed her.

And she disappeared from his arms.

I glanced over at the fainting couch. Nick was cradling Dolly, talking to her, and I could see her nodding absently as she turned toward Dante on the opposite side of her.

Fiona and my father came to me. Fiona had, of course, seen what happened.

"Walk me over there, will you?" I asked them.

"How are you, Dolly?" I asked when I got there.

"Full of anticipation," she said, and she winked.

A Tip for
the Vintage Handbag Lover

PETIT POINT SCARLET FLORAL
ON LUSH BLACK

Purchased at the Cottage in Amesbury, Massachusetts, a bag that came from a former handbag museum in Maine, this structured handbag is startlingly beautiful in full black with a gorgeous red floral centered front and back.

At nine inches high, it's eleven inches wide at the top and twelve inches wide at the bottom, covered by a black trellis-like background, front and back. The trellis is either petit point or applied with a fine, thin band of petit point-like trim. I can't tell which.

As far as the petit point, front and back, the center is a top-to-bottom oblong trellis that takes up one-third of the bag, the trellis itself centered by a Jacobean bouquet of three red flowers, each with a black center. Either side of the trellis is plain black.

This handbag closes with a swirling, floral clasp that is

one and one half inches wide and three quarters of an inch tall, as beautiful and ornate as a gold floral broach.

Inside, the bag is lined in black satin with a zipper pocket and an open pocket. The zipper pocket is lined in pink tricot. There is no maker's name in the handbag. The straps and bottom are likely a quality mock leather. The flat bottom is twelve inches wide and four inches deep. It has four gold feet.

I haven't been able to find this specific bag in either Anna Johnson's *Handbags: The Power of the Purse*, Judith Miller's book *Handbags*, or anywhere on the web. However, judging by the embroidered purses of this style, with a costume jeweled clasp, and taking the tricot into consideration, I'm dating it as coming from the sixties or seventies.

**This handbag can be seen at
www.annetteblair.com.**

Make Your Own Clutch

AN ENVELOPE PURSE FOR
THE NON-SEWERS AMONG YOU

❦

Pick out an envelope, either a number ten, business-sized envelope, or an envelope that came with a greeting card. Try to pick one with a wide overlap. This will be your pattern, so it should be a size that you'd like to carry as a purse.

Take the envelope gently apart and lay it out on a piece of self-binding fabric or leather—black, natural, colored, your choice—just make sure it can be cut cleanly without the need for hemming.

After your leather envelope has been cut out, fold it the way the envelope was folded. Purchase fasteners at your local leather or fabric store that you think will add to the charm of the design. Make sure they're small enough to fit the width of the overlap. Rather than gluing your leather envelope clutch together, use fasteners, about a half inch apart, or closer, to attach the front.

To fasten the envelope point to close your leather bag, choose snap fasteners, Velcro, or magnetic fasteners. If you use Velcro, make sure the sticky side will adhere to leather.

Floral pieces of leather can be added with the fasteners as centers for decoration. The fasteners alone could also be applied in other locations and designs to give your clutch character.

An alternative to the design is, of course, to sew the leather envelope together for a clean look. Try sewing it with contrasting thread.

**A sample can be seen at
www.annetteblair.com.**

Turn the page for a preview of the next
Vintage Magic Mystery
by Annette Blair

Death by Diamonds

Coming soon from Berkley Prime Crime!

One

❧

Vintage Magic is my shop for designer vintage fashions and designer originals. When I arrive every morning, I can't believe I'm looking at my dream come true.

I faithfully believe every customer who tells me that my restoration of the funeral chapel carriage house added a certain cachet to the charm of historic downtown Mystic.

I believe it and I wallow in it.

The designer originals I sell are my own, under the Mad Magic label. You see, I'm an escapee from the highest levels of the New York fashion industry. You can call me Mad, or Maddie, unless you're my father, Professor Harry Cutler, in which case you will call me Madeira whether I want you to or not.

As for the Magic, I'm also my mother's daughter, not a witch, precisely, but I have a whole psychic thing going on that feels like magic, which I evidently inherited from her. I can't ask for confirmation. She died when I was ten.

So, vintage clothes occasionally speak to me, often about dead people. I see snippets of greed, jealousy, hate, revenge . . . motive. But since it's been quiet on the vision front for a couple of months, I'm hoping that was only a phase.

As I parked in my lot, my best friend Eve's Mini Cooper sat beside a *Wings* overnight delivery truck. Eve, aka, the Man Magnet, had already taken to charming the driver's socks off.

"Hey," I said, when I joined them. "Am I late?"

"No, I'm early," Eve said. She handed me a caramel latte and the morning paper, signed for, and accepted, the box from the driver, then slipped her business card into his pocket. "Later," she said with a wink.

I don't know if he winked back. His billed cap was tilted forward to shade his face, his jacket collar stood high and zipped tight, and his dark glasses protected him from . . . snow glare?

We watched his truck turn onto Main Street and disappear. "You're my idol," I said. "Did he join your stud of the month club?"

"He will."

In the shop, Dante Underhill, former undertaker and hunky house-bound ghost, waited for our morning chat. Nothing like catching up on seventy years worth of gossip.

Today, however, he saluted and disappeared. Eve couldn't see him, and since she could get a bit edgy where ghosts and magic were concerned, I'd never told her about him.

None the wiser, she relaxed in the chair Dante vacated to read the morning paper while I opened the box. Leery about touching a potential vintage item, because of my visions and the murders they'd dragged me into, I carefully parted the layered tissue.

I recognized the dress immediately but could hardly believe my eyes. Some years ago, in fashion school, I won the opportunity to design this awesome gown, trimmed in pricey cubic zirconias, for an actress, now a dear friend. But since *she* collected designer clothes, I couldn't imagine why she sent it to me.

Dominique was a note writer, so I fished through the tissue, careful not to touch the dress, and finally opened the parchment envelope that had slipped to the bottom of the box. "Mad, Sweetie, I always wanted you to have this. I hoped someday to give it to you myself. If you have it, I'm dead. Use your talents wisely. Love, Dom."

"Oh my stars," I said. "Dominique DeLong died."

"No kidding. It's all over the front page of the Times," Eve said. "She collapsed during an Off-Broadway performance."

"She would rather have died *on* Broadway," I muttered, aware that I was in shock.

"At least there were witnesses," Eve said. "Hundreds of them."

My stomach flipped while Dominique's note trembled in my hand. "Witnesses?"

"You know the infamous diamonds she wore around her eyes during each performance? They disappeared sometime between her death and her arrival at the hospital. She was D.O.A."

I removed myself from the vicinity of the dress, my stomach lurching. "When did she die?"

"Evening performance. Last night."

I lost my breath, looked back at the dress, re-read the note, and considered the feasibility of a legit ten-hour delivery.

Dominique's words, swimming before my eyes, echoed in her voice. "Use your talents wisely."

She did *not* mean dress design.

Two

Eve's brows furrowed. "Hey, how did *you* know she was dead?"

I handed her the note and weighed the possibilities. "Why someone would send *me* the dress, I can't imagine. Unless the box was already packaged and addressed to me. Though it wouldn't be, would it, if Dominique wanted to hand it to me herself?"

Eve focused on reading Dominique's note. When she finished, her head came up fast, her face a mask of confusion. "Huh?"

"Right."

"Does this mean you're going to New York?"

"It means that I'm going to Nick's to lock this gown in the cold storage unit he had installed in his basement for me."

"Why at Nick's? Why not here?"

"Because Nick's an FBI agent who lives closer to me than his partner, my brother Alex, does. Because the storage unit's a safe, it's a closet, it's climate controlled, and it's where I keep my furs, unless I get a call for them. Because my shop, and my Dad's house, are too obvious for a safe. Nick's a Fed, so his house is naturally safer, and because—"

"You keep half your clothes there, anyway, since Nick moved back to Mystic?" Eve had raised a brow, her mouth pursed in disapproval.

I chuckled inwardly at the snarky relationship between my on-again, off-again Italian Stallion, Nick Jaconetti, and Eve, my best friend since kindergarten. "Can you keep an eye on the shop while I go lock this up?" I asked putting on my black, Sonia Rykiel coat with a capelet collar, and going for the box carrying Dominique's gown.

Eve checked her watch. "Sure, I don't have to proctor end-of-semester exams until two."

With the gown box igniting a stress ulcer that felt a bit like the lit end of a ciggy butt in my gut, I'd barely gotten to the door when Detective Sergeant Lytton Werner, my nemesis, walked in. "Miss Cutler, Miss Meyers," he said, tipping a nonexistent hat.

This was so not the man that Eve and I got drunk with on Mexican beer a couple of months ago. Werner had crawled so far back into his stiff, unfriendly shell—as far as we, the enemy, were concerned—he was going to crack his tail bone bending over backward to be polite.

I so wished I hadn't called him Little Wiener in third grade. Who knew the name would stick like frickin' forever? As had the animosity between us, with the occasional foray into a shadowy land of sexual awareness, on the few occasions we were forced to try to solve a crime together.

I pulled myself from my deer-in-headlights trance. "To what do we owe the pleasure, Detective?"

"We found an abandoned *Wings* truck in the Mystic Seaport parking lot."

"And that's of interest to me, because?"

"It's empty. Key in the ignition. No fingerprints. No cargo. Nothing inside except an Internet map starting in New York City and heading straight to this address. Your name and the name of your shop are written in miniscule handwriting—very unabomber—on the top of the printout."

I shrugged. "We did get a seven A.M. delivery."

No need to share my concerns. If there was a murder, it took place in New York City, not Lytton's jurisdiction.

"Damn," Eve said. "I guess my date with that driver is off."

"You saw the driver, then?" Lytton pulled out his trusty notebook.

We both nodded.

"Hair color?" Lytton asked.

"Er."

"Um." I described the whole face cover-up.

The detective growled.

Fortunately, Eve had the uncanny ability to describe the rest of his body, his "squeezable tush and quarterback shoulders" included, in detail.

"Any identifying marks?"

"He wore gloves," Eve said.

"Emporio Armani, logo labeled. Men's dark brown Nappa leather."

Eve and Lytton looked at me like I had two heads, *both* designer originals.

After giving me a double take, Eve turned back to Werner. "He had a tat at the edge of the glove on his right lower arm. I wouldn't have seen it if I hadn't nearly dragged the glove off, trying to pull him closer. It was a capital B or an 8, in blue with red and yellow fire around it."

"Why so interested in an abandoned truck?" I asked.

"A.P.B. It was stolen last night around midnight in New York."

Oops.

My thought processes were having a parting of ways. Should I admit that I knew Dominique, a Broadway star, not a movie star, or that I was carrying a dress that might—if one had a wild imagination—be construed as evidence? Or should I let it ride because the crime, if there was one, had been committed in New York City?

My decision: Shut up, Mad. "If we've answered your questions, Detective, I have an errand to run."

Werner nodded toward my package. "Is that the box the pseudo driver for *Wings* delivered?"

Out of the corner of my eye, I saw Eve slip the note from Dominique into the folded newspaper.

I handed Werner the box.

He opened it and whistled. "This is primo designer, isn't it? Big bucks?"

"Why thank you, Detective."

"Why thank *me*?"

"I designed it for Dominique. That's why she wanted me to have it."

That took Werner aback. If I didn't know better, I'd

think he suddenly regarded me with a touch more respect. "It must have cost her a fortune."

"Today, it'd cost a fortune, because of its age and provenance, not the least of which was the linking of Dominique's name with mine, and our resultant friendship."

"That's why your eyes are red," Werner said.

I hated that my nemesis noticed these small, personal things about me. I raised my chin. "Yes, I lost a dear friend last night, and she left me this dress to remember her by."

"Too bad somebody felt the need to steal a truck to bring it to you."

Scrap. "There is that."

I'd never been so grateful to hear my cell phone ring. I answered right away.

My caller identified himself and shocked the Hermes out of me. "Kyle," I said. "I'm so very sorry to hear about your mother. She'll be deeply missed."

Werner kept mouthing "speaker phone," so I had no choice but to set the phone down so we could all hear it.

"It's chaos here, Miss Cutler, but Mom left strict instructions about what she wanted after she died."

"Funeral arrangements, you mean?"

"Uh, no, not that. They're not releasing the b—her until the investigation is cleared up. No, this has to do with her vintage clothing collection. She wants the collection to make the charity rounds, fashion shows and such, while she's still news, and she wants you to arrange the events. She left a list of locations and causes. Can I count on you Aunt Mad?"

Oh, sure, play the Aunt card in front of Werner. Damned kid's nearly as old as me. "Of course, Kyle."

"After the charity events, I have permission to sell her collection at a private auction—all except for a dress she wanted you to have. And don't worry, I'm sure I'll find it eventually. Mom included a list of the people she wanted to invite to the auction. Your name's at the top. She wanted you to have first pick before you hosted the event."

"Kyle," I said, "it sounds like your mother *knew* she was going to die."

Magic or destiny, Annette Blair's bewitching romantic comedies became her first national bestsellers. Now she's entered a world of bewitching mysteries and designer vintage, a journey sure to be Vintage Magic. You can contact her through her website at www.annetteblair.com.